HIS
LAST
NAME

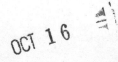

Also by Daaimah S. Poole

Yo Yo Love

Got a Man

What's Real

Ex-Girl to the Next Girl

All I Want is Everything

A Rich Man's Baby

Somebody Else's Man

What's His is Mine

Another Man Will

Pretty Girls in the VIP

Diamond Playgirls
(with Miasha, Deja King, and T. Styles)

HIS
LAST
NAME

DAAIMAH S. POOLE

KENSINGTON PUBLISHING CORP.
www.kensingtonbooks.com

To the extent that the image or images on the cover of this book depict a person or persons, such person or persons are merely models, and are not intended to portray any character or characters featured in the book.

DAFINA BOOKS are published by

Kensington Publishing Corp.
119 West 40th Street
New York, NY 10018

All Kensington titles, imprints, and distributed lines are available at special quantity discounts for bulk purchases for sales promotion, premiums, fund-raising, and educational or institutional use.

Special book excerpts or customized printings can also be created to fit specific needs. For details, write or phone the office of the Kensington Sales Manager: Kensington Publishing Corp., 119 West 40th Street, New York, NY 10018. Attn. Sales Department. Phone: 1-800-221-2647.

Dafina and the Dafina logo Reg. U.S. Pat. & TM Off.

ISBN-13: 978-1-4967-0158-9
ISBN-10: 1-4967-0158-5
First Kensington Trade Paperback Printing: October 2016

eISBN-13: 978-1-4967-0159-6
eISBN-10: 1-1967-0159-3
First Kensington Electronic Edition: October 2016

10 9 8 7 6 5 4 3 2 1

Printed in the United States of America

To Robin Sampson and Auzzie Poole.
Thank you for all your love and support.

Acknowledgments

Thank you, Allah, for the gift of writing.

Thank you to my sons, Ahsan and Hamid Poole. My mother Robin Sampson and father Auzzie Poole, and stepmother Pulcheria Ricks-Poole. My sisters Daaiyah, Najah, and Nadirah Goldstein. My grandmothers Dolores Dandridge and Mary Ellen Hickson.

Many thanks to my friends and family: Keva Dandridge, Ieshea Dandridge, Tamika Wilson, Carla Lewis-Shelton, Sharon Long, Gina Dellior, Daryl Fitzgerald, and Elaine Shanae Pettit.

Special thanks to my agent, Sara Camilli, and to my mentor and friend, Karen E. Quinones Miller. Allison Hobbs, thank you for everything. You always have my back.

Thank you to everyone at Kensington Publishing and to my editors Mercedes Fernandez and Selena James.

Readers, thank you so very much for purchasing and reading my books. I appreciate your comments and e-mails. Please keep them coming.

DSPBooks@gmail.com and DSPBooks.com

Much Love,
Daaimah

CHAPTER 1

Tiffany Holcomb

"Don't answer the door," my husband, Damien, shouted. He ran into the living room as a loud, continuous knock became even louder.

"Why, what's wrong? What's going on? Who is it, Damien?" He snatched my arm and pulled my petite body to the floor. I had no choice but to follow his lead and kneel next to him on our marble floor.

Moments passed, but the relentless pounding did not stop. Damien hadn't answered my question, so I asked him again, "Who is at the door? Who would have the audacity to drive onto our property and up our driveway?"

"It's the people from the bank. They're trying to serve me more court papers."

"Why are they coming here, banging on our door? I thought you said your attorneys were handling everything."

"They are. He is. He said they may start coming around, but not to sign or accept anything. As long as they aren't able to personally serve me, it gives me more time."

"Okay." I took in a deep breath and tried to make sense of

what was going on. Damien saw the defeated look in my eyes and comforted me with a kiss on the cheek. His kiss only made me sadder. I tried to hold the fear in, but a stream of tears flowed down my face.

He wiped my face with his thumb. "Babe, don't do this. Don't make me feel any worse than I already do. It will be okay. I'm in the process of getting this all under control. My lawyer put in all the paperwork with the creditors. He's taking care of everything. It's all going to work out. Trust me."

"I don't understand, Damien. One day you say we're okay, and the next day someone is at the door trying to serve us papers. What's going on? Tell me the truth. Can we afford to stay here, or do we have to move?"

"I told you already. We don't have to move. Once the bankruptcy filing goes through, everything will be back to normal. I'll get one payment to pay all the creditors, and they will leave us alone. I promise you. I told you I will take care of you, and I will. Do you believe in me?"

"Yes, I do."

He turned to face me. "Then know that I won't let anything happen to you."

"I understand, but my mom saw something on the news and people are sending my sister stories they've found on the Internet."

"I don't want to talk about this anymore. People owe me money. I have investments out there that will pay back eventually and hopefully I will get a job covering sports somewhere. I don't know—maybe I'll get a scouting position. And in the meantime, I will be in the gym. I can have a comeback. Teams are still interested in me. I have a plan, Tiffany. Believe in me—I got us," he rambled on. "Believe. All right?"

I shook my head and told Damien that I believed in him, but I was lying. I didn't believe him or even like him at that moment.

After five long minutes, the knocking finally stopped. I got off the floor, walked to the window, and watched the man who'd been knocking as he got into a navy blue SUV. *How did we get here? What happened in our lives that led us to this awful place?* I thought to myself as the SUV pulled out of our looped driveway.

Since I was a teenager, my mother, Helen, told me that I was never to be with a man who could not take care of me. She gave me detailed instructions on how to have a man provide for me. She had used the same rules to land her wealthy husband.

So I'd followed the blueprint step-by-step, but now I needed a new set of plans.

The first half of my life, my mother was a hardworking single mom. She worked as a secretary and was struggling. Then she met high-powered attorney Wilson Miller, Jr. at a convention and everything changed.

My brother, Charles, and I knew our mother quit her job, but instead of having less money, she had more. She went on long trips for weeks at a time, and we moved in with our nana. That lasted for about two years, from the time I was in fifth grade until the end of seventh grade.

Then out of nowhere, my mother came home and said she was married and we would be moving to North Carolina. My brother and I were happy for our mom, but totally shocked when a tall white man walked through our grandmother's door.

"*That's* Mr. Wilson?" I asked my nana. She shook her head and instructed me not to say anything about him being white.

We moved into a house right outside of Charlotte, North Carolina, in a suburb called Huntersville. Our new home was four times the size of Nana's row house back in Baltimore— and that didn't even include the trees and grass that circled the gigantic house.

I remember how I walked into the house in amazement with my mouth wide open. All of the furniture was new, bright, and beautiful. I couldn't believe we were actually moving into a house that nice. Then my mother walked us to our rooms. I had a white canopy bed with pink sheets and my brother's room was blue and filled with toys.

The next day, we went shopping for school clothes. Unlike other school years, there wasn't a limit to what we could get. If we liked a pair of jeans, my mom allowed us to buy them in every color, along with matching shirts and sweaters.

That night, as we unpacked all of our new clothes, my mom sat me down and said, "Look around, Tiffany, This is how you live. A man is supposed to treat you like a queen. Like royalty. And if he can't, then he doesn't deserve you." That conversation stayed with me the rest of my life.

Life was great in North Carolina. However, Charles and I learned to stay out of Wilson's way. He was our stepfather, but not our dad. Our dad was the lazy black motherfucker who left us in Maryland. Our mother reminded us of this all the time. Wilson didn't speak to us a whole lot, but he kept our bills paid. I always got the impression that he loved my mother, but tolerated us. He set up a small trust fund for my brother and me. He even made sure my tuition was paid in full and I didn't need any loans for school. My teenage years were great, but I was happy to go back up north for college.

My mother drove me to Syracuse University. It was a long twelve-hour drive up the east coast. The entire ride, she talked to me about planning and taking advantage of the opportunities that were being presented to me. She said that I only had four years to succeed. Initially, I thought she meant to complete college, but my mom was already thinking beyond college. She told me not to eat too much, to study hard to earn my degree, but, most important, to find a wealthy husband: a life partner who had the potential of making a six-figure income and also came from a good family. She warned me to stay away from future teachers and all art majors. My mother thought I should also date outside of my race, because black men weren't any good. It was a lot to take in, but I took notes.

One day during my third week of school, I met Warren Michael Joseph as I left the library. He was double majoring in both political science and finance. Check. He was from a good family. Check. His father was a pastor at a mega-church and his mother a principal in Memphis, Tennessee. He was black, but I had checked off three out of four of my mother's requirements. The bonus was that he was also a football player. We dated freshman through junior year. He interned at Wilson's law firm in the summer. We planned to get engaged and married after we graduated, but then something changed during homecoming weekend of our junior year.

That something was his teammate Damien Holcomb. We met at a party one night and connected instantly. I remember it vividly. I arrived at the party early and Warren wasn't there yet. He didn't answer his phone, but Damien was there and wouldn't take no for an answer when he asked me to dance. Something was so ruggedly handsome about him. He had deep, fudge-colored skin, a chiseled athletic frame with a sexy, aggressive New York swagger and the talk to match. He was so confident. He didn't just simply ask me to dance, he took my hand and pulled me toward the dance floor. We danced and he held me for six songs straight. I left the party with Damien. A few days later, I broke up with Warren.

Warren didn't handle it well. He tried to win me back by sending flowers, crying, and begging me to come back to him. Everyone on campus knew that Damien had stolen his girlfriend, and he couldn't handle the embarrassment. I didn't know if he wanted to get back together because of his male ego or because he actually wanted me. When his pleading didn't work, he became depressed and transferred schools.

I felt bad, but Damien was everything that Warren wasn't. He was one hundred percent authentic and knew who he was. He was also everything I was supposed to stay away from. He was on scholarship, and his major was physical ed-ucation He was a football player who didn't come from a good family with money. Actually, he didn't have any family. He was brought up in the foster care system and only had cousins and an aunt and uncle in Brooklyn, all of whom he rarely spoke to. He said the only person who was there for him was his social worker. She was the one who told him he had a good head on his shoulders and should be in college.

She was right. He did well in college and was excellent on the field. Everyone wanted a piece of Damien and they were all trying to put in their bids in advance. He wasn't supposed to take any gifts from agents or teams, according to NCAA rules, but they didn't know that his girlfriend was accepting things on his behalf.

Soon after we became an official couple, untraceable gifts would arrive at my parents' home from sport agencies and future sponsors. To my surprise, my mother was very accepting of Damien because even she knew he was destined for the NFL. And she was right. That next spring, Damien and I were married and he signed a contract with the Denver Broncos for thirty million dollars over five years and a five-million-dollar signing bonus.

Immediately, we were thrust into an entirely new world of privilege. The other side of a million dollars was something new for both of us. While he was out on the field making the money, it was my responsibility to furnish the house and plan the vacations. We traveled to every continent in the world during the off season. We owned three homes. Our main house was in Alpine, New Jersey, but we also had a home in Denver, Colorado, and a condo in Orlando, Florida.

We owned five cars: a Bentley, a Mercedes-Benz AMG convertible, a BMW, a classic 1967 Chevy Camaro, and a custom Tahoe. Our life was great and money wasn't an issue. When I shopped, I didn't look at tags or turn over a pair of shoes to check the price sticker before I charged them. We always picked up the tab at a restaurant when we went to dinner with our friends and we never had any financial worries. We had everything. We were the couple that other couples aspired to be. I was the beautiful wife with the handsome millionaire husband.

Things changed when Damien had a career-ending injury. It happened right before his new contract was finalized. He was on the twelve-yard line about to go into the end zone, and the Saints linebacker charged him. His body fell backward, but his leg went forward. From the stands, I could almost feel his leg as it cracked in half. I screamed as they led him off of the field. Damien went straight to the hospital and into surgery. I prayed and prayed, but I already knew he would never play again.

That was two years ago, and that's how our lives went from boarding private planes to creditors trying to knock down our front door. Our accountant hadn't been paying the IRS or filing state or local taxes—he was too busy investing our money in various businesses that never turned a profit. He thought he was going to be able to put the money back before we noticed, but Damien's injury prevented that. Damien also liked to gamble and lend money out, and he made horrible business decisions. Then Damien decided to get drunk and drive home. When a police officer tried to arrest him, he gave the cop a hard time. Not only did he get a DUI, but he also got a court date for resisting arrest.

All we had left was eight thousand dollars in the safe in our guest room that I had put to the side. I wasn't even sure if our car notes were paid that month. Damien would tell me to keep the cars in the garage, so I had to assume they weren't. We voluntarily turned in the Bentley and the Mercedes, which left us with only my BMW, his truck, and the classic Chevy.

Things were rough right now, but Damien was a hustler. And I knew that I could find a job if I had to.

On our wedding day, I vowed to love him in sickness and in health, for richer and for poorer . . . but what did they say about repossessions and foreclosures?

CHAPTER 2

Monique Hall

"**G**uard your man! Guard your man, Kadir! Come on, guard your man!" I shouted from my seat to my six-foot-four-inch son who was running down the court at the packed and noisy Liacouras Center. He was a sophomore shooting guard for Temple University's basketball team.

"Don't make the boy nervous, Monique."

"Be quiet, Carl. He needs to be pushed. These are the last few games before the draft. June is only three months away."

Kadir's teammate made the shot, taking their lead from three points to five, and then the time ran out for UCF. The Temple Owls won eighty-three to seventy-eight.

My son, Kadir, started to play basketball when my boyfriend, Carl, placed the ball in his hands. He was only two years old, but he never put the ball down. Some kids had blankies, but Ka-Ka had his ball. He slept with the ball and started dribbling it when he woke up every morning. He would say, "Ma ball. Ma ball." It went everywhere with him. In the tub, at the playground—he even tried to take it to day care.

I knew he loved basketball, but I realized he was good when he was about ten and teenage boys would knock on the door to play with him. By sixth grade, there was always a league, tournament, or summer camp. If he missed a game, his coaches would call and offer to pick him up because they needed him in order to win.

Five summers ago, Kadir grew from five foot seven to six foot four in three months and schools began to call. Prep schools and colleges started ringing my phone at work, at my house, and even on my cell phone. How they got my numbers, I'll never know. I let Carl talk to most of them; I didn't know much about the schools. I just wanted Ka-Ka to have the best opportunities possible.

It was important for Kadir to go to college and become someone because I missed my chance. I wanted to go to college, but I had Kadir at seventeen and had little support. His father was killed before he was born, and my parents made it known that they would not be my babysitters.

My mother, Dottie, told everyone in our family that nobody was to help me since I had embarrassed the family by getting pregnant. There was no baby shower or happiness at the hospital. There was only one thing that I remember my mother saying when Kadir was born: "You better be glad I'm not making you give this baby up for adoption."

My mother was upset about my pregnancy, but she never told me how to use a condom or what birth control was. Her only rule was no sex before marriage, because if you have sex, you will get pregnant and your life will be over.

That summer, it was just me and Ka-Ka. I took him everywhere with me. My mother was so mean to me and even refused to pay my tuition at school. She said, "Teen moms don't go to Catholic school." According to her, I wasn't going to amount to anything anyway.

For eleventh grade, I attended Simon Gratz High School instead. It was down the street from my home in North Philly.

Gratz was so different from the all-girls Catholic school that I had attended for so long. The biggest difference was that they had day care at the school. There were a bunch of other teen moms just like me, and some even had two babies. It wasn't a big deal. No one judged me and everyone was supportive. Kadir was safe while I went to class, and I was able to visit him during my lunch period.

That's where I met my best friend, Celestine, whom everyone called CeCe. She also had a son, who was three months older than Kadir. We liked the same things and bought a lot of the same clothes for ourselves and our boys.

We took our sons to the park, and I spent a lot of time at her house. Her mom was the complete opposite of mine. Ms. Laura would watch the boys for us while we went to the movies or any parties.

CeCe had two younger sisters and one older brother, Carl. In CeCe, I found my sister, and in Carl, I found unconditional love. From the very beginning, Carl accepted Kadir as if he were his own son.

We were committed to each other for more than eighteen years. He was a good guy, but not perfect. Carl and I never had any children together, and sometimes I felt we acted more like siblings than an actual couple. We loved each other, but we weren't "in love" anymore. I never would have left him, though. I didn't know what I would have done without him. Besides, I couldn't afford to leave him even if I wanted to. I worked a part-time job to make sure I was there for all of Kadir's games.

After Kadir's win, I met him and the rest of the team at Maxi's, the pizza shop on campus. It was a tradition after each home game to go there. All of the cheerleaders and coaches were sitting at the tables in the front of the restaurant.

Once he saw me, the head coach stopped mid-sentence to greet me. "Hey, coach! Good game!" I responded.

"Thanks! Enjoying the last days while we still have Kadir. After this, he's off to the big leagues . . ."

"Yes, absolutely! Praying and crossing my fingers," I said proudly.

I looked around the back of the restaurant for my son, when a young man approached me and said, "Who you looking for?"

"Kadir."

"Forget Kadir. You can have me, beautiful. I'm B, Allen Richardson's cousin."

"Really? Well, I'm Kadir's . . ." Before I could get "Mom" out, Kadir came over and interrupted the barely legal boy's game.

"Bryan. B, that's my mom, man!"

"Oh, for real? My bad. She look good, though. I might have to be your step-pop."

"What you say?" Kadir looked like he was ready to punch the boy in his throat.

"I was joking."

"Yo, I'm not, man. Say something else about my mom."

"I was giving your mom a compliment. We good, Kadir. Relax." The young guy playfully smacked Kadir's arm and walked away.

"Mom, what I tell you about dressing like that?" Kadir said as he looked over at my outfit. I was wearing a black sheer shirt and tight jeans. He steered me to the table past his other teammates.

We sat down at the table and I picked up a menu. Carl joined us. Carl was two years older than me, but looked his age. He was still handsome, but he had picked up a few pounds over the years. His fuller light brown face was complemented by his trimmed beard and brown eyes. His five feet ten inches almost seemed short now next to Kadir's six-four. He gave Kadir a fist bump.

"Son, I saw you make that three in the fourth. You have to keep that up. All eyes are on you."

"No. Right now, all eyes are on Mom. Dad, tell her to stop dressing like that. She's not going to the club."

"What I'm wearing is fine," I protested.

"No, those pants are too tight, and your shirt is see-through. You are showing too much. And you're wearing high heels. Most moms wear sneakers and sweatshirts to the games."

"Most moms don't look like me."

"But, Mom, you are thirty-eight."

"And I still look like I did when I was twenty-five." Kadir hated when anyone except for his dad paid attention to me. I couldn't help it, my wheat-toast-brown skin didn't have any blemishes nor were there bags under my eyes. I usually wore my hair in a weave with a part in the middle; even when I tried a different style I still looked young. I didn't necessarily eat well, but I had a toned body and I didn't mind showing it off. Kadir would have to get over the way I looked and dressed.

"Whose father are you, Kadir? Don't worry about what I have on. You should be more focused on your game. I saw that pass you threw away."

"I know. I didn't see it coming."

"Exactly. When you go to the pros, there is no missing passes."

"I know, Ma."

"I'm not getting on you. I know you are great, Kadir. But you have to make sure you're always ready."

"I'll be ready."

"Enough. Tonight, let's relax, eat, and count our blessings," Carl demanded. "Say your prayers, Kadir, and leave your mother alone. Mo, start dressing your age."

"Amen to that," Kadir said as we laughed and talked about the future.

There were so many sacrifices over the years that we all had made. Carl worked two jobs, and I made the money stretch. We scraped, saved, and did whatever we had to do so that I could be there to cheer Kadir on at every home game as well as some away games. I was the coach's extra set of eyes, the baker, the therapist, and the surrogate mom for kids whose parents never made it to any of the games.

Now, everything we worked so hard for was about to happen. Kadir just entered the NBA draft, and when he walks across that stage and the commissioner shakes my baby's hand, I'm going to be right there.

CHAPTER 3

Shanice Whitaker

A lot of girls dream of one day being famous. They work on being sexy daily. They get ass shots and breast implants, trying to achieve the perfect body. Some even think all it takes to be a model is to post pictures all day long on social media. But me, I'm sexy effortlessly. I was born that way. My ass and titties are all mine. A few years ago, my only dream was not to have to worry about my rent every month and to be able to fill my refrigerator.

That was then, and this is now. Who would have ever thought I would be where I am today? My name is Shanice "Shani Amore" Whitaker and I am a video vixen, men's magazine cover girl, and model, a.k.a. your boyfriend's #WCW (Woman Crush Wednesday). I'm living a life I didn't even think was possible. I'm traveling all over the country and making good money just to pose or host parties, but I know it won't last forever, and that's why I'm trying to expand my brand. I know there are other girls with cuter faces, longer weaves, and super snatched waists, ready to try to step into my heels. That's why I'm transitioning into commercials and acting. I never want to be known for just one thing.

My career began when I worked in a Philly nightclub called Belize. There, I met a lot of powerful people and made a lot of connections. I worked for this lady named Adrienne who knew everyone. I also met my homegirl Darcel, who put me on to do video shoots. From there, it was on. I started appearing in music videos and getting more modeling work and hosting parties. I also met the love of my life, Jabril Smith, who played basketball for the Oklahoma City Thunder. He had a girlfriend, but he still invited me to his games and flew me out to his city. From then on, I humbly accepted the position as his main side chick. He bought me a condo and gave me a nice monthly bag and shoe allowance. Yes, he was in a relationship and had a baby on the way, but he was kind and I didn't have to lie about who I was and what I did. I was a girl from North Philly, with a daughter that I had at sixteen and a mother in jail. I didn't graduate high school, and I fucked him and his teammate the same night I met them. He knew all of that and still loved me and treated me like a princess.

I loved Jabril so much I took a case for him. One of his boys left some weed in the car and we were pulled over by the cops. I claimed it as mine and for being his down-ass chick, Jabril rewarded me by never calling me again. At least he was nice enough to hire me a lawyer, who got all of the charges dropped. He also sent me twenty thousand dollars in "thank you" money. None of that meant anything to me, because all I wanted was him.

Our breakup devastated me, but I still had to move on so I could eat. Tears don't pay bills. I picked myself up, and I've been hustling hard ever since.

Since then, I landed six magazine covers and was both the lead and love interest in eight music videos. Life was good and about to get even better. My management was in talks to have our modeling agency be a part of a television show.

But until then, I was in New York City rehearsing lines in my head for a national flavored-yogurt commercial audition.

I prayed that I booked this commercial. It was my third audition this week and I was a little discouraged.

"Shanice Whitaker," a woman with a clipboard in her hand called out.

I walked into the audition and introduced myself. There were two young white women and a black guy with orange-blond hair. The woman who called me into the audition told me to begin while the black guy and a blond woman read over my résumé. I cleared my throat and began. Thankfully, I had memorized the lines on the train because they didn't give me a script. I smiled and then began: "Yogi Fat Free Yogurt, it's just what I need after the gym. Only ninety calories with a lot of flavor—without all the bad stuff." I smiled again and held up the yogurt. I added my own twist on the commercial by holding up the yogurt at the end.

"Very good," the man said. He looked over my résumé again and asked me what my measurements were.

I hesitated. Although I took yoga and spinning classes and had slimmed down from a size ten to a size eight, I was still a little self-conscious about my weight.

"I'm thirty-eight–twenty-seven–forty."

"Yeah, I think you are beautiful, but . . ."

The other lady interrupted him. "To be honest, your photo made you look a lot thinner. In person, your look is too pinup-girlish. But thank you."

"I think I look like the average woman."

"You do, but we are looking for slim and athletic. Thank you," the woman said. She dismissed me and called in the next person.

I walked out, and the man from the audition ran up to me. "Listen, your look is good for music videos, but to be taken seriously as a commercial model or actress, you need to lose thirty pounds. I know a trainer in Brooklyn. His name is Marco."

"With that much weight gone, I would look anorexic."

"No, you would look like an actress." He handed me a card.

I thanked him and left the audition depressed. They made me feel like I wasn't good enough—something I dealt with all of my life. I balled the trainer's card up and walked out of the building. I felt so alone again, like I always did.

I had family, but none living with me. My daughter, Raven, had lived with her grandmother since she was born. I got to see her when my schedule allowed me to. My mom is in prison and I don't know when she will be released. I didn't speak to my aunt—who raised me and my cousin for years—because my cousin was a hater. My cousin Courtney went to blogs and radio stations talking shit about my relationship with Jabril. She said that I was a former stripper and that I fucked old men for money. It was true, but as my cousin, she should have kept my secrets and tried to build me up. Instead, she wanted to bring me down. She was so jealous and set on destroying me, but all she did was raise my stock. Dumb bitch. I missed spending time with Courtney and my aunt, but I can't forgive a disloyal bitch.

Well, Jabril ain't loyal, either, but I was still in love with him. I watched his games a few times and checked for him on Twitter and Instagram. I wondered if he ever thought about me. I didn't want to hurt his girlfriend or their daughter, but I had feelings, too. I just wanted for him to look me in my eyes and tell me what we had didn't mean anything to him. I knew what we had was real, and I knew that one day we were going to have our face-to-face. Until then, I knew it would be hard to give any man my all.

Chapter 4

Zakiya Lee

"Jabrilah, what are you doing? Give mommy back her necklace!" My daughter ran clumsily through my spacious living room and down the hall with my necklace in her hand. I chased her and caught her. We both giggled. I gave her a bunch of kisses on her cheek, and she kissed me back. My baby was a beautiful miracle. I know all moms *think* their babies are cute, special, and smart, but I *knew* mine was from the moment I held her.

Not being able to carry a baby full term made me long for a healthy baby. Once I had her, I just wanted to be the best person I could be. I loved becoming a mommy. It was the best thing that ever happened to me. I wanted to ensure that I gave Jabrilah everything that I didn't have—like a mother, a father, and a happy home. So far, so good. Today, my fiancé and I are still in love and going strong—even though everything and everybody tried to rip us apart. I suffered a stillborn baby, and then there were the side chicks and groupies, the breakups, makeups, and setbacks. Him being in the NBA meant many women threw themselves at him daily. Knowing that, I tried to keep our communication open. Over the years,

I learned so much from other players' wives. I used to hang out with Nichelle, the wife of Jabril's teammate Lloyd Deburrows. Nichelle's advice for me was to look the other way when it came to cheating and have my own life. Then Christie, the girlfriend of one of Jabril's teammates, told me the key to keeping a man from straying was to be freakier than him. She said that if you fucked him all the time everywhere, he would be too tired to cheat. But she was really crazy—she had me throw a baby shower for a nonexistent baby. So I couldn't really take her advice and I'm not looking the other way either. I listen to my own advice but I have learned from their mistakes.

We are a young couple—I'm twenty-four, he's twenty-five—and I know that there is a lot of temptation out there. So I have to make sure he doesn't get caught up. And I have left him before. When we first met he was out there with a lot of girls. And I lost our son and just got tired of it, so I left him for like six months. He couldn't live without me, so he came to Philly and brought me dozens of roses and all this jewelry to win me back. At first I wasn't impressed, but then I realized I loved him. I knew he would do right when he begged me for another baby and we planned the second pregnancy—but he didn't. Instead, he had this video chick named Shani something who thought she was special, but I shut that down and got rid of her. He was parading her around everywhere while I was in the house, pregnant with his child. I didn't have any other choice. I planted drugs in his car and then called the cops. I don't know what I thought was going to happen. He could have lost everything. Luckily, she took the charges for him and he cut her off. So it was a good thing . . . but I would never do it again or tell him the truth. His near miss to jail gave him a wakeup call. We got engaged, he doesn't smoke weed anymore, and he barely drinks.

I know he is faithful now and I love my man, but I'm not naive enough to think that there aren't other women who will lie, cheat, and steal to be in my situation. Before, his traveling drove me crazy. I would be texting and calling him all day long. I don't do that anymore. We talk and pray, and that has made the biggest difference in our relationship. Now I am preparing for our wedding and honeymoon in three months.

Initially, Jabril said my budget for the wedding was two hundred and fifty thousand dollars. When he gave me that figure, I told him, "No. I don't need that much. I can have a great wedding for a hundred thousand." Then I started to become a bridezilla. One visit to an amazing venue will do that to you. I started flipping through bridal magazines and got so many ideas and was so inspired that I almost lost my mind. My simple wedding turned into a circus. I wanted doves, a horse-drawn carriage, and fireworks. I even called John Legend's management to see if he was available to sing at the event. Unfortunately, he was already booked. Then my sister brought me back to reality and convinced me that a wedding was about celebrating love—not a show for the guests. I agreed and came back to my senses.

I put all my focus back on our relationship and our day of unity. I still wanted a one-of-a-kind dress, so I pieced together different dresses that I liked. Then I had a new up-and-coming designer sketch the dress and design it. I scaled back the wedding a lot and even shortened my guest list and decided I wasn't even having bridesmaids.

My nanny, Lena, walked into the living room "Time for lunch, Little Ms. Jabrilah!" She grabbed Jabrilah out of my arms.

"She should be hungry," I said, getting up from the floor.

"I'll make her a sandwich."

"Okay. I'll just be out for a few."

"No problema."

When Jabril initially hired a nanny, I was against it. I'm from Philly, and I didn't know anyone who had a nanny. We raised our kids ourselves. But then I realized Lena was there to help me, not take my place. Plus Jabrilah loved her. Lena was in her fifties—an older Mexican woman. I loved her because she was great with my daughter, she'll never be after my man, and she doesn't care about material things. Once, she even found a pair of diamond earrings in my pants pocket and gave them back. I hired her sister to work on Lena's days off, and her son to do our landscaping. They were all really good people, and I admired their work ethic.

A lot of things that came with being engaged to a professional athlete had to grow on me. I now can say I've adjusted to the fabulous life God has blessed me with. Sometimes, I would come home to twenty dozen roses just because he missed me. Jabril spoiled me and our daughter with everything. Even now, I still don't care if it's a designer name or not. If I like it, I like it. That's one of things Jabril says he loves about me—that I'm a regular girl. I don't have to cake makeup on to look good. My caramel skin tone has its own glow. I'm very low-maintenance. I get my shoulder-length brown hair blown out every week and get a simple manicure. I'm naturally slim, so I get to the gym when I can. I'd rather spend time with my daughter and Jabril than have money any day, but he insisted on giving me money and buying me things. I put most of the money up for our daughter, I send money to my sister, and still have enough to go on shopping sprees if I care to. I have two engagement rings. I lost the first one, so Jabril replaced it with a bigger and better one. Then I found the first one under our bed. My focus is on my family, but once Jabrilah is in school, I want to start our foundation and complete my degree.

I exited my gated community and my phone started to ring. It was my baby Jabril.

"Hey, Bril. What's up, baby?"

"I wanted to FaceTime with Brilah. I'm on my way to the airport now."

"She's home."

"All right. Well, I'm just checking in on y'all."

"How is your knee?"

"It's better."

"Love you. Can't wait for you to get home."

"I'm going to get there around midnight. When I get there, be ready. It's been a week, and I'm overdue."

"I'll be waiting for you."

It was 12:30 a.m. when I heard Jabril pull into the driveway. I walked down the circular staircase in six-inch stilettos and a purple-and-black corset. I stood in the doorway and waited for him. He came in, slammed the door shut behind him, and grabbed me. He pushed my body up against the door. I turned around and kissed him passionately. His hands roamed every inch of my body.

"I missed you, Kiya."

"I know you did, but I missed you more." I slid down on to my knees and unzipped his pants. He released a long moan as I placed his manhood into my mouth. I had become pretty good at pleasing my man. When I first met him, I was a virgin and didn't have any skills, but after watching videos, reading books, and practicing, I had improved a lot. Once he was fully hard, I moved him to the floor and straddled him, placed him inside me. I began to slowly stir my hips in a circle over his pelvis. He grabbed my breasts and pulled my hair while I moved up and down, bringing the two of us to a simultaneous climax. Once we were done, I helped him up off the floor and joined him in the shower for round two.

We had our hard times, but I knew there was no other man I would ever want to be with for the rest of my life. I couldn't wait until we were an official family and all of our names finally matched.

CHAPTER 5

Adrienne Sheppard

Staring at the ceiling, I kept asking myself where I went wrong. I had a baby by a millionaire, I married him, then divorced him, and had a five-hundred-thousand-dollar cash settlement . . . so why was I broke and hundreds of thousands of dollars in debt? I'd lie in bed and ask myself this question almost every morning.

A year and a half ago, I realized my dream when I opened the doors to Belize, my very own VIP club in Philly. Celebrities, athletes, professionals, and beautiful people frequented my establishment. My club was so hot I was turning people away every night. Then my dream became my nightmare. My ex-boyfriend, Ian, and his cousin decided it would be a good idea to extort my customers and sell them drugs. When the feds arrived at my door with a case against them, I had to make a choice. Either I could testify against Ian and his cousin or go to jail with them. Orange is not the new black for me. I testified and did what I had to. Besides, Ian wasn't loyal to me. He not only ruined my club, he was also fucking and living with one of my employees in my Miami condo.

After I lost everything, it was difficult to rebuild my life.

The first few months after the trial, I went into seclusion. It was devastating to find out that the person I thought had my back was the person who had been betraying me all along.

Instead of being up and having it all, I was back to scrambling with nothing. When the club closed, it left me at a loss. It was crazy getting bills in the mail that I couldn't pay. Most of my creditors and vendors were threatening me with lawsuits and liens. Eventually, I lost my condo to foreclosure, and I moved back to Philadelphia permanently.

I got up out of the bed and tried to start my day. I pulled my naturally dark curly hair back into a ponytail and noticed my cocoa butter skin was paler than usual. Thirty-two years young, but I felt at least fifty. I was under so much unnecessary stress.

Ian tried to reach out to me, but I never responded to any of his calls or messages. There was absolutely nothing he could say to me that would make up for all the damage he caused. I had a hard time taking care of my daughter because of him.

My five-year-old daughter, Malaysia, was my life. My ex-husband and I shared custody of her. She lived with me, but spent time with him in Atlanta. We made our exchange at the airport. We took turns flying back and forth. It was a crazy arrangement, but it worked for us.

My daughter's father, DeCarious Simmons, retired from the NFL and opened up a chain of sports-themed burger and wing spots. My sole income was my monthly child support check. I got seventy-five hundred dollars a month, which was just not enough anymore. Asia was going to start private school in September, and I needed an increase. When I picked up my daughter in Atlanta on Friday, I also made a stop at family court.

My flight had a two-hour delay, so I ran slightly behind for my one o'clock court appointment. Traffic on I-85 north was crawling toward the Atlanta skyline. I picked up my rental car and checked into my hotel room.

I arrived fifteen minutes late to the courthouse. DeCarious was in the waiting area with his wife, Cherise. I hated her. She was a reporter on the news and my daughter's ugly step-mom. I tried to be cordial, but she was still mad that I took DeCarious from her four years ago. He dumped her and married me, because I lied to him and told him I was pregnant with our second child. When he learned the truth, he divorced me and went back to her. I spoke to them, but they looked up and gave disapproving glances. I guess they weren't happy about my three-thousand-dollar-a-month increase request. Oh, well. I looked over and watched my baby girl as she played with her favorite doll. Asia saw me and screamed, "Mommy!" She ran over and gave me hug. I kneeled down next to her and took in all her affection. I noticed white bandages swaddled around her arm.

"Hey, Asia girl. What happened to your arm?" I asked.

"Mommy, remember the burn? It hurts bad. Right, Daddy?" she said, looking in her father's direction. He looked down, and I turned my attention back to my daughter.

"What are you talking about, Asia? Are you okay?

"Yes."

"So, did you miss me?"

"Yes, Mommy. I've missed you so much, but I've been having so much fun."

"That's good, Asia. Are you ready to come home?"

"I can't, because I'm going to my school now."

"Yes, you are going to kindergarten after the summer."

"No, Mommy. I go to my new school now."

"You go to your new school now. Huh?"

How is that possible? I thought as I eyed DeCarious and his dumb wife. We agreed that Asia would be going to school in Philadelphia during the school year and spend the summers with him. Before I could react to the information that Asia had given me, we were called into the courtroom. Asia and Cherise stood in the waiting area, and DeCarious and I walked into the small courtroom. A sharp young guy in a well-fitted suit entered the courtroom behind us. He sat his briefcase on the table and sat next to my ex. It became instantly obvious that DeCarious had hired an attorney. He should have saved that money because he was going to lose. I shook my head in disgust when an older judge entered the courtroom with his black robe slung over his robust frame. The judge reminded me of an easygoing grandfather who would have sympathy for a struggling young mother. I smiled at him while we were sworn in and told to be seated.

The judge placed his glasses on his crinkled brown face before speaking: "Today we are here to hear the petition to modify the support payments for one minor child, Malaysia Simmons, age five, as well as an emergency custody hearing filed by counsel for Mr. DeCarious Simmons."

DeCarious's only emergency was that he didn't want to give me any more money. He was always so manipulative and conniving. Instead of trying to reach an agreement with me, he wanted to out-lawyer me. I didn't have representation, and I wasn't about to try to argue against his without my own. I raised my hand to get the judge's attention. He looked over at me.

"Your Honor, may I speak?" I asked.

"Yes, you may."

"I would like to ask if we can please postpone this hearing."

"For what reason?"

"Because I do not have an attorney, and I wasn't aware of an emergency hearing for custody. I thought we were here for the support case. I am not prepared for any of this."

"Ms. Sheppard, I understand your concern. However, this hearing has been scheduled for several months."

"Yes, the support case. But not anything else."

"Paperwork was sent to you, ma'am. I'm not sure why you didn't receive it. Due to the current circumstances, we combined both hearings. I'm sorry. I have to deny your request to postpone."

I sat back down and I looked over at DeCarious and his attorney. I didn't want to go through with the hearing, but I didn't have a choice.

"Counsel, are you ready?" the judge questioned.

"Yes. We are, Your Honor."

DeCarious's lawyer sprung up and said, "Your Honor, we filed for an emergency custody hearing because my client believes his daughter is in grave danger. His daughter, Malaysia, suffered severe burns and bruising on her left arm." He slapped enlarged pictures in front of me and then handed one to the judge. I took one look at the picture and almost laughed. Grave danger? Really? He knew what he was trying to pass off as abuse was an accident. A few weeks ago, I heard the loudest scream come from the bathroom. I'd accidentally left my curling iron on, and it fell on Asia's arm. I rushed her to the hospital and was told she had a second-degree burn.

After Asia was all bandaged up and ready to go, I was confronted by the hospital's social worker. She asked me if it was okay to speak with Asia alone. I cooperated that night, but that didn't stop them from making a surprise visit to my house to inspect and interview Asia again a few days later.

I was cleared of any abuse and told by the caseworker it was standard procedure to investigate burns because it was an early sign of child abuse. I had explained the situation to De Carious, but I never imagined he would try to use it against me.

In the small courtroom, DeCarious's attorney was performing like he was trying to sway a jury in a capital murder trial. I just shook my head at the ridiculous lies. After his long spiel on how I was a neglectful, abusive mother, he began questioning me about why I needed an increase in support.

"How are you supporting yourself, Ms. Sheppard?"

"I'm currently unemployed."

"I see. May I ask you, what is your highest level of education?"

"I have a degree in nursing."

"Nursing. That's a prestigious and rewarding field. Why are you no longer practicing?"

"I started a business."

"Okay. I understand. Were you the owner of the now defunct club Belize?"

"Yes."

"For what reason did your nightclub close?"

"Business declined."

"Declined? Is that a nice way of saying the federal government shut it down?"

"No, but that's partly true."

"Your Honor, the club closed after a federal investigation. Ms. Sheppard's boyfriend was convicted," he said as he presented him with paperwork. "Ms. Sheppard is still in communication with Ian McKinley, who is serving ten years in prison. Isn't that true, Ms. Sheppard? Remember, you are under oath."

"He is no longer my boyfriend, I don't talk to him, and no charges were ever filed against me."

He then moved on to his next round of questions and continued his relentless attack on my character.

"Now, you said you needed an increase in child support due to your daughter's private school tuition and other expenses associated with her schooling—or is it that what you need to pay your own bills? Please explain to the court why it is so difficult to take care of a child with seventy-five hundred dollars per month."

"I never said it was difficult. I said that Malaysia's tuition was twenty-five thousand a year and that I couldn't afford to pay it on my own and also pay my bills."

"So, you are using your daughter's tuition as an excuse to get more money from Mr. Simmons to pay your own bills."

"No, that's not what I said."

"Are you sure? Because according to your correspondence with my client, you said—and I quote—excuse me, Your Honor, some of the language is a little colorful—you wrote: 'Fuck you. Pay me.' Is that correct, ma'am? In response to my client's simple request to keep the current support order the same?"

"No, I don't recall writing that," I said, dumbfounded.

"Are you sure? I have a copy of the text message right here."

I thought about it. I knew I wrote it, but I didn't think De-Carious's dumb ass would bring it to court with him. "I'm not sure. I may have said that."

"So your daughter is no more than a paycheck to you?"

"That is not true."

"Did you burn your daughter with the curling iron because she was disturbing you while you were getting high?"

"No, I don't do drugs. And I left the curling iron on by accident."

"Accident, but didn't it take you days to inform her father about the injury? And didn't you try to conceal it?"

"No, that's a lie. I called him as soon as it happened. And now he is using this against me." I turned to DeCarious and screamed, "You know the truth. Why are you sitting here lying?"

"Ma'am, you need to address the court, not my client."

I started to lose it. "I am addressing the court and you."

"Please, control yourself," his lawyer snapped at me.

"You control yourself. I can speak, and he knows what the hell he is trying to do."

"Ms. Sheppard, you have to watch your language in my courtroom. I'll have you taken out," the judge barked at me.

"I apologize, Your Honor. I just don't like to be lied on."

"As you can see, she is extremely irrational. My client feels his daughter is not safe and that she is not being properly cared for. The minor child is beginning kindergarten this September, and my client has already enrolled her in pre-K. Mr. Simmons would like to give his daughter stability. The mother has questionable behavior and associates. We are requesting drug testing, and rehab if the test comes back positive. Also parenting classes for the mother to deal with her anger."

I stood still in shock. I wanted to cuss DeCarious and his attorney out, but I knew I had to do the opposite. I took in deep breaths to keep myself calm. Then I was prompted out of my daze when I heard the judge say: "Do you have anything to say, Ms. Sheppard?"

"Yes, only that I was totally caught off guard with all of these lies, but I am a great mother. My daughter has spent the majority of her life with me. I am a responsible parent. When I do not have my daughter, she is with my mother. She is never in harm's way. She was burned by a curling iron, but it was an accident, and I immediately took her to the hospital. I believe that Mr. Simmons is trying to railroad me, and is simply making up all of these ridiculous allegations so that he won't have to pay child support."

"Thank you for your testimony, Ms. Sheppard. Let me examine the information and then make a determination."

Fifteen minutes later, the court officer called us back into the courtroom. The judge put his glasses back on and began reading his decision.

"Based on the information I received today, I do not see any reason why Ms. Sheppard's custody order should be altered at this time. The current support order will remain the same. Both parties should enter into family counseling."

I felt relieved. I didn't get any more money, but DeCarious lost. It was over, and I was ready to go home when DeCarious started sobbing loudly. I wanted the judge to hit his gavel on something to officially end the case, but instead he asked De-Carious if he was okay.

"No, judge, I'm not okay. I want to beg the court not to think of my money right now, but to think of an innocent child. I don't know if you have any children."

"I do."

"So you should understand. My daughter, Asia, has never

had a stable home. Her mother moves all around. Philadelphia, Miami, and Atlanta. She has no sense of stability. She dates criminals, drug dealers, and she's using drugs. I just want the opportunity to raise my daughter. I want to give her a schedule and a home-cooked meal every night. I've already enrolled her in a pre-K at a private school that she loves. My daughter shouldn't have to catch a plane and be moved all around the country. She shouldn't be being burned. It wasn't an accident. Please review the facts. Please. I'm begging the court to make the right decision."

"What? Don't listen to him, Your Honor. You have already reached your decision!" I shouted.

The judge took off his glasses, and it almost looked like a tear was falling down his face. I could not believe that he fell for that dramatic act.

"Ma'am, just give me a few moments. Sir, you have made some valid points. Let me look at the case once more."

The judge returned again. This time, his position was a lot more stern.

"I have examined the claims today, and the minor child has always been in the custody of her mother. I didn't see any reason to modify that. However, after further review, I have changed my decision. Ms. Sheppard, you don't have a job and you are educated, which means you should be able to watch your daughter without the child being injured. I have been provided with evidence that your establishment was closed and that you associated with criminals. I also think it is unfair to transport a minor child over seven hundred miles every couple of weeks. It is this court's opinion that children should be in a stable, loving home. Ms. Sheppard, I do not feel like you are stable at this time. I'm going to award temporary custody to Mr. Simmons for one hundred and eighty days. You, Ms. Sheppard, will be required to take parenting classes, find a job to prove to the court that you are not using your child for monetary gain, and undergo drug testing."

"But, Your Honor. When will I see my daughter? I live in another state."

"Again, this order is temporary. You can have one supervised visit every other weekend. The child is not to leave the state of Georgia until this case comes back to me."

"But, Your Honor, I can't afford to fly back and forth."

"Well, ma'am, if your child means that much to you, you won't leave the state, will you? You have six months to get yourself together. Put this on my October calendar. I will bring the case back without prejudice. We will review the case again at that time. This order is effective immediately. Also, because the child is in the custody of the parent paying support, support is now terminated."

I was in total shock. He had stripped me of my parental rights, and I could only have visits with my daughter for six hours on every other Saturday.

I walked out of the courtroom angry, confused, and disappointed. I ran over to Asia and gave her a kiss. I told her that I loved her and that I would see her soon. I heard DeCarious call my name, but there was nothing to discuss. I knew I had to get out of that building or I would threaten, hit, or kill someone and be put in jail. I couldn't afford that.

The next day, I couldn't get out of my hotel bed. How had this happened to me? I thought I was going to get more child support. Instead, I lost my child and my source of income. I had to figure out a way to get them both back.

CHAPTER 6

Adrienne

The first three days after the court hearing, I kept asking myself "Why?" Why would the judge rule against me? Why would he believe DeCarious over me? Why wouldn't DeCarious just admit that I was an excellent mom and a good person? I had already booked my flight back to Philly, and I was sickened that I would not be taking my daughter with me. I had no family in Atlanta, and in order to get my life together and get stable, I had to go home.

Before I left, I was going to make sure I saw Malaysia. I packed up my stuff and checked out of the hotel. From the expressway, I dialed DeCarious.

"DeCarious, I'm about to leave and I want to come and see Asia before I go. My flight leaves at five." It took a lot for me to call and ask his permission to visit with my own daughter.

"When I wanted to talk yesterday, you didn't want to talk."

"You know what you pulled yesterday wasn't right, and I had to get out of there."

"Well, today is not good for us. We're taking Asia to Disney World and we won't be back until next week."

"Next week? I'm leaving today."

"We're already on the road. We're taking a family vacation."

I ignored his asinine family vacation comment, asked him how far he was, and if it was possible for him to turn around.

"No, we already left. You should have called earlier."

"You shouldn't have made up lies in court and separated your daughter from her mother."

"Well, you should have been a better mother."

Instantly, I snapped back, "Fuck you. I'm going to appeal this order. I'm a great mother."

"Adrienne, I wanted to work things out with you and split custody, but you were being greedy and look what it got you."

"If you wanted to split custody, you still could."

"I can't now because my attorney said that we can't go against the order. I'm listening to the judge. I'm sorry, but Malaysia needs to be in a stable home. And you need to find a job and get yourself together. I don't know what else to tell you."

I paused for a moment and gathered my thoughts. I was so angry and thankful that he wasn't home, because if he was, I would have driven to his house and killed him . . . which would have proved his allegations that I was unfit and unstable.

"DeCarious, you are going to regret that you did this shit to me. I'm my daughter's family, not you or your stupid-ass wife." Before he could utter one dumb remark, I ended the call.

I flew back to Philadelphia, saddened that I left my daughter behind. Suddenly, my anger turned into fear. I had an immediate reality check about my financial situation. No child meant no support. I started calculating my bills. I needed at the very least five thousand a month just to cover the basics. I wasn't even sure if he was going to give me my last child support payment that was scheduled for Thursday.

When Thursday came, I was petrified. I checked my account and the available balance was four hundred dollars. If my child support check didn't go through, I didn't know how I would pay my bills.

At one a.m., there was nothing. At 4:55 a.m., I refreshed and saw that the money was there. I took a deep sigh of relief and thanked God. I paid all my bills and decided I had to make some changes. When I went in front of that judge again in six months, I was going to be ready.

I called a few attorneys, and I settled on one who took the time to advise me on exactly what I needed to do. He recommended that I schedule parenting classes, get a job, and contact him once I had done both. He also charged five thousand dollars. Once we met in person and I paid his fee, he would attach himself to my case. Five thousand dollars wasn't a lot of money to get my daughter back, but I didn't have it at this time.

I knew I had to get it somehow. To save money, I decided I was going to move in with my mother, rent out my house, and go back to work. If I got with the right temp agency, I could work sixteen hours a day and have enough to pay my bills and hire an attorney. I contacted an agency and set up an interview. If everything worked out right, I could be working by the weekend.

The Nursing Tech employment agency was located on the third floor of an office building right outside of Philadelphia. I walked in and filled out an application. I had a seat and waited for my name to be called. The receptionist scanned my application and asked me a few questions.

"Have you worked for this agency before?" she questioned me.

"No."

"Okay, would you be interested in private residences or nursing homes?"

"I would prefer a private residence." I didn't want to tell

her how much I hated nursing homes, but I had to do what I had to.

"I just need your license number. It's in Pennsylvania, correct?"

"Yes." I gave it to her. She typed it in, and then asked me to repeat my name and my number again.

"Okay, is all your information correct?" she asked, turning the computer screen to face me.

"Yes, that's it."

"You haven't practiced in a few years. Are you aware that your license is suspended?"

"It is?"

"Did you forget to renew it?"

"Well, my ex-husband and I moved around a lot with his job. Can't I just renew it online?"

"If it hadn't expired, yes. But because it did, you have to take the boards over."

"I do?" I sighed hopelessly.

"Yes. I need people immediately. I would say to take a refresher course and go take the test again. Give me a call afterwards."

The nursing state boards weren't for another three weeks, which meant I couldn't make any moves until then. In the meantime, I moved in with my mom and put all my furniture into storage, then I put my house on Craigslist for rent. In my neighborhood, everything was renting for fifteen hundred dollars. I listed mine at twelve hundred. I wanted thirty-six hundred to move in. That would cover the first month, security, and last month's rent.

Being separated from my daughter hurt, and living with my mom at thirty-two years old was worse than living with her as a teenager. She was annoying and asked too many questions. She complained about me not cleaning my room and leaving her lights on. She came in my room daily and asked me if I was asleep. If I was sleeping, then I wasn't anymore because she had awakened me.

"Are you up?"

"What's up?"

"I have a letter here for you. It is from someone in Florida." I knew she already looked at the return address on the envelope. "Who's writing you from Florida?" she asked, peering over my shoulder.

"I don't know." I opened the tan manila envelope to see my ex, Ian's, name.

"How nice, a letter from that convict boyfriend of yours."

"Ex-boyfriend, Mom."

Ian had tried to reach out to me many times before. I never opened any of his letters and usually wrote "RETURN TO SENDER" on the envelope. Being slick, he sent the letter to his stepmother, who repackaged and sent it to me. It read:

> *Dear Adrienne,*
>
> *I know I have hurt you, but I need for you to forgive me. I put you in a horrible position and for that I am sorry.*
>
> *Since I have been here I've been thinking a lot. And I don't know how I will ever make this up to you. The one thing I keep thinking about is how I said no to that company that wanted to buy my script. I should have sold it. If I did, I wouldn't have been tempted to make money and I wouldn't have hurt you and destroyed your business. I am writing you to ask for you to sell "Falcon Hall Boys." We can split the money. You can set up a meeting with Blackground Films, because they will still want it and they can make any changes they want; I don't care. Sell it for whatever you can. You can give my half to my dad and stepmom. Once again, I'm sorry Adrienne, and I do love you.*
>
> *Love,*
>
> *Ian*

I balled up his letter and chuckled out loud. Don't nobody want that bullshit.

"What did he want?" my mother asked.

"Forgiveness, and for me to sell his script. Neither one is going to happen."

My mother left my room, and I became angry. Ian should just leave me the hell alone. Getting his letter was a reminder of how much in a shambles my life was. I hated living with my mom, missed my daughter, and I didn't have a man in my life. I needed a huge change. I called DeCarious and blocked my number. I was shocked that his bitch-ass wife answered the phone. She said, "Hello?" a few times, but I couldn't bear to ask another woman's consent to talk to my child. I was happy I had blocked my number. I hung up and decided to just study for my boards. Once I passed that test, I knew everything would be back to normal. I was going to get my baby and bring her home.

CHAPTER 7

Monique

The day had finally arrived and my stomach was in knots. I was seated in the third row in Barclays Center in Brooklyn, New York, at the NBA Draft. Everything around me made me feel extremely nervous—the crowd, the noise, the cameras flashing. I sat next to Carl and grabbed onto his shoulder as each name was called. They were announcing the fourth pick. I heard the commissioner say, "The Charlotte Hornets select guard from Temple University . . ." I shouted, "Thank you, Lord! Thank you!" I clasped my hands together in praise before he completed his sentence. I knew the next two words would be "Kadir Hall." He was the only first round draft pick from Temple. By the time I finished praying and stood up, Kadir was proudly walking across the stage putting on his teal and purple Charlotte Hornets hat. He shook the commissioner's hand and smiled for the cameras. My son had just become an instant millionaire. My phone immediately chimed with dozens of congratulatory texts and phone calls. I couldn't respond because I was too excited and full of joy. Carl brought me into his arms, and we both began crying and hugging each other. Everything I worked for had paid off. My boy did it. He was a professional basketball player.

Kadir walked off the stage and was bombarded by ESPN and other networks. He grabbed my arms as the reporters asked him questions. The first reporter asked him how he felt. I was proud that I raised a young man who could handle himself and speak articulately. But then, I heard his response: "My parents were always there for me and especially this man right here. I am who I am because of him and my faith." He pulled Carl closer to him and continued speaking. "He is the one who held our family together. He worked two jobs so I could be raised right." Then he must have seen the shocked expression on my face. Yes, it was true that Carl had paid the bills, but I was at every game. "Oh, and my mom, too! She is my rock and sacrificed her life to get me here." He then took his hat off his head and placed it on mine. *That is more like it*, I thought as I smiled for all the cameras and prayed again.

After the official draft, there was a party at the 40/40 Club. The club was beautiful and crowded with reporters, agents, players, fans, and celebrities. We were able to get right in, there was no waiting in line. It was a little overwhelming when I realized that people knew who Kadir was already. They were coming up to him, shaking his hand, and asking him for pictures and autographs. A group of young girls in short dresses that made me blush, with weaves that touched their asses, followed us to our table and were salivating all over my baby. One out of the pack was very bold. She came over and asked Kadir if I was his girlfriend. My son's eyes were fixated on the girl's curves.

"No, that's my mom." She waved at me then asked to take a picture with him. He took the picture and then said, "Oh, can I get a dance?"

"Sure." He told the girls he would be right with them, and then whispered to Carl, "They might want a drink or something, Dad. I need some money." Carl pulled out a couple hundred dollars and slipped the bills into Kadir's hand.

"Thanks. Soon, I'm going to be giving *you* money."

"Don't worry about it, son. Have fun. We will be over here."

"Don't go off anywhere with those girls. They just see dollar signs, Kadir," I cautioned.

"That. And this body. And my smile. I'll be back," Kadir said with a big grin.

I was hesitant about letting my son leave with a flock of girls, but Carl held me back.

"Relax, Monique. Let Ka have some fun."

"What if they try to take him somewhere?'

"He won't go. He's smart, and he knows better. He's just dancing. Look at him."

I looked over and saw my son in the middle of a circle of girls. "Okay, if you say so. I need a cigarette."

On my way to smoke, I ran into Kadir's agent, Eric Turner. He was a young black agent with the Daniel Ready Agency. Kadir wanted an agent who he could relate to, but who would also represent him well. Other agents had fancier presentations, but we chose Eric because he knew exactly who Kadir was and who he wanted to be. He came over to me and gave me a big, warm hug. I think he was more excited than I was.

"I told you we were going top ten."

"You did."

"Now we have to get Kadir ready for North Carolina. He leaves in the morning. He needs to head back to the hotel and be ready for his eight o'clock flight. The Hornets jet is flying us down to visit and introduce him to the GM and coaching staff. Then, once he signs tomorrow, they should have his first check wired into his account in a few weeks."

"That soon? That's great! So, is this a good team?"

"Yeah, they really don't have anyone like Kadir, so he will be a star. You can start looking for a house and get him settled. It's important that he stays focused and has a breakout season."

"Of course. He'll be ready. I'll let him have a little fun, then he'll be out of here no later than twelve."

"Good. See you in the morning." Eric walked off to talk to some of his other clients.

I walked out of the club and up the block to have a cigarette. With Kadir dancing, no one could tell me I shouldn't be smoking. It was a bad habit that I'd stopped, but when I was nervous I had to have a few. And I was nervous about all of this. Who knew that my decision to raise a little boy on my own at sixteen would lead to this?

My phone was still ringing, and I had a bunch of unanswered messages. I scrolled through my texts. Some of the numbers didn't have names, and I didn't know who they were. The texts ranged from "Congrats!" to asking Kadir to call them. Then my phone rang again. It was my bestie, CeCe.

"Hey, best friend! God is good!" she said.

I responded, "Yes, he is!"

"Where is my nephew? I want to tell him how proud I am of him."

"We're at a party. He is signing autographs already. They have Ka flying on a private jet to North Carolina to meet the team and everything."

"Really? That is so nice! This is so wonderful."

"It is. I can't believe it. I knew it was coming, but it is finally here."

"Don't get yourself all worked up. Tell Ka-Ka we love him, and that his cousin Faheem and I have lost our voice screaming!"

"I will. Hold on, someone is calling." I looked down at the screen. It was my mother. Our relationship had been strained since I was a teenager, and she never called me. I pushed the red decline button.

"That was my mom. I bet she wants to talk to me now. Everyone wants to talk. And guess what? Now I don't have anything to say."

"That's still your mom, Monique."

"I'll talk to her when I'm ready, because today is not the day." I laughed and told CeCe I would call her back. I put out my cigarette and walked back into the club to join Carl at the table. Kadir was dancing with another group of women.

"I spoke with Eric. He said that the team is sending for Kadir in the morning and he will get his first check in a few weeks."

"I was going to go to work tomorrow."

"Carl, you don't have to work anymore. Your son is rich."

"I don't know if I should retire just yet. We still have the mortgage."

"Kadir is going to pay that house off. Me and him already talked about everything we going to do, and who we're going to help."

"But I'm not living off of my son. It's his money."

"Well, forget about that souped-up Cadillac Escalade you always wanted. Ka said he was going to surprise you with it, but I'll tell him never mind. I'll tell him that you would rather drive your Hyundai."

"No, no. I'll take a new truck, but I want him to know his money is his, not ours."

"Hmm, it is just as much my money as his. He's been telling us he is going to take care of us since the sixth grade, and I'm damn sure going to take my son up on his offer."

"Let me think about it. Right now, let's get Kadir back to the hotel."

Chapter 8

Tiffany

Damien and I exited the courthouse. My dark frames covered my tear-filled eyes as I held Damien's hand. Damien was found not guilty of the DUI, but was found guilty of resisting arrest and ordered to do three hundred hours of community service. That was one issue behind us, but up next was the bankruptcy meeting. I knew there was a possibility that a few cameras might be outside, but I wasn't prepared for the sea of news reporters that were sticking microphones in our faces. They asked all types of idiotic questions that didn't make enough sense for Damien to answer.

One older white male reporter said, "Mr. Holcomb, why did you resist arrest?" Another female reporter asked, "What did you do with thirty million dollars? Why are you broke? Will you ever play again?" Then someone else called out, "What are you going to do now?" In every direction we tried to walk, more questions were thrown at us. His lawyer finally spoke up and said, "Mr. Holcomb has no comment." His attorney then turned and held open the SUV door, and we shut it on the nosy reporters. Right then and there, I wanted to break down. Once the door closed, I did. Tears came pouring down my face. Damien comforted me, and I wept in his arms.

The next day, we met with the bankruptcy attorney, Mr. Morrison. We went to his office and he explained the process to us.

"You are fifteen million dollars in debt." I knew we were in a bad financial situation, but this was far worse than I ever fathomed.

"Fifteen what?" I almost passed out. "How is that possible?"

"Well, you have multiple high interest loans in default, credit cards, and your mortgage alone is five million dollars. There are years of unpaid taxes and other debt. That's the bad news. Here is the good news, Mrs. Holcomb, you will not be involved in the filing. Your name was not on any of the loans or debt. You never filed joint taxes. You are in the clear." Hearing that information did little to calm me. I wasn't in debt, but my husband was. What was the difference? Damien got up from the table and walked away. I sat dazed in disbelief. Mr. Morrison asked Damien to come back and sit so he could go over our options.

"We can file two ways. One is you could file Chapter Thirteen, where we settle with your creditors and you get to keep everything—but you will have to enter into a repayment plan."

"That sounds good. How much are the payments?"

"With that plan, your payments would be around twenty-seven thousand a month for five years. Do you have anything put to the side?"

"No, and I don't have a job. All I have is about eight thousand dollars," Damien responded.

"I thought that was probably the case, so what I would suggest is for you to sell all your assets and file Chapter Seven. You will lose everything, but be done and be able to move on with your life in less than six months."

"I thought we could keep our house if we caught up on our payments," I said.

"You have two hundred thousand dollars of equity in the house and your creditors want their money. You definitely must sell the house. And I usually charge three hundred dollars per hour, but I'll charge you a flat fee of ten thousand dollars, which will include all the filing, preparing of documents, and court dates. I'll give you some time to think this over, but make a decision as soon as you can so we can complete your paperwork."

"Okay. We will."

The day couldn't possibly get worse, but it did. We pulled into our driveway to see that a tow truck was placing Damien's red 1967 custom Chevy Camaro on the lift. My husband had been hit by the biggest linebackers in the game and stood with his head high in court with no emotion, but seeing his prize possession being escorted down the driveway broke him. My big man jumped out of our car without putting it in park and ran over to his baby and yelled, "Don't take my car!"

The car was his first big purchase when he first signed. I didn't know he had gotten a loan on a car that was already paid off. He was so stupid.

The young black tow truck driver paused and recognized him. "DH, I'm sorry, man. I'm just doing my job.

"Don't take my baby. You can't take her."

"Look, we don't give it to the bank right away. If you come up with some of the money and make a deal, you can come and pick it up."

"Nah, let me call them. I can work something out over the phone."

"No. Sorry. I can't do that. You have to step away or I'm going to have to call the cops."

"All right." He stepped away and finally let the tow guy take the car.

Once in the house, I walked into our bedroom, passed my closet packed with racks of designer bags and shoes from tons of shopping sprees. I felt like throwing them all away, because they were meaningless now. Instead, I took off my suit and fell on the bed. I turned on my iPad and swiped through the news and entertainment websites. As I suspected, we were on every gossip blog. From the picture, I looked like I had everything under control. My hair was perfectly curled, my Birkin bag was coordinated with Louboutin heels, and my dark shades gave me a hint of glamour. Reality is so different than perception. The reality is I didn't know how I was going to get through the day. This was the most embarrassing thing I had ever been through. Damien entered the bedroom. I closed my iPad case because I didn't want him to see more bad news.

"We are going to make it through this. I'm going to come up with something."

"I know you will, babe. I'm going to take a shower."

"All right. Uhm, I'll order us Chinese. Tiffany, I love you."

"I know you do."

The shower jets hit my body from above, left, and right. The powerful steam spray was calming and exactly what I needed. Damien knocked on the bathroom door, but I acted like I didn't hear him. I'd locked the door on purpose. The last thing I wanted was Damien touching me. Right now, I wasn't attracted to him in the least.

During the course of our marriage, I forgave a lot. I looked the other way when he was playing and had random women who were "friends." The condoms hidden in his suitcases, the middle-of-the-night blocked phone calls. Even the maybe-baby whose mom settled with him for a million and half dollars and signed a confidentiality agreement to go away forever. I didn't make a big deal about any of it because I was his wife. I was the one who would be taken care of. The casual women were fun for one night, but I was there for a lifetime. Funny how life goes. I was the one who was plastered all over the Internet looking crazy. The one who stood by her man's side. Where were all his women? They should have to deal with this devastation and humiliation, not me. They were smart and had already moved on to the next player. I was the stupid one who said, "I do" and was stuck in the nightmare.

The next morning, the Chinese food we ordered the night before was half eaten on the nightstand. Damien was awake looking at his phone, but his back was turned toward me. Instead of dealing with him, I went into our home gym and worked out.

I watched *The Wendy Williams Show*. Her hot topics were funny and I was able to get my mind off of my own incredibly disastrous life.

After my workout, I checked my phone. I had thirty-two missed calls. My mother and brother called a few times, and so did some friends from college. They all were probably just checking on me, but I didn't want to talk to anyone. Then I heard loud knocking at my door. I was terrified. Who was it now? Maybe they were coming for my car. I peeked out and saw a petite woman walking toward a car. She saw me and waved. It was Erin Baxter-Jones. Why was she at my house? I opened the door.

"Sorry for coming without calling. I tried you a few times, and I was in Jersey for a couple of days. I wanted to talk to you." Erin and I were acquaintances when her husband played for the Broncos with Damien. We were friendly, but not friends. We were definitely not close enough for her to show up at my door unannounced.

"Can I come in?"

"Sure." I invited her in and told her she could have a seat.

"I know you are probably wondering why I am here."

"Honestly, I am."

She grabbed my hand and said, "I just wanted to tell you, I was where you are four years ago. There is a lot of uncertainty now, but you are going to make it. Me and Anthony had everything taken from us. I mean, they came in my house and took my *china*. We were so broke that we had to catch the bus. We were living on my mama's sofa in Trenton with our two kids." Tears starting falling from her eyes. "So, I know, okay? I've been there. It's hard, but you are going to make it out of this."

I got up off the sofa and grabbed a box of tissues and handed them to her. "This means a lot," I said.

"You're doing better than us. We didn't have a house or cars left."

"The house, huh? I don't know how much longer."

"What matters is that you have each other, and anything material you got once, you can get again. I'm sorry I just came to your home, but I wanted you to know if you need me for anything, you can call me. It is not going to be easy, but you can get through it."

A single tear slid down my cheek. She gave me the tissue box back.

"Trust me, the pieces will come back together. Just have your man's back. Stand by his side. He needs you. You are the only person that knows what he is going through."

"I will."

CHAPTER 9

Adrienne

My phone kept ringing. Whoever was calling was insistent on speaking with me. I lifted my head from under the covers and grabbed my phone from the bottom of my bag.

"Hello?"

"Are you okay, Adrienne? It's Zakiya."

"Yeah, I'm fine. I just have a lot going on."

"You are still coming to my wedding, right? It's a month away I haven't received your RSVP."

"Zakiya, I'm not sure I will be able to make it. I have so much going on, but how are the baby and Jabril?"

"They both are good. Everything is great. But is there anything I can help you with?"

"No, but I'll try to get there. If I don't, I wish you and Jabril the best."

I immediately looked up flights; the cheapest I found was nine hundred dollars and I didn't have that. She used to be my live-in nanny and looked up to me and now I was too embarrassed to tell her I couldn't afford a flight. Her wedding was the least of my worries. I had to sign up for a nursing re-

fresher course, take the boards, and find a job. In the meantime, I had to meet with prospective tenants.

A couple pulled up in front of my house in an older black
Toyota Corolla. They appeared to be young. They looked like
they shared a lot of meals together. The woman was short and
chunky, and her boyfriend was tall and husky. They got out of
the car and introduced themselves.

"Hi, I'm Talene, and this is my fiancé, Devaughn. I called
you to see the house. I'm sorry. We are a little late."

"That's fine." I showed them my empty house. As we
strolled through, I saw that I should have painted and that my
carpet could use a shampoo, too. I noticed the imperfections,
but the couple seemed oblivious to them.

"Look, sweetheart, a washer and dryer," the woman pointed
out. "No more trips to the laundromat. And look—two bath-
rooms! The place we live in now is a real dump," the girlfriend
said.

They didn't see any of the imperfections, but I still needed
to see if they could afford my home.

"Where do you work?" I asked as we came back down the
stairs.

"I work at Starbucks and bartend. We're in college. I'm
working on my master's, she's in undergrad and a waitress,"
the boyfriend answered.

"Oh, okay. Well, it's twelve hundred a month and you
need thirty-six hundred to move in."

"Twelve hundred? Our budget was around ten-fifty. Can
you bring it down a hundred dollars at least?"

"No, I can't," I said assertively. "Let me give you two
some time to think."

I left them in the kitchen to make a decision. I hoped they
got the house. I would be able to pay my mortgage for two
months, have enough money to book my flight for Zakiya's
wedding, and put money toward a lawyer.

I waited, and the boyfriend walked in and said, "We really like the place, but we have a few other places we have to look at. So we will be in touch."

"Okay." Damn. I thought about taking the $1,050, but it was too late, they were already in their car.

An hour later, the couple called back and asked if my house was still available.

"It is."

"We really like it, but we have been only able to come up with two thousand dollars. Would it be okay if we could give you that as a deposit today and the rest in two weeks?"

Two thousand was better than nothing, I thought.

"That's fine. You can move in with that. And just make it up when you move in."

I liked the couple because they didn't have any children to write on my walls and they were in college, so they would be busy studying and going to work.

I took the refresher course like the agency suggested. Truthfully, I didn't even mind. I felt better equipped to handle patients. Plus, I knew that once I got back on the floor, I wouldn't really have to do anything anyway.

The boards were held in the state office building in Harrisburg, Pennsylvania. I sat on the train for an hour and half and studied the entire ride. I walked into the test confident and ready. I was led to a computer. I had a seat and began the test. There were a hundred questions. They were pretty easy until I got to about the ninety-fifth question. I got a few wrong in a row, and then the test stopped. I tried tapping the screen a few times. I walked over to the test monitor and asked for assistance.

"Excuse me, something is wrong with my computer. My test cut off."

"No, I'm sorry it automatically does that when you answer more than ten questions incorrectly."

"But I only had three more questions to go out of one hundred."

"Yeah, I know. I'm sorry. I've seen people get to the last question and the computer shut off. Sorry. You can take the test again in ninety days." She took my paperwork, and the next person behind me approached her.

I stood to the side because I had another question to ask, but after five minutes, I decided I would just call.

I couldn't believe I failed the board. I didn't know how I could go another ninety days without a job.

CHAPTER 10

Shanice

I met up with my manager, April, in her Brooklyn condo. She was the main reason I was successful as a video model. She stuck by my side when I had drama, and I was grateful for her being one of the people who changed my life.

A few of the other girls she managed were there, too. I was the last to arrive because they all lived in the city. I came in, spoke to the other ladies, and sat at April's table. Some were new girls, and others I had worked with either on videos or hosted parties with.

"As you know, Eye Candy Queens have been offered a television show. Everyone here will be a part of it. It is a reality show, and we start filming this fall."

I was confused. "Hold up, wait. A reality show? I thought when you said we were getting our own show that we were going to be acting in it?"

"I did say that, but who in this room has taken professional acting classes?" No one raised her hand.

"Exactly, so we pitched them one show idea, but they came back with this. Once the reality show goes well, then I can get you movie roles and—"

"But people be looking down at reality show stars. They're all ratchet and fight," one girl stated.

"Ratchet, but getting paid fifteen to twenty stacks a night to show up at a party. That's about five or six times more than what I'm getting now," Ashley V answered.

"True. I could use that money," I said.

"Who's in?" April asked, and everyone raised their hand.

"Good, I want to introduce you to Doug Housley. He is one of the producers." Doug walked in. He had on khakis and a black t-shirt and was short with curly brown hair.

"Nice meeting you, ladies. Here is the premise for the show. The cameras will follow you as you go on auditions, modeling, hosting events, and behind the scenes with your family. You will talk about current events. What's going on in your lives, who you are dating, etcetera. So, think *Love and Hip Hop* meets *America's Next Top Model*."

"What is the name of our show?" I asked.

"It will be called *Eye Candy Queens: The Come-up*. Think about what it would take for the come-up. What do you need to do to get money and be seen?" Doug asked if we had any questions. No one did.

"Well, ladies, that's it. Shanice and Ashley V, you need to post about the event you're doing tomorrow in New Orleans. Text me as soon as the promoter drops you off at the hotel," April said.

I took an Uber back to the train station. I was so excited about the future. Maybe I would be moving to New York sooner rather than later! Once in the car, I posted the flyer for the club in New Orleans with me and Ashley V on it.

Right after I posted the flyer, I had four hundred likes and thirty comments. I read through the comments and there was one that stood out: *I love you. Call me cousin it's important.* Lately, my cousin Courtney had been stalking my page. I instantly deleted her comment, and then she wrote another: *Don't delete! Shanice, my mom wants to talk to you. Very important. Please call us.* I deleted it again. I had pushed them out of my life, and I didn't have any plan of letting them back in. She left her number in my comments six times in a row and asked me to call her. I hated her, but she wouldn't stop harassing me until I called her back.

"Hello?"

"It's Shani. What's up?"

"Oh, my God, cousin! How you been?"

"Good. What do you want?"

"Mom, it's Shanice on the phone. Here, talk to her. My mom wants to talk to you."

"Hello? Hey, baby! Wow! It is good to finally talk to you. Just in time, too."

"Hey, Auntie. Just in time for what?"

"I have some news about your mom. Won't you stop by? We will talk then."

"What about my mom—you know what? Don't tell me. I have to catch a flight in the morning, and I don't want to hear anything bad until I get back."

I had to be in New Orleans in the morning, so I called my daughter and checked in on her. Raven's grandmother, Valerie, has been raising my baby for me. They live right outside of Philly. Her son, Ray, was a career student and a spoiled grown man. Although his mom took care of our daughter, he still had very little to do with her. I was saying for years that I was going to bring my daughter to live with me. But it would have been hard for me to take her away from her great life with her grandmother and grandfather. They were stable. I, on the other hand, was in one city on Thursday and another one on Saturday. One day soon, I would get her. Just not right now.

"Miss Raven, did you do your homework?"

"Yes, Mommy."

"What did you do today?"

"I went to school and I read my books and now I'm watching television with my mom—I mean my other mom."

"Okay, make sure you say your prayers. I'm coming home in a few days and me and you are going to go out and have fun."

"Can we have another sleepover at the hotel?"

"Maybe. Just be a good girl, okay?"

"Love you, Mommy."

"I love you, too, baby."

CHAPTER 11

Zakiya

My sister Lisa was flying in from Philly to help me to finalize the wedding, and I couldn't wait to see her. Sometimes I wished she lived here. I missed her and my twin nephews. I picked her up from the airport.

"Another new car, Zakiya? Where's my brother-in-law? Tell him I need a car!"

"He's out. He will be probably be there by the time we get home. And this is old. He bought this, like, a year ago or something."

"I'll take an old Mercedes. I have to tell Jabril. His nephews be at school every day, saying, 'That's my uncle! Jabril Smith! He plays for OKC, and he is rich!' Hah, they almost get in fights because no one believes them."

"Really? I miss my babies."

"They miss their auntie, too. Why did we just speak your nephews up?" she said as her phone began to ring. "Why do they act like they can't live without me?"

She spoke to them as I drove to the dress shop. I was ecstatic to have my sister in town. There wasn't anything like having family around. We were even closer because our mother committed suicide when we were younger, and we had to raise ourselves.

"Before we go to the dress shop, I need something to eat. Maybe a cheeseburger or something," Lisa said.

"No cheeseburgers. If you have one, then I'll want one and I won't be able to fit into my dress!"

"One cheeseburger, Zakiya?"

"Yes, one cheeseburger can ruin it all. We can stop and get salads, but no fast food."

We arrived at the bridal shop and met with the woman who did the alterations. She brought my dress out, and I was excited to try it on for Lisa. The pictures I sent her didn't do it justice. When I came out of the dressing room, Lisa's face lit up and tears streamed down her face.

"You look so pretty, Zakiya!"

"Thanks. Now stop it, before I starting crying too!"

After showing her my dress, we came back to the house and went over the guest list and the menu. Lena had our lunch waiting for us, a spread of fruit and chicken Caesar salad.

"Thank you, Lena. That was so nice of you to make us lunch."

"You are so welcome, Ms. Zakiya. I will be leaving for the day. Do you need anything else before I leave?"

"No, have a good day."

Lena left and gave Jabrilah to my sister, and I turned my attention back to her and my menu.

"You are so blessed, Zakiya. You know that, right?"

"I know most nannies don't cook, right?"

"No, you are lucky because you live here and have a nanny. Period."

"Oh, yeah . . . that, too. Let's get back to the menu and list. Now more people want chicken than fish, but do you think we should have extra fish just in case? Or do a buffet? I wanted a buffet with chicken and fish, but the wedding co-ordinator said that it was tacky to have a buffet."

"Since when is a buffet tacky? Everyone gets to eat and go back if they're hungry."

I agreed with Lisa. My husband-to-be walked through the door. Jabril was six-five with chestnut colored skin and eyes. He had muscles, but they were covered with all his tattoos. "Look, Daddy's home!" Jabrilah jumped out of my sister's arms and ran over to her daddy's leg. He picked her up and kissed her, and she gave him a hug. He gave my sister a quick hug, then looked in the refrigerator.

"Bril, fish and chicken or a buffet with both?"

"It's your big day. Get whatever you want. I just want to be at the honeymoon," he said, as he slapped my butt, then poured a glass of grape juice.

"Stop! Not in front of my sister!"

"Did she tell you right after this wedding she's getting pregnant again?" Jabril asked Lisa playfully.

"You are, Zakiya?"

"No, I'm not."

"She is. She just don't know it yet. The practicing begins tonight. This time I want twins. Jabril the second and third." He was playfully kneeling, patting my stomach.

"Jabrilah, beat Daddy up. He's talking about having more babies. Get him, Brilah!" Jabrilah started tapping her daddy's face. We were all laughing when his phone rang. He looked at the screen and said, "Hold up, babe, it's my agent, Dave." I took the baby from him, and he stepped out of the room. I continued to play with Jabrilah and a few moments later he came back in the kitchen with a confused expression on his face.

"What's wrong, babe?"

"Dave said they traded me."

"What?" I said as I covered my mouth. Lisa grabbed Jabrilah and took her upstairs to give us some privacy.

"They had to free up some of the salary cap."

I was speechless. We had our life already here in Oklahoma.

I walked over to him and comforted him and said, "It's going to be all right. You are going to be able to handle this."

"This is crazy. I didn't even hear any rumors out there."

"It's probably a better team and better situation."

"A trade is never good, Zakiya. When they do trades, it is to improve the team and get something better. The bull they traded me for is garbage. He doesn't have anything on me. I didn't do anything wrong. I've been working out, being a team player, and putting up my numbers. And for all my hard work, they send me to North Carolina? There's nothing there."

I didn't want to agree with him. I didn't know anything about the Hornets and we didn't know anyone there, but it couldn't be any worse than Oklahoma. I immediately went into supportive fiancée mode.

"Bril, it may be a good thing. Now we will be on the East Coast again, closer to our families."

"Yeah, that's true."

"So, how soon does everything happen?"

"Dave thinks it is a good idea to get down there and start my workouts as soon as possible."

"Did you tell him you have a house to sell and you were about to get married?"

"Yeah, and they don't care about any of that. We may have to switch some things around."

My brain was still trying to process everything that had occurred in the last five minutes.

"Jabril, what do you mean switch some things around? I don't understand."

I wanted to be supportive, but I couldn't keep it together. I ran upstairs and broke down. My dream wedding was weeks away. I had the location, vendors, and dress all lined up, and now none of that mattered. I ran into our bathroom and I bent over the double vanity sink and began to cry some more. I turned the faucet on and washed up to remove any sign of tears. I looked up and told the woman in the mirror to be strong. She had to be. Jabrilah needed her; I needed her. I had to ask her what was more important, the wedding, or the marriage? I told her that no matter what, she needed to be by his side and make sure she was there for him. I prayed, and fifteen minutes later, I went back downstairs and found my fiancé.

"Why are you crying, Zakiyah?"

"Because you said the wedding was cancelled."

"I didn't say that we weren't getting married. We just won't be able to take a honeymoon right away."

"Oh, I thought you said to cancel the wedding."

"No, you weren't listening. I said change some things around."

"Jabril, wherever you and Jabrilah are is where I'm going to be. This is our family. I don't care about a honeymoon; I just need you. You are going to be great in Charlotte. You are going to make them regret that they traded you."

Chapter 12

Monique

Kadir had been staring at his bank account on the computer for the last two hours. I hadn't seen my son so excited since he was a little boy on Christmas Eve, waiting for Santa Claus to come. I tried not to be too nervous. I told him that the money would be in there soon and to just relax, but secretly I was just as excited as he was. Kadir would be getting seven million dollars in the next hour or so.

"So this is my plan, Mom," he said, looking down at his list "First, I want to go buy a car. I got to get my G-Wagon. Then, I want to transfer money to your account. I want you and dad to buy whatever you want. Give dad money for his truck and make sure you pay off the house on Nineteenth Street. Then buy you a car, pay off Grandmom Laura's house, give her some money, and then give Faheem and Aunt CeCe some money. Oh, and give Mom-mom Gloria some money . . ."

We waited and waited. Finally the seven million dollars appeared in his account. It was an indescribable feeling to know that you would never have any more worries in life.

I made one phone call to my job. It was official—I could

quit. I said something like, "I won't be returning." My manager said he understood and asked if I could get him tickets when we played the 76ers. I told him I would.

"Mom, let's go; the sales guy is waiting on me. I already talked to him. He knows who I am and told me to come through," Kadir said.

"Hold up, Kadir. You need to pray and then check your list again."

"I did, Mom, and the first thing on my list is to buy myself a car. Let's go get it."

"Right this moment?"

"Yes."

Kadir didn't even let me grab a jacket. He picked up his ID and ran to the car. I texted Carl and told him we had the money. He just texted back "Good," and said that he would call us on his lunch break. I got in the car, and Kadir was on the phone with Faheem. He told him we were on our way to the dealership.

"So, how does it feel?" I joked with my boy millionaire.

"I don't know yet. I will let you know when I'm behind the wheel of my new car. Now, chauffeur, to the dealership," he joked as he put on his sunglasses.

"Kadir, you can't go Hollywood on me."

"Yes, I can. What's your name again?" He laughed and gave me a side hug. "But seriously, Mom, thank you for having my back and making sure I went to practice even when I didn't want to."

"You're welcome, Ka."

"Mom, remember the time you drove two hours to Delaware, so I could play in my lucky t-shirt?"

"Yes, I remember you called me crying. I think I still have that dingy thing with the yellow armpit stains. But you have to be proud of yourself, Kadir. You made all of this happen. You believed in yourself, didn't give up, worked hard, and look, you made it. I'm proud of you, Ka."

"Thanks, Ma."

"I just want you to pray, remain humble, and when you get on that floor at the arena, just let them know that you belong and that you are just as good as they are."

"I will. I'm going to make you proud, Mom."

Whoever said money isn't everything was a goddamn liar. It changes what kind of car you drive and what zip code you live in. It also changes the way people treat you. Kadir had been doing a lot of interviews with the local news stations and everyone was making a really big deal over him. More and more people were asking for his autograph. When we went to the bank, the tellers' eyes widened and their smiles became huge. And the bank managers—men twice Kadir's age—started calling him "sir." Then you also had people who you don't know, but who know you. I bought Kadir about a hundred condoms and let him know I was too young, hot, and poppin' to be anyone's grandmother and to be careful of all of the girls he was meeting.

After Kadir got his G-Wagon, he bought himself two more cars: a white and blue i8 BMW and a black-on-black Range Rover with custom rims. He said they were his night and day cars, and he would drive his wagon when he was going out. He also treated himself to a diamond-encrusted Rolex watch that cost thirty thousand dollars. While we were in the jewelry store, he treated me to a diamond necklace and earring set. I was happy, but Carl thought he was spending too much money too fast. I didn't agree. He worked hard and deserved to enjoy the fruits of his labor. Kadir could get the excessive spending out of his system and save the rest of his career. I wouldn't let him go too crazy, but he could have a few shopping sprees. We found a seven-bedroom home with a pool house just outside of Charlotte. It was a rental, but it had everything that Kadir wanted. The first thing on his list was a pool. The house was seventy-five hundred square feet. It belonged to a family from Turkey. Their father was retiring and going back home and they weren't ready to sell their house yet. We decided that we would stay here for a year and then buy in the area. Kadir's agent said a few of the other players lived in the neighborhood.

Everything was good, but we did have a whole new set of problems. We were both still adjusting to having money. For the first week, I went shopping every day just because I could. I was picking up things I didn't need, but the fact that I could afford them gave me a rush. I had a junk room of things I needed to return. Kadir bought another Benz, but in white. He said he always wanted white-on-white. I had to tell my Ka that four cars was enough. I was going to yell at him, but he knew it was a dumb decision and took the car back without me even saying anything.

I had to change my phone number twice. I knew people were crazy, but not as crazy as my neighbor who asked me to pay for her father's funeral. She didn't even speak to me when I lived on the block. I felt bad for her, but I didn't know him. Then two ladies from my old job told me they wanted to start their own day care and asked if I could help them with an initial investment of fifty thousand. I'm just learning people are insane. I would never ask anyone that wasn't family for anything.

CHAPTER 13

Tiffany

Damien had been lying in the bed lifeless for weeks. My once handsome, clean-shaven, ripped husband had turned into an average looking, scruffy-bearded, unkempt man. As each day passed, I was becoming more aggravated and disgusted by him.

He barely got up to go to the bathroom and would hardly eat. When he was up, he was staring at the ceiling or at the television. I wanted to not care, to give up and hide away from the world in the house, but I couldn't take it anymore. I was being suffocated by his depression. Being crazy wasn't an option. There had to be one sane person in this marriage. Somebody had to get up and make some money. I came to the realization that I had to get a job and feed us.

He filed for bankruptcy, and we had to move out in six weeks, by August 15. I began packing, but I didn't know where we'd be moving to. That's one of the things that frustrated me about Damien. He kept me in the dark about everything, and that's why we were in the predicament we were in.

I couldn't live like that anymore, so I applied for a few positions at various companies and even some temp agencies. I worked at an agency when I was in college, so I knew that their hiring process was fast and I would get paid quickly. I used my maiden name on my résumé. Damien's name was plastered everywhere, and I didn't want anyone to know I was his wife.

I got a call back from an insurance company, and I was on my way to interview with the company. "I'm going out. There's some soup and crackers on the table if you want it. I'll be back after my interview." I stopped and came back. I felt like I had to say something reassuring to him. "When I get back, you better be up."

The interview went well; I was hired on the spot. I thought I would go right into management or something, but I didn't have any experience anywhere doing anything, so the only position that I was qualified for was entry level, which meant I would be answering telephones and informing people of their benefit options. I would make two dollars more than the people who didn't have a degree. Which didn't make any sense, but it was what it was.

I dialed my mother, and my stepfather, Wilson, answered the telephone. "May I speak to my mother, please?"

"Your mother is out in the garden. Do you want me to get her?"

"What is she doing in the garden?"

"Telling the gardener what to do, of course." He laughed, and I gave a fake laugh. I was used to his dry humor.

"Yes, I really need to speak to her. She is not answering her cell phone." He called out for her and then she came to the phone.

"Tiffany, what is it? Is everything okay? I see I've missed your calls."

"Yes. Mom, have you seen my degree?"

"No, I haven't. I think it may be upstairs in your room. I'll look for it. What do you need it for?"

"I got a job and they need a copy of it."

"A job? Oh my," she gasped.

"I'm working for an insurance company. I'm going to finally put my business degree to use."

"I'll look for it and if I see it, I can overnight it. But this is insanity. It is embarrassing enough for me to have my friends call me and say that my daughter is on the news with her broke DUI husband, but now you are working at an insurance company? So I suppose you're trying to take care of him now?"

"No. He's looking for a job."

"Enough is enough, Tiffany. I raised you better than this. I will not have my daughter stuck in a dead-end job for the rest of her life and taking care of a no-good man. You showed your support for long enough. It's time for you to leave him." The tone of the conversation was harsh—even for my mother.

"I can't just leave him. He's my husband and I love him."

"Love doesn't pay the bills. Get off of that train, Tiffany, because it is about to crash."

"Mom, we are going to be okay. Damien has a plan."

"You are not going to sit here and waste your life with him. You are getting a divorce."

"Mom, I can't believe you. How could you say something like that? He bought the car you are driving and has sent you on plenty of vacations. And now—just because he is down and out—I'm supposed to leave him."

"You would if you were smart. Do you need any money?"

"No, we will be fine. Everything is going to work out."

"I sure hope so."

CHAPTER 14

Shanice

I was hosting rapper Don Santos's mix tape release party with Ashley V in New Orleans. The front desk at our hotel called to tell me our car was here.

My wand curls flowed past my breasts and I was wearing a cream bodycon dress with a plunging neckline. I thought I looked great until I saw Ashley V. She looked gorgeous in a black one-piece. She had all ass with no stomach and the tiniest waist. She walked over to me, told me to fix my hair, and said that I had lipstick on my teeth.

"Thanks."

"No problem. We represent the Eye Candy Queens. I can't have you out here looking a mess."

"Thanks. So what do you think about the show?"

"I think by this time next year everyone will know our name. So get your business together right now."

"What do you mean?"

"I mean, girl, you have to get these coins while you can. I have a t-shirt and swim line, I act, and I have a cell phone store back home in Dayton. I'm saying while we got this opportunity you better start yourself a business, so you can eat forever."

"Okay. You're right. I have to think of something to sell."

I heard that Ashley V was stuck up, but she wasn't. We talked the entire ride to the release. She was smart and sweet and shared a lot of information with me.

We entered the club, and the promoter, Jahti, took a picture with us and said, "So, ladies, we're sold out. Everybody in the city is here to see the lovely Ms. Ashley V and Shani Amore. Make sure y'all work the room."

The music was blasting, and the entire club was filled over capacity. Santos's people made sure we were taken care of. People wanted to take pictures with us and Don Santos.

"Hey, beautiful. Don't I know you?" a deep, sexy voice asked. I turned to see a handsome guy who could be the rapper Common's cousin. He had a rugged beard against his almond-colored skin. I wasn't interested in meeting anyone, but my mind could be swayed by the right man.

"I don't think so," I responded.

"I do know you. You're the chick from the 'Slide It Down' video with the fat ass."

"Yeah, that was my first video."

"How could I forget that ass? Damn," he said, eyeing every curve in my dress. "Can I get a picture?"

I struck a sexy pose, leaning over the cute guy's shoulder. I thought he was going to ask me for my number, but he didn't. Instead, he tried to grab my ass and asked, "How sweet is that pussy?" Before I could answer him, he said, "Let me buy you a few drinks. I bet you take it in that big ass?" I thought about slapping the fuck out of him, but I remembered I was working. Instead I whispered in his ear, "Don't worry about it. You can't afford it."

"You sure I can't?" He pulled out a stack of twenties, and I laughed. I knew he was flashing his paycheck that took him two weeks to make. Dudes like him were the reason I was single. I looked around the club, and in every direction I saw couples. Loving couples who were dancing and hugging each other. Watching them dance reminded me of Jabril. Suddenly, I became jealous, because me and my bae used to club together. I don't know why I was in my feelings, but I was. Five glasses of champagne does that to you. Alcohol brought out true feelings. I wished I could stop thinking about him. I missed his scent and his touch. I used to love the way we would go at it all night. He would fuck me so good that I couldn't think straight. Besides the good sex, he was my friend and just an all-around good person. I couldn't believe he wasn't in my life anymore. I looked on his Instagram, and I saw pictures of him, his daughter, and his fiancée. That made me sadder. I was hoping to see pictures of him being single, not as a family man. At least then I would have thought I had a chance. Seeing him happy let me know it would never happen.

I had thirty minutes left at this club, and then I would be on my way back to the hotel and hop on a plane home in the morning.

"Excuse me," a voice said, as I felt a tap on my shoulder.

"I'm not taking any more pictures tonight."

"I don't want a picture, I want to introduce myself. I'm the owner and producer of Don's label. Deuce."

I turned around and said, "Okay, nice meeting you." I wasn't interested. He smelled good and was handsome, but he had about a hundred and fifty extra pounds on him that I didn't find attractive at all.

"So, how long are you in New Orleans?"

"Tomorrow I leave."

"Shanice Whitaker, when you get home, you need to let me take you out." He thought he was special because he knew my real name.

"You don't even know where I live."

"It doesn't matter. I can fly you to me from anywhere. You have to give me your number."

"Is that so?" I liked his confidence, but that was all. I've never been into big guys. I liked my men in just about any shade of brown, but I had an over five foot eleven requirement and a nice body was just one more category on the checklist. With my heels on, I was taller than him. He couldn't have been over five foot seven. "All I have to do is stand here and look good."

"I need to take you out, and you will lose that little Philly thug attitude."

"That was kind of funny. You sure know a lot about me, Deuce. Are you a stalker?" I smirked at him.

"I'm not. I just know things. But I'm serious. When you get back, I want to take you to dinner."

"I'll think about it."

"Now, *that* was funny. Let me see your phone." He grabbed my phone and stored his name and number. Then he called himself. I had to admire this confidence and how he stole my number.

"I'll call you tomorrow."

The next day, I hopped on my flight, and after we landed, I powered on my phone, only to see five text messages from Courtney. She was a pain in my ass. I posted a picture on Twitter with the caption: "Just landed!" and two minutes later my phone started ringing. It was Courtney again, stalking me. I knew I should have blocked my number when I called her.

"I see you're back in Philly, can you come to the apartment?"

"Courtney, tell your mom I'll be there."

"Like, what time?"

"By four." I wanted to tell her to stop harassing me, but I just hung up instead.

I pulled up to my aunt and cousin's apartment. There was trash on the ground and a few dudes in front of the corner Chinese store. I got out of the car, and one of them shouted if I could give them a ride and did I have a man. I ignored them and banged on the door. Courtney answered. I hated my cousin, but she was still pretty, skinny, and cute with a short blond haircut. She forced a hug on me. "Oh, my God, I'm so happy you're here!"

I looked around, and everything was still in place like how it was when I left years ago. I was so happy the apartment no longer felt like home.

"Have a seat, cousin. I am so proud of you." She immediately started taking pictures and behaving like I wasn't the same person who shared a bedroom with her all her life.

She pushed some mail and a blanket off the sofa so I could sit down.

"So, cousin. I missed you. What's up? How you been?"

I didn't bother to hold in my dislike for her. I yelled out, "Bitch, I still don't trust you."

"Why, Shani? I've changed. I swear on my kids."

"Kids? You have one daughter."

"Well, you know what I mean. But, no, I go to church now. I really have changed. I have a job at a day care and everything. When I was dropping my baby off, I asked the lady if she needed help. She hired me. And I'm helping my mom."

"So, what's going on? Why are y'all contacting me?"

"My mom will tell you when she gets here."

"Where is your mom?"

"She went to the store. She will be right back. Sit down. So how you been? What's going on? I see you still doing videos and parties. That's so good. Remember when we were kids, we said we were going to grow up and become famous? You really did it!"

"Courtney, you said your mom had something she wanted to tell me about my mom. I don't have time to sit here with you and reminisce. I didn't forget all that trouble you started, or how you talked about me to the radio stations and blogs."

"Whatcha mean? I never started trouble before! I know we went through what we went through, but I'm different now. I don't even go out anymore. I don't drink and I have a

boyfriend. I just be chilling with him. Back then, I was getting high and drinking. You know that."

"Smoking a little weed doesn't make you tell your family's
business."

"I was on more than that, but that's another story."

I missed my cousin Courtney, but she wasn't trustworthy. I
knew she could strike again. Courtney's daughter, Ayana,
came up the steps, carrying a white plastic bag with bread in it.

"Where's Grandmom?" Courtney asked her daughter.

"She is coming up the steps." I ran up to give her a hug. She
pulled back. It was messed up. Her daughter was acting like
she didn't know me.

"Shanice, oh my! I'm so glad you're here. You look so
beautiful. I am so very proud of you!" my aunt Rhonda said,
coming in behind her granddaughter.

"Aunt Rhonda, why are you walking so slow?"

"I'm sick. I'm going to be okay, though. My doctor said I
just have to slow down and take my medicine." I let her have
my seat. She coughed before speaking and said, "So, the
news I have for you is that your mother was given parole. She
is coming home next month."

Next month? I hadn't seen her since I was six years old.
She killed my stepfather for abusing her. I didn't think I
would ever see her again, and now she would be home?

"What? How?"

"She knew she was up for parole, but didn't want to get
her hopes up high. I couldn't believe she called me. I was so
happy to hear my only sister's voice. We caught up for over
an hour on the telephone. I told her you were out here being
a model and making lots of money."

"What did she say?"

"She said she couldn't wait to see you and meet your little
girl. That's why Courtney been trying to get a hold of you."

"So where is she going to live?"

"Here. I know we don't have much room, but we will

make do. Courtney is going to go on the sofa. And I'm going to put her in her own room. And when she gets on her feet and starts working, maybe we can afford to move."

I hadn't seen or heard from my mother in more than twenty years, but I couldn't imagine her leaving jail to come home to a dusty apartment. I loved my mom, even though she wouldn't talk to us. I knew I had to get her and my aunt a bigger place, but I didn't know how.

CHAPTER 15

Adrienne

I could not sit in Philly for two more months. I was thinking about going back to Miami, or to Atlanta to be with Malaysia. I needed to get my old life back. My current life of deprivation had to end. I sat on the bed, undecided. What the hell was I going to do? At least I had a tenant who could pay my mortgage, but I needed another stream of income. I was not used to being broke. I needed to find a rich older man or something. I couldn't live like this forever.

The mail came and another letter from Ian arrived with another copy of his script.

> Dear Adrienne,
>   I don't know if you have read any of my letters I've sent. If you have, you haven't responded. I want you to take my script and sell it. It is the only way I can pay you back. You don't have to do any work, all you have to do is get it to Blackground Films. And if they don't want it anymore, hire a film agent. The minimum it should sell is for fifty thousand dollars. You can take sixty percent and give the other forty percent to my

*dad and stepmom. She is going to invest it for me, so I
can have something when I come home. Please, I'm
begging you. If you don't do it for you, do it for
Malaysia, give the money to her. Please, I know you
need this money. Let me make it up to you and this is
the only way I know how to do this from where I am.
I pray that you both are okay. I think about you constantly and hope that you take advantage of this
opportunity. Adrienne, please write me back.*

    Please respond,
    Ian

The script sat on my dresser for several days, and I finally
got around to reading it. Pages one to ten were good. Then
eleven to thirty-five caught my attention and made me want
more. I kept reading. Within an hour, I finished reading all
one hundred and twenty-five pages. I remembered it being an
excellent read, but I think my hate for Ian made me discount
his work. The script was about five guys who all lived in the
same dorm, Falcon Hall. They made a vow to each other that
they would all graduate college no matter what. Some made
it, others didn't.

The more I thought about it, the more interested I became
in *Falcon Hall Boys.* Maybe Ian was right. This could be
what got me out of all my debt. If I was going to sell it, I
needed to register the script with the Writer's Guild of America. It belonged to whoever registered it, and then it would be
me. I did a little research, and I learned that I should make a
minimum of fifty thousand dollars—maybe a million. It was
worth a try. He fucked me out of my dreams and hundreds of
thousands of dollars, and it was only right that I got some of
my money back. I took the liberty of changing a few things
and making it my own. I read a bunch of articles on screen-
writing and selling scripts. I contacted Blackground Films,
like Ian asked, but they had merged with another company
and weren't accepting any unsolicited scripts. So I submitted

Falcon Hall Boys to some other small film companies and a few agents and hoped that someone would be interested in it.

A couple days later a producer from Aviera Films reached out to me. He had read the script in one night and asked if I was in L.A. and available to meet. I lied to him and told him I was. I scheduled a meeting with him at the end of the month. I checked out the company's website and read that they had produced a few indie films that made it to the Sundance Festival and were purchased. I needed to meet with him, sell him the script, and start recouping my losses. And if I did sell it, I would give Ian twenty-five percent, not forty. He didn't deserve anything.

I felt excited for the first time in months. Things seemed like they were possible again. I booked a flight with my child support money and decided my bills could be paid when I returned.

"Mom, I will be going out of town and I need you to do something for me."

"What do you need me to do and why are you going out of town?"

"I have to take care of some business. I'm going to L.A. to sell Ian's script at the end of the month and I need you to pick up my rent money."

She shook her head and said, "You are a horrible mother. You should be where your daughter is."

"How? I couldn't stay there. I didn't have any money. All I can do is get a new lawyer and fight to get my custody back. I can't go kidnap Asia, or I will go to jail."

"Well, no court would have been able to tell me what to do with you . . ."

"Remember my dad and his family did not want to be bothered with you or me. You were just his white ex-girlfriend with his biracial child. So you didn't have that problem, now did you?"

"Adrienne, life is not about running from one dream to the

next dream. People get up and go to work. When are you going to wake up? You've always been a dreamer. It is time you get real about life. Get your daughter, get your old job back, and get your life together. Marry for love and not for money, and stop living in a fantasy world."

"Uh huh, Mom. Fantasy world? Whatever."

I was trying to remain respectful, but I had to say something back to my mother. She hit a major sore spot. Why did she have to bring Malaysia into the conversation?

"What the hell do you want me to do? I have to make something happen, or I'm going to be stuck with your ass for the rest of my life."

"Don't curse at me."

"How about you mind your business and when I come back, I'm moving out. How does that sound? I have better things to do than waste away at the same job for twenty years. Do you understand that I'm hundreds of thousands of dollars in debt? How long do you think that will take to make at a regular job? If I don't take a chance, how will I come up with that kind of money?"

"I don't know, but you'll wake up one day, because life has a funny way of catching up with you."

"I *am* awake, and it already has. And now it is time for me to get ahead of it again."

CHAPTER 16

Zakiya

I was finally Mrs. Jabril Smith. Our wedding was wonderful: it was a perfect July day filled with family, friends, and love. I had the big day that I had dreamed of since I was a little girl, but the next day Jabril flew to Charlotte to meet with his new team. Jabril sent Jabrilah, Lisa, my nephews, and me on a Disney Cruise vacation and told us we could go on two vacations after he was settled in with his new team.

So far, I liked Charlotte. It was like a city, but still had Southern charm. Instead of renting a big house, we opted for a condo. It was beautiful. It came already furnished. We had twenty-foot-high ceilings, hardwood flooring, and gigantic windows overlooking the city, and two terraces. I liked the coziness of having only four bedrooms and two baths. I hung up an oversize wedding picture in a gold frame and a few pictures of Jabrilah to make it feel more like home. Since we were only nine hours away from Philly, Jabril's mom and uncle visited twice shortly after we moved. It was great having the company and help with Brilah, because I missed having Lena around. I had asked her if she wanted to move with us, but she couldn't leave her husband and children.

I didn't want to tell Jabril yet, but I liked this move. The team colors were pretty, and the people were nice. The only thing I wasn't excited about was the new set of wives and girlfriends that I had to encounter. Would you believe one of the wives of the players sent me a message on Facebook just a week after moving, welcoming me to the team? She wanted to set up a lunch date. I had no intentions of getting to know her or anyone else on this team. For what? I decided that I didn't want to be bothered. All of the drama that I experienced with the last set of ladies was enough to teach me a lesson. "Hello" and "Goodbye" would suffice this time.

CHAPTER 17

Monique

Carl didn't quit his job, but he took a leave of absence. If he wanted to work hard every day when he didn't have to, that would be on him.

CeCe, Faheem, and Mom Laura came down to our new house for the big cookout that I was throwing for Kadir. He would be leaving for rookie camp in two days, and I wanted my son to enjoy his family and friends before the real work began.

"Y'all made it! Welcome to Charlotte," I happily shouted to my family as they came through the door.

"I'm so happy you sent that driver to the airport for us. The man was so nice. He had a sign with our name on it, and he put the luggage in the trunk and opened my door," Mom Laura said as she walked in the house and gave me a warm embrace.

"That's nothing, Mom Laura. You're welcome."

"Faheem, look at you! I see that mustache and facial hair! Come on in."

"Philly in the house," my best friend playfully hollered,

dropping her luggage off at the door. "Wow, this house is beautiful."

"Thank you! Let me show you guys to your room."

Kadir ran down the steps and over to Faheem. "What's up? Y'all finally made it. Let me show you my new car." They ran to the garage like two little boys.

"I can't believe this house. You got this house together quick. Wow, I can't even get up these steps! How big is this place?" Mom Laura huffed. "How did you find it?"

"The real estate agent showed it to us, and I said we'd take it. We had to hurry up and find something so Ka could be comfortable and ready for work."

We reached the top of the steps, and I walked to the bedroom closest to the stairs. "Mom Laura, here is your bedroom. I didn't get a chance to complete it yet. I ordered the curtains, but they are on back order."

"This is plenty fine. I might not go home. I'm moving in here with y'all."

"You can stay. You know Carl and I don't mind."

"Where is Carl, anyway?"

"He went to Lowes to go pick up the grill."

She sat on the bed, and then CeCe and I walked down the hall. I showed her to her room.

She closed the door and shouted, "Mo, I am so happy for you. You did good, girl. Like, really, look at your baby. The one we used to take to the park."

"We did good, just like we said we would. Faheem and Kadir made it. They graduated high school without any babies and went to college."

"Well, Faheem is not going to be a millionaire, but I'm proud of him. He made the dean's list and has a little girlfriend."

"A girlfriend? Did you tell him that you don't want to be a grandmom?"

"Yes, I told him. I'm too sexy to be a grandmom. I can't

believe we made our moms grandmoms so early. Now we would die if it happened to us."

"I already had the conversation with Kadir. I said use a condom each and every time. Don't bring home any babies, strippers, or white girls. I'm going to be the only woman waiting outside the locker room for my boy. It's either me or Carl. So, what else is going on with y'all?"

"Nothing, only thing I'm stressing a little over Faheem's school balance. He's going back next month and I'm just hoping all his scholarships and financial aid come through."

"Don't stress about no scholarship money, girl. I will pay the balance."

"It's six thousand dollars."

"No, problem, Cee. I got it."

"But . . . I wasn't telling you so you can pay it . . ."

"I know you wasn't, but it's no big deal. Tell Faheem his aunt Mo hooked him up."

"Damn, just like that you just solved a big problem for me. Thank you, Mo. We will pay you back."

"No need. I'll write the check now." I ran into my room to get my bag, took out my checkbook, and wrote her a check for eight thousand dollars. "Here, and get my nephew his books and a few pairs of sneakers, too."

After everyone was settled in, we sat by the pool and Carl cooked on the grill. He had rows of salmon, chicken breast, turkey burgers, and a few beef ribs cooking. I was on margarita duty. "Who wants a drink?" I asked, pouring more tequila into the frozen strawberry mix.

"Mom, let me get one?" Kadir asked.

"No, boy. You can't drink. You're not twenty-one yet."

"Hah. You're still a kid even though you're rich." Faheem laughed.

"Let the boy have a drink, Mo. Don't let me tell them how you and CeCe used to get drunk off my Johnnie Walker and put water in it."

"Yes, the good old days," CeCe said.

Mom Laura shook her head. "Y'all were drinking my liquor. That's why I was always running out."

"Here, take a margarita to make up for it. Oh, Kadir, go get the jerseys and give everybody one."

Kadir ran into the house and came back and handed everyone his teal jersey with "Hall" written in purple big letters and the number 45 under it.

"I'm so proud of you, baby. I'm wearing mine to work," Mom Laura said.

"You know I'm wearing mine on campus," Faheem said.

"And we all are wearing these at his first game. One day everybody is going to be rocking number forty-five."

"They will, but, Mom, you make sure you don't turn yours into a dress. I'm not joking. Seriously."

"Whatever, boy." I played around with the jersey, being silly and dancing to a Beyoncé song.

"I can't believe she came again and I missed her. Every time she comes to the city, I miss her," CeCe sighed.

"Who, Beyoncé? Me too. Maybe we need to go to her. Look and see where she is going to be next. We can fly out to wherever she is."

"Oh, really? Okay? We're just going to fly to see Beyoncé?"

"Yeah, we are."

CeCe pulled up Beyoncé's tour dates and then passed me the phone and said, "She's not going to be in the States again for another seven months."

I looked at the phone. "She's going to be in England. That's not that far. We can fly to London to see her."

"No, that's crazy. We can just see her next time she comes. Plus, I have to work."

"Call out from that job, let's get our passports and go to see Bey in London!"

CeCe and I went into the house and booked our reservation. Carl said I was doing too much, and Kadir and Faheem called us Stans. Who cares? We would be leaving for Europe in two and a half weeks. It felt wonderful wanting to do something and being able to do it as soon as you wanted to.

The party continued. Carl was taking a break from the grill, playing spades with Faheem and Kadir. CeCe was helping me straighten up the kitchen when the doorbell rang. We didn't know anyone in our neighborhood. We thought that maybe our music was too loud and the neighbors wanted us to turn it down.

I opened the door, only to see my crazy mother, Dottie, and Aunt Jean. I hated my mother and my hate was even stronger for my aunt. During my pregnancy with Kadir, her nickname for me was the "Pregnant Prom Queen." She and my mom made my pregnancy miserable. They both told me I wouldn't be anything. They were in church every Sunday, but still did and said every wicked thing possible to make my life hell. As religious people, they weren't supposed to be so mean but their mental abuse could have very well driven me to suicide.

They both yelled in unison. "Surprise!"

"Huh? What the hell?" I did not hide the fact that I was highly annoyed. I walked away from the open door, leaving my aunt and mom in the doorway. I walked back to the yard to confront Carl. I knew he was behind the awful surprise.

"What the fuck, Carl? Why the hell would you invite her?" Everyone turned around to see why I was so upset.

"Mom, invite who?"

"Ask your father." We both looked over at Carl. He put his hand of cards down and pulled me to the side. He began confessing before I could interrogate him.

"Yeah, I invited her. Be nice to them." I couldn't believe Carl would do this to me, especially on a celebratory weekend for my child. My mom was such a negative person. She could find something wrong with heaven. She would probably say, "It's too peaceful in here, don't y'all have some noise?"

"Mo, I didn't feel right with my mom being down here and yours not. She should be here to celebrate Kadir, too!"

"Carl, how could you? I'm not ready to deal with them. Well, they can't stay here. There isn't enough room. You better book them a hotel room."

"There's two empty rooms upstairs."

"I don't care, she's not staying here." I was angry and minutes later, my mother and Aunt Jean came in to the backyard uninvited.

"So, you were going to just leave me at the door, Monique?"

"Hey, Mom," I said shaking my head and taking a deep breath.

"Kadir, look who's here!" I announced, pretending we cared. Kadir ran over to them and greeted them. My mother and Aunt Jean approached him like a loving nana and auntie, kissing his cheek and telling him how handsome and tall he had gotten, and how proud they were of him. It was unbelievable they had never showed up at games or sent any birthday gifts, and now they were his biggest cheerleaders.

"Y'all want something to eat?" Kadir asked.

"No, we ate at the airport waiting for a cab. Uhm, y'all got all those cars and nobody couldn't pick us up?" Aunt Jean questioned.

"We didn't know or we would have sent a car like we did for Mom Laura. Let me get your bag and show y'all to your room." Kadir came up and took their things. I followed them into the house.

"So, Laura get the special treatment, and we get the slave treatment," my mother mumbled under her breath.

It was hard for me not to cuss my mother out and tell her she wasn't invited anyway. I looked over at Carl and he waved his hands in front of himself, giving me the signal to chill. We followed them up the steps, and the first thing Aunt Jean had to say was something negative: "This is a whole lot of house, Monique. Hmm . . . you better hold on to some of that money. Put some up for a rainy day. If he gets hurt or something, he doesn't get that money."

I corrected her. "Yeah, basketball money is guaranteed. Even if he gets hurt tomorrow—God forbid—he is still going to have the money on his contract. We're good. We couldn't spend it all at once if we wanted to."

"I don't care what you say, it's easy to go broke. You hear me, Kadir?"

"Yes, ma'am. I won't."

"My son won't be going broke at all. He has a smart mother and great financial advisors," I lied.

"Mike Tyson went broke and he was ten times richer and better than Kadir," my mom said, joining the conversation. That last comment deserved to be ignored.

"So, Mom, how many days are you staying?" I asked.

"Until Saturday. I have to make it to church on Sunday. You have to praise the Lord for all your blessings. From the looks of things, you need to be praising God twenty-four seven."

"I do. Every day."

The weekend wasn't as horrible as I expected. As much as the Evileens were against spending Ka Ka's money, they had no problem accepting his generosity at the mall. He gave them both one-thousand-dollar Visa gift cards. They bought Michael Kors bags and Pandora bracelets, and Aunt Jean got herself some sparkly Uggs even though it was the middle of the summer. They were in a great mood on the way to the airport. They even thought about not going to church on Sunday, but I assured them that they should.

Carl and I dropped them off at the airport. Happily, I walked them to the TSA gates and wished them well. Then, the moment I was in the car alone with Carl, I cussed his ass out.

"If you ever invite them to my house again, I'm going to beat your ass. What the hell were you thinking?"

He chuckled. "It wasn't that bad."

"I'm not joking. It wasn't, but there better not be a next time."

"There won't. Everybody had fun, though, and that's what's important. Kadir's whole life is never going to be the same again. And I just wanted him to experience some normalcy."

With everybody gone, I would have some time to spend with Carl. We hadn't had one-on-one time in forever. I couldn't remember the last time he bent me over and made love to me. I wanted both to happen soon. It was time to rekindle our relationship.

"Let's get a drink and sit by the pool," I suggested. I wanted to get him tipsy and try to initiate some poolside sex. I poured what was left of the margaritas and had a seat by our pool.

"Isn't this nice, just you and me. We have all the time in the world," I said as I stretched across his lap and unzipped his pants. I began stroking his manhood up and down and then licked the top of his dick to get it wet. After he was well lubricated, I stood up and lifted my dress up and began to insert his dick inside of me, when he stopped me and nudged me off of him.

"Why are you stopping me?"

"Just stop, Mo."

"What's wrong?"

"All of this. I have something to talk to you about. I have been thinking about moving here and I've decided I'm not quitting my job."

"Why not?"

"Why would I retire at forty? If I quit my job I'll have fun for a month or two. Then I'll be bored, and what am I going to do for the next thirty or forty years? A man needs a purpose. Without a purpose, you don't live. Maybe you should think about getting a job, too."

"I paid my dues already. I'm not working anywhere."

"I don't feel that way, and I'm staying in Philly. Kadir is

grown, and he won't even be here. And if he needs me, he will call."

"So how does that work? Me here and you there?"

"Mo, I don't know; that's what I want to talk about. I love you, but . . ."

"But what?"

"You know we haven't been right for a while, and now we can stop pretending. You don't even look at me in that way anymore."

"I do, Carl. I was trying to look at you like that right now."

"Now you want me? Monique, all your concentration has been on Kadir and basketball for years. You haven't been thinking about me."

"Carl, this isn't making any sense. Is there anybody else?"

"No, not at all. I love you and we aren't breaking up. We're just taking a break."

"A break? Okay." It was sudden, but everything Carl said was true. I couldn't disagree. However, it didn't make any sense that now that we had everything we fought for, we would give up on each other.

CHAPTER 18

Tiffany

I was at this pathetic job for almost a month, and I still wasn't adjusted to waking up early, having a set lunchtime, or having to ask for advance permission to take the day off. I had to endure training with a bunch of dumb people who didn't have any phone etiquette. How unintelligent did you have to be not to be able to answer the telephone? That took up the first two weeks, and now we were live on the floor answering phone calls.

Every morning, I parked my car around the corner and walked to the office building. The last thing I wanted was anyone to see me driving an expensive car. I wanted to blend in like everyone else.

At lunch, I sat by myself. Making friends was not on my to-do list. That didn't stop a young girl named Shanae from sitting next to me. She was brown-skinned with dimples and long braids.

"I love your bag. Your ring is nice also."

"Thanks."

"It almost looks real. Where did you get it from?"

I gave her a dumb smirk. "It *is* real."

She laughed. "Yeah, I know. It is a good copy. Tiffany, where are you from?"

"Baltimore. Well, really, Charlotte, North Carolina."

"How do you like the job so far?"

"It's okay."

"That's what I said, a paycheck, right? My commute is an hour and fifteen minutes. I make four dollars an hour more here than at my last job at the mall."

"Interesting," I said, looking at her, not the least bit interested. "Do you know how much we make and when we get paid? I forgot to ask."

She laughed again, almost spitting her food out. "Sixteen an hour."

"That's it?"

"Girl, what's wrong with you? That's the first thing you are supposed to ask. After they take out taxes, we should clear like nine hundred or so depending on how many dependents you claimed. I claimed five. I rather get my money now than later."

"Yeah, of course." I smiled, still wondering why she was so friendly. She made me remember that I had to pay our cable bill. My phone buzzed. "Excuse me, I have to take this call." I stepped out of the cafeteria area and took the call from my mother.

"Hey, where are you?"

"Mom, I'm at work."

"You really are working? If you need money, I can transfer some money into your account."

"No, we are fine. I'm working."

"Are you sure, Tiffany?"

"Yes, I am. Yeah, if anything changes, I will call you later in the week."

"Well, I'm very proud of the way you are handling everything. God knows I would be crying every day if I was living under those conditions." My mother was always good with her backhanded compliments.

"Thank you, Mom. I have to get back to work. I will talk to you later."

At the end of the day, they handed us our paychecks. I ripped it open, and I couldn't believe the amount. I made nine hundred and seventy-five dollars. All of that getting up early and driving for a half hour in traffic, and this was my paycheck?

Besides my paycheck, I was even more irritated when I saw Damien standing outside of my job, leaned up against his car. He had this big smile on his face. I walked over to him and pulled him to the other side of the parking lot.

"What are you doing here, Damien?" I asked, looking all around. The last thing I needed was for someone to recognize him and my mediocre job cover to be blown.

"I have good news. I have a job."

"Where?"

"At the dealership. I was getting the car serviced. I sat in the showroom, and I was talking to the owner. Then someone came in and I started showing him a 550. You know I know my cars. So then the guy asked if we could go for a test drive and the general manager said go ahead. We took the car out, and when we came back in, the man bought the car. As soon as he left, the GM, Chuck, said, 'Damien why don't you come on board?'"

"That's nice, Dame. How much does it pay?"

"Do you know for that one car I made two thousand dollars? He said they had it for a long time. It was a target car, and I came right in there and sold it."

"Two thousand dollars? Just for one car? It took me two weeks for nine hundred."

"Let's go to dinner and celebrate. We both have jobs now."

"No, I'm too tired. You don't have that money yet, and I'm not sure if my paycheck is enough to pay our cell phones, cable, and buy groceries."

"We have enough, and I get paid in two weeks. I want to take you out to get a steak from Fernando's."

"We can't afford Fernando's."

"Yes, we can."

"No, we can't. Our bill is always three hundred dollars or more. We don't have that kind of money. And we can't afford this car anymore. You shouldn't have been getting it serviced. Don't you get it? This is our new life, our new normal—getting up and going to work every day, not steak and lobster dinners. Plus, I have to get up for work in the morning."

"I don't know why you're getting upset. I told you, you didn't have to work. I have a job now."

"I'm upset because we have to move everything out of our dream home, but you want me to pretend like none of it is going on. I can't do that. You're still in living in a dream world and I'm thinking realistically."

"You're right, Tiffany, but the way I see it is I'm so good at selling cars that I can probably open my own car lot in a few years. I know it's not millions, but some of the guys make a hundred fifty thousand a year. That's a nice living if it's managed properly. So, it's all going to work out."

"I still think we should go buy groceries. I'll meet you at the house."

I went to the market, came home, and started cooking. Just because we couldn't go to a fancy restaurant didn't mean we couldn't eat like we were at one. I bought us steak, potatoes, shrimp, and lobster tails already steamed. After thirty minutes of fumbling around the kitchen I was done cooking.

I did the best I could. The lobster was okay, but my steak was kind of overcooked. Damien came in and ate my mess of a meal like it was something delicious. We ate dinner and watched a little television. We snuggled on the sofa until the late news went off. I was happy he had a job, but I wouldn't feel completely safe until we were in our new home and we had some money in the bank.

The next morning, Damien got up early, showered before

me, and was out the door on his way to the dealership. He wished me a good morning and kissed me on the cheek before leaving. He was no longer moping around and down and out. I was proud of him. I saw a hint of light finally coming through the dark clouds. That was pure luck, him getting his car serviced and then landing a job without even trying.

CHAPTER 19

Adrienne

I landed in the City of Angels, and I had to admit to myself that I was probably crazy. I'd just traveled across the country to have one meeting. It was the most spontaneous thing I have ever done. However, I was confident that it would be well worth it. Before I left, I apologized to my mom. I was wrong for cussing her out, but I needed her to stay out of my business. Truth be told, she is the only family I have besides Asia.

I rented a car and checked into my hotel and had a little to eat. After watching some television, I pulled out my clothes for the next day. I selected a simple black dress and navy blazer. I turned in early, so that I could be well rested for the next day.

The next afternoon walking out of my hotel room, I felt a bit nervous. But after drinking coffee, I was fine.

I was meeting Carlos Peters from Aviera Films at a small café. I arrived ten minutes early, and he was already seated at the table, dressed in a very nice suit. I tried to hide my enthusiasm. My phone rang just as I was about to have a seat. It was my mom, so I sent her to voice mail.

"Hi, I'm Adrienne Sheppard."

He stood up and said, "It's very nice to meet you, Adrienne." He asked me what I was having for lunch. I ordered a salad, because I was too nervous to eat anything else. Our food arrived, and we made small talk before Carlos began talking about my script.

"Ms. Sheppard, I and my associate read *Falcon Hall Boys*, and we absolutely loved it."

"Thank you, I'm glad you enjoyed it."

"We also are interested in representing you. We have many connections at film studios such as Sony, Columbia Tri-Star, and Warner Brothers. With that said, the script is good, but we need it to be great. We just need you to fix up the script some."

"Okay, that's fine." Ian said he didn't care what they changed this time around, and I wasn't going to object to anything.

"Perfect, so in order to get *Falcon Hall Boys* to be great, it needs to go to a script doctor. They will give it a little polish and then it will shine and be more sellable." I nodded in agreement. I was just waiting to hear how much he wanted to buy it for.

"Adrienne, it will be twenty-five hundred for the script doctor. Will that be a problem? It doesn't have to be cash. They do accept credit cards."

"Okay," I responded. Here it was. I thought I was at a meeting with a legitimate company, but I was in a meeting with a scam artist who was trying to hustle me for money. Pay twenty-five hundred to fix a script? Did he really think I was going to fall for that scheme?

"Do you want to pay by credit card today or cash?" He pulled out a credit card adapter for his cell phone. *Isn't he an optimistic scam artist?* I thought. I couldn't take it anymore. I wasn't rude, but I told him thank you but no thank you.

Although my meeting was a bust, I decided instead of rushing back home and having to fly back out I would stay in L. A.

a little longer. All I needed was a month to make something happen.

I tried to find an extended stay hotel, but they cost just as much as an apartment. So then I began searching for apartments that had month-to-month leases.

Luckily, the next day I found a small place in a neighborhood called West Adams. The leasing agent gave me a discount for paying for all four weeks at once. I didn't have any furniture, but the last tenant left a kitchen table and chairs. I had my laptop and phone and I would buy an air mattress. I didn't have any plans of resting while I was there. The apartment was fifteen minutes from downtown Los Angeles and right by the I-10 freeway. As I brought in my luggage, a young guy dressed in all blue held the door open for me.

"How's it going, miss lady?"

"I'm fine."

"If you need anything, I'm right down the hall. My name is Rico."

"Thank you Rico."

I settled into my small apartment and began coming up with a plan. My rent was paid, I had a few dollars in the bank thanks to DeCarious, and my mom planned to pick up my rent check from Talene and put it in my account. While I was out here, I planned on being in the gym so I could get my body back.

I called my mom and she answered on the first ring. "Mom, did you get a chance to pick up the rent?"

"I did, but when I went there that young lady didn't answer the door. The window was broken and there were four cars in the driveway."

"Okay, I'm about to call her. Then I will call you back." I hung up with my mom and called Talene. Unlike my mom she didn't answer immediately. I had to call her back three times before she finally picked up.

"Ms. Adrienne, sorry I didn't answer, my ringer was off."

"Talene. My mom came passed the house today, and she

said there were several cars in my driveway, a window was broken, and you didn't have the rent? What's going on?"

"Oh, I had a few friends come through and Devaughn had locked himself out. So he had to break the window to get in, but we are going to fix the window this week. Yeah, I told your mom I didn't have the rent yet, but I should have it by next week."

"Our agreement was you were going to pay the balance when you moved in. You have to make sure you pay your rent and don't damage my house."

"I'll have it next week. I promise."

After a shower, I remembered to call my mother back.

"Mom, she said she'll have it next week. I'm glad you went over there for me. Thanks."

"That's fine. Everything okay out there?"

"Yeah, I had a meeting yesterday. And I've decided to stay out here for a little while. I found a little cheap apartment—" I was interrupted by the sound of gunfire. "Hold on."

"What was that, Adrienne?"

"Hold up, shh. It sounded like gunshots outside. I have to check it out."

"Don't go to the window. You might get shot."

I took my mother's advice and peeked out the window, only to see the Wild, Wild West outside. I hung up on her. There was a black car with a man hanging out of the window, shooting at guys who were standing in front of my building. They were shooting back. My heart began racing, and I ducked down to the ground. For at least ten minutes, I heard rapid fire. I felt like at any moment a stray bullet would come flying into my apartment. I fell to the floor. Then there was a pause. I heard the car take off and someone yell out, "Derk Gang!" I wondered if it was safe to go to the window. I lifted my head and glanced over the windowsill. I watched four men as they jumped into a white Buick sedan. One of them was that guy Rico who had opened the door for me. I couldn't call my mother back and tell her that a gang war was going on outside of my new apartment building.

For the next three hours, I tried to convince myself that I wasn't living in a gang-infested apartment complex and that I wasn't going to die. I was lying to myself. I heard people walking past my door and loud noises all night. I looked out my peephole and saw a guy with two guns drawn. I guess he was the security. I was too frightened to leave the apartment, but more afraid to stay. I wanted to call the police, but what would I say? And how did I know the cops wouldn't tell them who called? I decided I would just wait until the morning, get my deposit back, and find another apartment.

I stayed on the floor with the kitchen table against the door. I figured if the bullets came through, they would hit the table and not me.

At exactly ten a.m., I was at the rental office. Kelly, the bubbly rental agent from the day before, greeted me with a smile as she invited me in the office.

"Good morning!"

I didn't have time for her pleasantries. "There are Crips and Bloods living in my building. I can't live there. They were shooting, and I need my deposit back."

"That's not possible."

"It's very possible. It happened last night."

"They are not Bloods, they're Crips. Crips wear blue. Bloods wear red, and they would never live in the same complex. Conflict of interest." Was she serious? She was giving me a lesson in gang affiliations 101. Did she think I cared?

"So, you are aware gangs live in my building, and they have shoot-outs at night? I want a refund."

"No, ma'am. We don't give any refunds. Didn't you see the sign?" She pointed to a raggedy handwritten sign on yellow stationery that I didn't notice previously.

"I gave you a full month's rent yesterday and today I'm telling you I don't want to live with gang members and you're telling me I can't get my money back?"

"Yes, unfortunately. I don't make the rules, but feel free to write your grievances and send them to the building owner. Here is his e-mail address." She scribbled down his address on a piece of paper. I snatched the paper from her hand, and I walked out of the office, slamming the door. I didn't know what to do. I considered just packing up and leaving. I walked back to my apartment. The sun was bright and shining. Children were running, and an elderly woman was pushing her shopping cart down the street. It was in stark contrast from the previous night's warfare. I wanted to ask them if they heard the shooting. Was it every day? Or maybe it was just a one-time occurrence? I called other hotels and apartment complexes, but there weren't any available until next month. I couldn't move in anywhere else until Talene sent the rest of the money anyway, since Kelly refused to give me back my deposit. I would have to deal with the gang activity, or die trying.

CHAPTER 20

Shanice

Deuce was the dude I met in New Orleans. Ashley V said he was someone I needed on my team. She said he had a lot of connections and just knowing him I could get a lot of jobs, and if he could help my career, I knew I should at least give him a chance. I was in New York already, so I figured what did I have to lose? He had a black SUV pick me up from my hotel, and said that the driver would bring me to him. His office was located on the Avenue of the Americas.

The driver opened my door and I walked into a large office building. I took the elevator to the fifteenth floor. I exited the elevator, and a petite, older African-American woman was behind the receptionist desk. Before I reached her desk, she said that Mr. Stewart was expecting me and would be with me shortly. Behind her was a large plaque that read "Regal Records." I had a seat and took in the scenery of the record label. Album covers lined the hallway. It was the end of the day, and people were leaving while I was sitting in the lobby in a low-cut blue dress, wearing stiletto heels. I felt very inappropriately dressed for an office setting. They gave polite nods and hellos, when I knew they were wondering in the back of their minds what I was doing and where was I going. I stopped chewing my gum and brought my legs together so I would appear more sophisticated.

"Sorry I kept you waiting," Deuce said, coming out of an office. He said good night to the receptionist and pressed the down button for the elevator. He smelled good and looked nice in his suit, but I still couldn't help but notice his bulging stomach.

"No problem. So, you work for Regal or Dominant Records?"

"Both. Dominant is my record label, and it is a division of Regal. I've been in the business for nineteen years. I started when I was eighteen. I've been working since you were still on the playground."

"Yeah, I guess." I did the math in my head. *Thirty-seven? He is twelve years older than me. I didn't know he was that old. He seems a lot younger,* I thought.

"You look nice. I like those shoes, too. You have any ten-inch heels?"

"Ten-inch heels? Only strippers wear them."

"I know. It was a trick question. I was seeing if you were paying attention."

We went outside, and the driver was still there waiting for us. He drove us to a dimly lit restaurant with small tables draped in heavy white tablecloths. Huge crystal chandeliers hung above each table.

"So I'm on a date with Ms. Shani Amore. I'm not going to lie, I'm a fan. I've seen you in a few things."

"Yeah? What are you a fan of?"

"That beautiful smile and cute face."

"That's it?"

"I mean it's a few other things. Your curves are nice, but I'm really into a person's spirit."

"So you could see my spirit from me dancing in a video?"

He paused and then said he could. I told him I didn't believe him.

Deuce was interesting. He was from the Bronx, raised by his mom and his grandfather, and he knew a lot about the music industry. He told me how he started his record label in his granddad's garage. His mom was mad at him for dropping out of high school in his last year, but his grandfather saw his vision and gave him his pension check to put out and market his first artist's album. He said when he got his first royalty check he paid his grandfather back, bought him a Cadillac, and sent him on vacation. "So how is your modeling? Do you like your management?"

"Yeah, April keeps me booked, but it's a little hard because I just don't want to be just a video girl and it's been hard trying to switch over."

"Things get easy when you have the right people in your life."

"They do?"

"Yup."

"Maybe I'll find out. Maybe I won't," I said as I toyed with the noodles on my fork.

After dinner, we drove to this warehouse at the pier and took the elevator to the rooftop. At first I thought we were going to an exclusive private club, but when we reached the top floor I saw a helicopter. He grabbed for my hand and began walking toward the helicopter.

"What do you think you're doing?"

"I'm kidnapping you." He nudged me in the direction of the helicopter.

"I don't want to get in that thing." I walked away from him. *First of all, what are the weight requirements?* I thought.

"I know what you are thinking. This helicopter can carry up to three adults, and it's only two of us and the pilot."

"That's not what I was thinking. I don't like being up in the air. It's not safe."

The pilot assured me that it was totally safe, and I reluctantly boarded. Deuce lifted me up inside and fastened my seat belt. He sat next to me.

"If we crash, the seat belt won't do anything," he joked. I gave him a mean face. The helicopter lifted off the ground, and I wanted to scream "No!" but it was too late. I felt us flying, but I was too scared to look. I opened my eyes a little, and saw that we were flying over water. I saw tall building lights twinkling and the New York City skyline.

"This is nice, right?" Deuce questioned me.

"It's okay."

"Okay, why are you acting like you are not impressed?"

"I'm not. I'm scared." I laughed and put my head into his shoulder and he pried my head up. Once I opened my eyes fully, I took in the beauty of the city lights and the water below.

"Yes, it is nice, but in the future, let me know when I'm going to be flying so I can prepare myself."

"One thing you'll learn about me is that I'm spontaneous. So I can't promise you that I will."

"Then I can't promise you we are going on any more dates."

"I doubt that. This is the first of many," he said confidently.

We returned back to the pier and Deuce made it clear what he wanted. "What is it going to take for you to stay with me tonight?"

"I'm not staying with you. I have a hotel room. That's all you think it would take, dinner and a helicopter ride, to get me to fuck you?"

"I didn't say that, but I don't care what you say, you're staying with me tonight. Don't worry, I won't bother you. I just want to go to sleep with a beautiful woman in my arms."

I started laughing. "That was so corny."

"Corny, but true. I'll send someone over to pick up your things up from the hotel."

I told him I would come over, but he better not touch me. I wanted to see how his place looked anyway. He lived in a beautiful penthouse with a Central Park view. I never saw a New York apartment so big. I really underestimated who I was talking to. I searched his net worth and he was worth over twenty million dollars.

After a few drinks and more conversation, I felt comfortable enough to stay over. He held me all night and didn't try anything. I felt protected in his arms, and to my surprise, his extra fat was like a warm pillow.

The next morning I opened my eyes and Deuce was still asleep. I got up to check my messages and read a text from the agent I'd been working with. She asked me to call her as soon as I could because she had found a house she thought I would like. I jumped out of the bed and walked into the bathroom to call her.

By the time I came out of the bathroom Deuce was sitting up watching television. "Why are you in the bathroom using the phone? Did you have to check in with your man?" Deuce asked.

"No, I had to talk to the real estate agent. I'm trying to get a place for me and my mom."

"Oh, okay. So what do you want for breakfast?"

"I don't want anything."

"Don't be one of those girls that don't eat."

"I'm not. I ate last night. It's just that I have a lot on my mind. I have to go back home and go see this place."

"What's wrong with the place you have now?"

"It's too small. I have to get a bigger place because my mom is coming home."

"Where was she?" he inquired.

"Away."

"Oh, your mom did a bid. Damn, let me find out."

I jokingly hit him and said, "No, seriously, my mom's been in jail since I was like six. She did twenty years for killing her boyfriend."

"Oh, my bad. I shouldn't play like that."

"No, it's cool. So I have to find her somewhere to live."

"I got Realtors everywhere. I can get you a house."

"No, thank you. I had someone pay for a condo for a few months and then when they stopped paying for it, I had to move into a smaller apartment."

"I wouldn't do that to you. If I get you a house, your name will be on the lease and the rent would be paid for a year, but what will you do for me?"

"What do you want?"

"I need a very good friend. I live a hectic lifestyle. And I need someone to come home to."

"We could work something out. I guess."

"I bet we could. You're good, though, with your pretty ass. You have me talking about getting you a house on the first date. Damn, what am I going to do when I hit that? Buy you a plane?"

"Maybe."

"I probably will."

There was something about Deuce I liked. He was confident, powerful, and had a lot of paper, but he was humble, too. And there wasn't a woman's presence anywhere in his house. I could already see myself taking over and having him do whatever I wanted him to do. He wasn't perfect; I didn't like his stomach or the way it shook when he laughed, but he had everything else I needed. He was workable and maybe I could put him on a diet.

CHAPTER 21

Monique

With Kadir settled in and Carl back in Philly, I felt comfortable traveling. I booked first-class everything for CeCe and me. Our flight was departing from D.C., and I was waiting for her to get there.

I brought two weeks' worth of clothes for our five-day trip. I knew I was overdoing it, but I was excited. I wanted to make my trip memorable and look flawless doing it. Without looking, I answered my phone.

"Hello."

"You getting real funny since you got money."

"Who is this?"

"Monique, there you go acting like you don't know nobody. It's the woman who gave birth to you. Why do you keep changing your number?"

"Because I have to. What do you need?" I was aggravated by her already, and I didn't even know what she wanted yet.

"So what's this I hear, you're taking people on vacations? Huh? And you bought Carl's mom a car and not me. I'm that boy's grandmother; if anyone should get a car, it should be me."

"What? You deserve a car for what reason? Are you the same grandmother that told me I wasn't going to be shit because I had him? The same one who wouldn't watch him and never came to any of his games? Mom Laura looked out for Kadir since he was a baby. She bought me and Carl our first car. You didn't buy me anything."

"Don't go spending up all my grandson's money. It is not yours."

"Don't count my money," I shouted.

"It's *your son's* money," she said, correcting me.

"It's *our* money. My son is taking care of me. You know why? Because I took care of him. I was a mother that was there for her child. I can't say the same for you. You disowned me and made my life hell because the church people couldn't see Dottie's pregnant teenage daughter."

"I gave you a place to live, I helped you with Kadir. I made you strong. You owe me, too! And *she* gets a Cadillac, and I don't? People at my church are asking me why I don't have a car."

"I don't care what people are asking you. Don't you ever call me questioning me about what I do for people who love me and my baby unconditionally. Unlike you. Me? Buy *you* a car? Ha! Keep waiting on it, because it will never happen. I don't owe you shit. And don't call this number again." She had a lot of damn nerve. Everyone's hands were out trying to get a piece of my son's empire and they all could go to hell. After I hung up, I remembered I was in the middle of a busy airport and I noticed I'd attracted an audience. I looked up and saw CeCe standing over me shaking her head.

"Call your mom back."

"Hell no. Do you know what she called and said right before the draft?"

"What?"

"She said don't be upset when he doesn't get picked. She

didn't have any confidence in Kadir or me. Now she got her hand out? Fuck outta here."

"You didn't tell me that."

"That's why I didn't answer her call that night. Let me calm down. This lady got me cussing."

"Yeah, calm down before they say you too angry to travel. Forget her. Let's get ready to have a great time. Look at you looking like a million dollars. I love the hair, bag, and the shoes."

"Thank you, girl." I gave her a few poses. "I got my hair done yesterday, these shoes are Jimmy Choo, and this bag is a Celine. The sales girl said all the Housewives carry them. So you know I had to have one."

"Yes, girl it's nice."

We boarded the plane and sank into our oversize seats. The stewardess came, welcomed us aboard, and asked if we wanted to see a drink menu. I told her we'd like two glasses of champagne. When she returned with the champagne. I raised my glass, turned to CeCe, and joked, "Bon voyage!"

"Dummy, that's French and we are going to England." CeCe laughed.

"Well, we are going *somewhere*. So safe journey, fun times, good shopping, and cheers to you."

"Cheers to you, Mo. I've always wanted to go to London since I was a little girl. And now I'm going. This is a big deal, Mo. Really." Cee looked out the plane's window to hide that she was holding back tears. "I will pay you back one day. I swear I will."

"Don't start, you crybaby. You know you would do the same thing for me, and you do not have to pay me back anything. So stop saying it. We are going to have so much fun."

"Yes, we are. How do you think the people will be there? Oh, if I meet an English man like Idris Elba and he starts talking to me in that bloody sexy accent, I'm not going to be any good."

"Maybe I will meet someone, too, since your brother wants to stay in Philly and take a break."

"I didn't know y'all broke up."

"Yep, he said I never paid him any attention."

"Well, did you?"

"I don't know. You are my sister and sometimes I feel like he is just my brother. We've been around each other so much just existing. You know we don't act like a couple and we don't have sex unless I come on to him. And the last time I tried to give him some, he pushed me off him."

"TMI. Yuck. I don't want to picture Carl getting some."

"It's the truth. He has all this and does nothing with it." I gestured my hands toward my body.

"Y'all just been together so long that you just take each other for granted. He should have been on this trip, not me. Maybe y'all could have rekindled everything."

"No, he shouldn't have. So he could complain the whole time about spending money? No, thank you. He's a human calculator. 'Uhm, Monique you know you spent seven thousand on bags last week.' And I'm like, yeah, I know."

"You did? Girl, how many bags did you buy?"

"I think I have five. I went into Neiman Marcus and said give me one of each. But I still tore Marshall's and Ross up, too. I may have money now, but I didn't forget where I come from."

"Girl, you are so silly. Well, I hope it is just a break. This is the time y'all should be celebrating, not separating."

"I know. I said the same thing."

We arrived in London at the Heathrow International Airport. We went straight through customs and then to our hotel. We crashed as soon as we got to our room. We were both exhausted from the flight and traveling. It took almost two days for our bodies to adjust to the five-hour time difference.

The days leading up to the concert we did plenty of sight-seeing. We visited Buckingham Palace and shopped at Har-rods, the most famous department store in the world.

The night of the concert, the O2 Arena was filled with over-the-top fans of every nationality. We walked down to our seats in the Bey Hive section. The seats were so close to the stage that CeCe screamed, "I love you, Beyoncé," and I swear she turned around and winked at her. Her performance was full of energy and worth every dollar.

After the show, we went back to the hotel. We weren't sure where to go to have any fun. We sat at the hotel bar and no-ticed a festive African wedding going on in the reception area. A few women were dressed in vibrant blue head wraps and men in black tuxedos with matching ties. Two men from the wedding party sat at the bar. One looked extremely fa-miliar, but I didn't know from where. The men said hello, and CeCe asked what kind of wedding they were a part of.

"It's Nigerian," one of the men answered.

"Oh, that's nice. They are wearing beautiful costumes."

"They're not costumes. They are traditional aso-ebi gar-ments."

"Do y'all live here or in Nigeria?" CeCe asked.

"We are from Nigeria. And let me guess you both are from the States, aren't you?"

"Yes, our accents give us away?" Cee asked, giggling. "So whose wedding?" she asked, turning her attention to the ex-tremely tall, good looking second gentleman.

"Our brother just got married. His bride is from here."

"Are y'all married?" CeCe asked.

"I have a girlfriend, but he is single. I live in Ireland. He lives in the States," the shorter brother answered.

"I didn't know black people lived in Ireland." I laughed.

"Very funny." The shorter brother laughed. "Of course there are, there are a bunch of us there. I stay there, but he lives and works in North Carolina."

"Really? She just moved to North Carolina! You look familiar. How tall are you?"

"I'm six seven."

"Wow, do you play basketball?"

"Yes, in Charlotte. How do you know?" the taller brother asked.

"What a small world—her son was just drafted by the Hornets. His name is Kadir."

"Kadir Hall? The rookie. I would never have guessed a beautiful young woman could be the mother of such a big, grown man." He extended his hand. "Ayodele Cisse."

"Adolee."

"No, A-yo-de-le. Everyone calls me Dele."

"Okay, Dele. What does that mean?" I asked.

"Joy has come home."

"That is beautiful," I told him.

He thanked me.

"Do you like it here?" CeCe inquired.

"It's okay. Actually, our family is from Nigeria, but we did our schooling in Paris and came here for college."

"Are you a Beyoncé fan?" CeCe asked. "We came all the way here for the show. My bestie treated me."

"You're dedicated fans. When are you returning?" Dele asked.

"Tomorrow, but before we leave, do you know a nice place to eat nearby? We are starving for real food and we want to see more of the city," I asked.

"There are plenty near here. Let me get your information, and maybe I will show you ladies a little of London on your last night here."

"Sounds good," CeCe said, and gave him my number. He said he would contact us later.

Back in our hotel room, CeCe and I debated who Mr. Fine-Tall-Sexy-African-Man was interested in.

"CeCe, why did you give him my number? You were doing all the talking."

"Because you have the international calling plan, Mo. I loved his accent and he is tall. Can you believe he plays for the same team as Kadir? What a coincidence."

"It is. I thought he looked familiar. I don't know everybody on the team yet. Girl, talk to him," I said.

"I would, but I think he wants some Mo in his life. If you weren't my brother's wife, I would say go get that tall muscle-popping chocolate African king, because he was flirting with you."

"I saw him staring at you the entire time. And if I wanted to talk to him, I would. Carl isn't here, plus remember we are on a break. But he is gorgeous. Those eyes . . . those cheekbones . . . his beautiful skin . . . I would have fun with him." I laughed and CeCe agreed. We had a few drinks in the room and packed for our return flight. Grandmom CeCe took a shower and wrapped her hair and put on her scarf. She tried to stay up, but by the time a text message came from Dele saying he was still downstairs and asked if we wanted to have more drinks, Grandmom CeCe was fast asleep. But I told him I would come down.

I walked to the hotel lobby to see Ayodele waiting at the bar. He was even more beautiful than I remembered from two hours earlier. I couldn't take my eyes off his delicious-looking malt chocolate skin. He had three drinks in front of him.

"You already ordered. Thanks, but CeCe is asleep. I tried to wake her up."

"Hah. She retired early. That's fine. I'm glad you decided to join me."

"Plus, I don't know you and what you could have put in my drink."

"You are right, but I am not that type of man. I'll order you another drink." He ordered another round of drinks and then turned his attention back to me.

"You are so beautiful."

"Thank you," I said, blushing. His forwardness caught me

off guard. I felt his eyes roaming my body. I tried to pull my dress down an inch.

"I still can't believe that you have a grown man as a son. How old were you when you had him?"

"I had him at seventeen. He's twenty and turning twenty-one soon. That makes me almost thirty-eight. How old are you and where is your missus, Ayodele?"

"Twenty-eight, and she is nonexistent. The life of a bachelor suits me well. I travel a lot, and well, I haven't found anyone that I would want to spend the rest of my life with."

"Why aren't you wearing your wedding ring?" Dele asked.

"I was with Kadir's dad for eighteen years, but we never got married."

"Why is he not your husband? You have a grown son, and you're not his wife? I never understand why you American women stay with a man for years and years and never marry."

"We just didn't. And he is not his real father. He helped me raise him. And that isn't any of your concern. We loved each other and we raised a great son together and that's it." I tugged on my dress again and took a sip of the drink in front of me.

"I'm sorry if I offended you. I was just curious. Why do you keep playing with your dress?"

"I'm just fixing it."

"I think your dress is fine. You are beautiful, and your body looks amazing. I can appreciate a confident woman."

"I wish everybody did. All my son says to me is that I should start dressing like a mom."

"I'm glad you don't dress like a mom. And you're his mom, but you're a woman, too."

"Thank you. That's what I tell him all the time."

"No, thank you." He licked his lips and his eyes wandered up and down my legs again. This time he grabbed his chin and I felt myself staring back.

He told me he played basketball for France in the LNB and then was drafted in the NBA five years ago. He was on a few teams before coming to the Hornets.

We had three more drinks, and then he asked me to join him in his room. He whispered something French in my ear. I don't know what the hell he was talking about, but it sounded so sexy. He stood up and towered over me.

"Why don't you come up with me?"

I laughed at his aggressiveness. "No, I'm fine. Thank you for the drink. I'll see you at a game."

"No, come with me. I promise you we will just sit and talk."

"I can't. I have to get some rest. My flight leaves at six."

"It's only ten. That means I can have the next five hours."

"No, because I have to get to the room before my friend gets up."

"So you agree you will stay with me?"

"No, I don't agree." My mind was saying one thing, but my body was talking another language. It was speaking seductively to his. He paid our check and grabbed my hand and led me to the elevator. I pressed seven for my floor and he pressed nine. When I went to say good-bye, he pulled me back in for a hug and picked me up. He then let me down slowly and went in for a long kiss. His lips nibbled at mine.

"Look, you made me miss my floor."

"Yes, because we're not done conversing."

Once we were in his room, his extra-large hands touched every single part of my body. Suddenly, my dress was up and his long fingers were forcefully inside of me twisting side to side. I felt a rush of pleasure. I grabbed his dick, which extended like a long snake down the side of his leg. When he took off his pants and unleashed his massive dick, I almost fainted. I didn't actually think my body could accommodate him. He slowly pushed his way in, breaking down layer after layer. I moaned, enjoying the pain and the pleasure. Once he got all the way in, he moved in a way that made my insides climax numerous times. He knew exactly what he was doing and I was receiving what had been missing for so long. It became a competition who could satisfy the other more. He kept whispering I was amazing in my ear, but he was the one who was putting it down. In the moment it was great, but after we were done, I became petrified.

"Are you okay? Do you want something to drink?" Dele asked.

"No, I'm fine," I said shyly. He had just seen me naked, but suddenly I felt like I needed to pull the sheets over my body. *What did I just do?*

"Okay, so let me just say this. If I see you at a game, you don't know me."

"Why do you say that? Is it your husband?"

"No, I'm not married. It's my son. Let's just pretend none of this happened."

"I don't think that is possible. I will tell him myself your mother is amazing."

"You can't."

"I'm only kidding. Don't worry, I'm not going to say anything. So relax. We are adults and both have long flights tomorrow. Let's make the most of tonight. And tonight will be tonight and tomorrow is another day." He got back in the bed and wrapped his warm, long arms around me. He fell asleep and I left the room.

I snuck back in the room just before CeCe awoke and I got right in the shower. When I came out, she was sitting up. "What are you doing up?" she asked, perplexed.

"I wanted to hurry up and take a shower, so we wouldn't be late for our flight. You better hurry and get in the shower." I sat on the bed and began reminiscing about my night with Dele.

"What are you over there smiling about?"

"No reason, I'm just feeling really blessed. Look how amazing life is. We were able to just get up and go and fly to another country. People can't do that."

"That's true. Miss blessed, hurry up and get your clothes on."

"I will."

I never really knew how to keep a secret. CeCe knew everything that ever happened to me, but my night with Ayodele I had to keep to myself.

CHAPTER 22

Zakiya

Today was the first official event we were attending with the new team. The Hornets were sponsoring a Carnival for Cancer shoot-around. I was very nervous because Jabril was nervous. It was the first time he had to suit up. I already told myself during the ride over to the arena that I was going to be polite, but not too friendly to any of the wives I met.

I picked up my tickets from the will call office and I gave the young woman my name and ID.

"Ma'am, your identification says Zakiya Lee. The tickets are for Mrs. Z. Smith."

"Oh, I didn't change my last name yet . . ." I began to dig in my bag to search for proof that I was the wife of Jabril Smith.

"You don't have to look. I believe you. I see that ring. It's huge. You have to get your license updated."

"Okay, yeah," I said, looking down at the gigantic stone in my new wedding ring set.

It was early, and I saw children playing on the court. I didn't see Bril yet. I looked over my shoulder and noticed a tall, thick woman who had a waist-length auburn weave dipped with blond at the tips approaching me. I tried my best to ignore her existence, but then she tapped my shoulder. I turned around and mustered a smile. "Yes?"

"Hi. Dawn Franklin. Your husband was the trade, right?"

"Yes, Jabril was traded here." I was offended by the way she was referring to my baby as the trade, like he didn't have a name.

"Not like that. I heard he is good."

"Yeah, he is. He averages five rebounds, ten points, and six assists a game."

"That's good. We need a point guard. I contacted you on Facebook. My husband is Thaddeus Franklin, the team captain."

"Oh, you did? I don't really get on there," I lied.

"So, you two are from up north, right? Philly?"

"Well, I'm from Philly. Jabril is from Jersey."

"My husband is from Baltimore, and I'm from D.C. So, how do you like Charlotte so far?"

"It's okay," I said.

"A little slow, though, right?"

"No, not compared to Oklahoma. *That* was slow."

"Let's exchange numbers. When they're on the road, I like to get out every once in a while. I don't do it often because Thaddeus and I have seven kids."

"Seven kids?"

"Yes, I already had two before we met, he had three, and now we had two together."

"Wow, what a big family . . ."

"Yeah, we make it work. Only four are here with us. The other two are in Las Vegas and Tallahassee. You know, he was out there when he was young, and I was married and in the military. I can still go out, though. Have you been to any of the clubs here? My favorite is Estate."

I didn't want to be rude. I enjoyed her conversation, but how could I be clear that I had enough friends and was too busy to go out?

"I don't really go out."

"We can do lunch then."

"Yeah, lunch. I have to see. I'll take your number," I said, hoping she would get the hint. She gave me her number, and I saved it in my phone. That was harmless. I just wouldn't call her.

That's what I promised myself: no new friends. But by the time the charity game ended, I hated myself for breaking my promise.

Dawn and I shared chicken fingers and juicy stories about the crazy fans and things we had seen being at games. She invited Jabrilah and me to her daughter's birthday party the following week. There was something likable about Dawn, and the more we talked, the more I realized we had a lot of things in common. We were the same age—literally, down to the month—and our daughters' names both began with the letter J. I noticed she wasn't anything like all the other toxic wives I had met over the years.

Everything was calm and peaceful until a woman came and stood in front of us blocking our view to the court.

"Girl, look at her, can you believe some people. This is an event for sick kids, not the strip club. She could have put on a pair of jeans or something. At least some tights."

I looked to see who she was talking about. She was pointing to a woman in a tiny black shirt dress who definitely needed a pair of pants on.

"Whose wife is that?" I asked.

"She has got to be a groupie, looking that cheap. Look at that white sticker on the bottom of her cheap shoes while she has the nerve to be carrying a two-thousand-dollar bag." I couldn't help but laugh. Dawn was right, the woman looked a mess. We were giggling hard and were oblivious that the woman we were talking about could hear us. She walked over and stood in front of us.

"When you talk about people, you should be a little more discreet. My dress is short, but I'm not deaf and maybe if you could, you would wear a dress like this. But you can't, so mind your business." We both were shocked at the lady's boldness. I was speechless and didn't say a word. But that didn't stop the woman from coming to me and calling me out. She stood over me and put her hands in my face and said, "And just to let you know. I'm no groupie. Kadir Hall is my son and the reason this team will start winning some games."

Dawn stood up, taking the attention off of me and said, "Well, I don't know where you're from, but we don't dress like that down here. You might want to change into something more appropriate as the mother of a player."

The woman looked around, and then said, "How about you might want to hit the gym. But if you really have an issue with me or the way I'm dressed, we can talk in the parking lot."

Dawn walked closer to her and said, "We don't have to go outside." Then she lunged for the mom. I grabbed Dawn before she could swing. But the lady was still coming over toward her. Luckily, security came over and pulled her away. Dawn straightened her clothes and thanked me for holding her back.

"Girl, Thaddeus would have killed me if I would have fought at a game, but that lady better watch herself."

"I don't even know what just happened, but thank you for taking up for me. She was all in my face."

I wasn't even at my first game and already I had witnessed some drama. I left before the end of the event and all I could think was: different city, same shit.

CHAPTER 23

Adrienne

L.A. had several sides to it. The beautiful, glamorous wanna-be-actor, just-waiting-tables-'til-I-get-my-big-break side, and then there was also the poor, skid-row, gang-infested side. I lived in the second side of L.A., and I hated it. Every night, I blocked the door with the sofa and slept very lightly. During the day, I got up and went out early. Gang members need their rest, too, and usually aren't up at six a.m., when I left. Then, by the time I returned, around seven, they were just hitting the streets.

I spent most days in North Hollywood, nicknamed NoHo. There were many theaters, and it was the artsy district of L.A. I met a lot of people, but not one who could help me. And I needed some help *badly*. I was beginning to second-guess myself and my choices. I had to go home successful, and I wasn't sure if that was going to happen. At this point, I would have sold that damn script for two thousand dollars. I just needed money. Whenever I got down, I called and spoke with Asia. Hearing her voice made me know that I had to keep going, because she needed me to make it and I needed her home.

"Mommy, I can read books."

"That's great, Asia girl! Mommy misses you."

"I miss you, too, and my daddy said you can visit whenever you like."

"I can visit? You will be coming home soon, Asia. This is not forever." I heard DeCarious in the background, telling Asia to tell me she didn't want to leave. I started to tell her to put him on the phone. Then I decided that wasn't a good idea, because I knew I would say something that I would later regret—or that could be used against me in court.

After speaking with Asia, I called my tenant. She still hadn't paid the rent. If I was home, I would have gone to the house and put her and all her belongings on the curb.

"Miss Adrienne. I'm sending the money today. My boyfriend is going to go cash his check."

"Okay, you *must* send the money this time." I had to stress that I wasn't playing with her anymore.

"No, I understand. You can go to the MoneyGram around six."

"That's three my time."

"Yes, I promise it will be there."

At 2:45, I was outside of the MoneyGram. I waited until 3:15 to go in. I gave my name and identification, only to be told there wasn't any money waiting for me. I called Talene back, frustrated.

"Ms. Adrienne. So he thought he was going to get his first full check, but he only got one week, and then so we didn't send the full two thousand. I felt bad, so I sent you what I had."

"And how much was that?" I asked, annoyed.

"Three hundred dollars." I hung up on her. If I didn't need her to send the rest of that money, I would have cussed her out.

I came home from picking up the money and saw an argument going on in front of my apartment complex. Rico was arguing with another guy. Something told me to stay in the car. I watched as Rico stood in the middle of the street, looking around to see if anyone was coming. When he didn't think anyone was watching, he repeatedly bashed the guy in the back of his head with a gun. Blood poured from out of the man's head. He attempted to run, but Rico pointed a gun to the side of his head and ordered him to sit in his car. I ducked down. I didn't want to be a witness to anything. They were probably going to kill him, but I wasn't going to wait to find out. They pulled off, and I ran into my apartment and grabbed all my possessions. I couldn't live there anymore. I had had enough.

The rain kept awakening me and the wind shook the car. Who knew L.A. got this cold and windy at night. I pulled my jacket out of the backseat and placed it over my body. I was reduced to sleeping in my car. I could have gotten a hotel room, but I had to hold on to all the money that I had left. I couldn't believe how hard I had fallen.

The sun rose and I felt so tired. I hadn't gotten any sleep. It was my first time ever feeling like no one needed me and I didn't have a destination. I didn't know what I was going to do next, but I knew I couldn't take another day in this city. I always heard women plan on money they don't have, but you'll never hear a man plan until the money is in his hands. My planning didn't go well at all. I took a roll of the dice and crapped out. I got my ass kicked. Los Angeles was not for the weak. I couldn't make it, and I was taking my ass home.

I drove straight to the airport and strolled right to the Delta Air Lines counter. I asked for a one-way ticket to Philadelphia.

"That will be six hundred and ninety two dollars."

"I only need a one-way ticket."

"Yes, I know."

"Oh. Thank you." I had a seat, pulled out my phone, and searched for a cheaper flight, without any luck. I thought of who I could call to pay for my flight. I knew the only person who would not question me and send me the money immediately would be my mom. I was independent my entire life. I went to college and paid my own tuition and bills. And now, at thirty-two, I had to ask my mom to pay for my flight to get home. I dialed her and she answered right away.

"Mom, I want to come home and the flights are almost seven hundred dollars and I've run out of money."

I was expecting her to give me a lecture, but she didn't. Instead, she sighed and said, "I'll put it in your account right now. You sure are lucky I'm downtown near your bank." I was relieved and couldn't wait to get home.

The first thing I was going to do was put that bitch out of my house. Then I was going to sign up for another refresher class, pass my boards, hire an attorney, and get Asia home for good.

My mom texted me as soon as the money was in, and I walked back through the terminal, only for the Delta agent to inform me that the flight was full and the next one wouldn't be leaving until the morning.

"I was just here a half hour ago."

"Yeah, there were only two seats left. Sorry, seats fill up fast—especially on cross-country flights."

I stepped away from the desk feeling exasperated. I needed a shower and a bed. I couldn't spend the night at the airport. I reflected on my life. I wondered why everything was going wrong when I was trying to do everything right. I prayed to get my life back together and asked God to send me a sign— any sign—and lead my steps so I would know in which direction to walk. In the middle of my prayer, my phone beeped. It was a text message from Talene.

I sent you two thousand dollars. Sorry about the delay. My boyfriend borrowed money from his mom.

I reread the message again. I couldn't believe my prayers had been answered that quickly. Maybe Talene sending the money was a sign that I wasn't supposed to give up. I decided

I was going to give myself to the end of the week. Maybe something—anything—could happen before then.

I checked into a hotel room and took a warm shower. I slid down in the shower and let the water run all over me. The last forty-eight hours had been insane, but there was still a possibility that I could make it in L.A.

Chapter 24

Tiffany

Damien didn't come home last night. I wasn't concerned at first. I figured he was just working late. That was until I called his job, and they said he was fired weeks ago.

Then I became worried and called and texted him all night. He didn't answer and didn't bother to come home until the next morning. He walked into the bathroom while I was applying my makeup and getting ready for work.

"Where were you? Why didn't you call?"

"I stopped and had a drink last night. I must have had too much. My phone had died. I'm sorry."

"You spent the night out, didn't call me, and all you can say is that you are sorry?"

"You're right. I should have called. But I was upset because I didn't sell a car yesterday. I think I might even quit that job. It's not how I thought it was going to be."

"You might quit?" I repeated after him. Though I already knew the truth, I allowed him to ramble on with more lies.

"Yeah. So, after work I had about five or six shots of Jameson with Terry from the dealership. I was done. You know that always puts me on my back. I slept it off on his sofa. You know, I damn sure don't need another DUI and make the news again. Then his wife woke me up and I came on home." I kept applying my blush. Then I noticed red marks that resembled passion marks on his neck.

"Damien, you were fired weeks ago and you have red marks all over your neck. So do you want to start your story over again? As a matter of fact, don't worry about it. I have to go to work. When I get home, you can tell me what really happened."

I was ten minutes late, and I didn't care. These people clocked in like their life depended on it. God forbid they were a minute late and reprimanded by the big boss. The big boss could come out of his office and question me if he wanted to. I wasn't in a good mood and wasn't about to explain why I was a little tardy. My day only got worse when Shanae came over to my desk and shouted, "Girl, why didn't you tell me your husband is Damien Holcomb? Why are you working here? I heard of rich wives having jobs for fun, but come on, girl. Tell me you don't need this job. I know your man filed bankruptcy, but your man was worth all those millions."

"Please be quiet."

"Be quiet for what? You should be proud of who your husband is."

"No, I'm not."

"Okay, I get it. The millionaire next door. Working just to get out of the house. I won't tell anyone. It's our secret." She winked at me, and the moment she left my cubicle I packed up my stuff and walked out of my job.

I wanted to cry, but tears wouldn't come out. I was depleted of any emotion. Too much had happened. My husband was cheating. He was jobless. And so was I. And we were still broke.

I pulled up to Starbucks and ordered a venti Frappuccino with caramel. What's another five dollars spent when you owe millions? I reached into my pocket and handed the barista twenty dollars, when I noticed my emergency credit card in the back of my wallet. It was as if I found gold. My entire disposition changed.

For months I had felt starved and deprived of the finer things in life, but not anymore. I treated myself to a delicious meal at Fernando's. I loved their surf and turf lunch with truffle fries. From there, I went shopping for shoes and picked up a few dresses. Then I got pampered with a massage, manicure, and pedicure. After it was all done, I felt guilty and had no idea how I would pay the huge credit card bill at the end of the month, but I also didn't care. It felt good to be my old self, even if it was only for a few hours.

I was back at my house, and it was time to face Damien again and conceal my overindulgences. He wasn't home and I was happy I would be able to hide everything. I stepped in the house, turned the lights on, and nothing happened. I flicked the switch in a few rooms. Nothing. I dialed Damien's phone.

"Damien, there is something wrong with the lights. They are all off. Is the electric on?"

"It might have got cut off. It's sixteen hundred, but they said they were going to give me a few more days. Hold on, let me see what's going on. Don't worry, I'll handle it." I hung up and instantly I felt sad and depressed standing in the dark. All the joy from my shopping spree was gone. I cried and then I did the only thing I could think to do. I called my mother.

"Mom, so I do need that loan."

"What are you talking about, Tiffany?"

"You said you would loan me money. Our electric is cut off. We need sixteen hundred dollars. Can you transfer it into my account?"

"No, I'm sorry, I can't help you. When someone offers to give you money, you take it."

"But, Mom, things are really bad now. Last week we were okay."

"Tiffany, get out of there while you still can. You have

weeks to move out the house before they come and take it. He has all that debt, not you. Don't you know it is not going to get any better? It's downhill from here. Do you understand this is your new life? Despair, misery, and poverty. Forever. I told you from the beginning: marry a doctor, an attorney— even engineers make decent money—but you had to have a fast-talking New Yorker with a football in his hand. You should have married Warren. He was a football player, but one with a future. I was watching television the other day and saw a preview for his next movie. That's the guy you should have chosen. Not Damien—he was never good enough for you. He didn't come from a good home and that's the reason you weren't blessed with children, because God knew this union wouldn't last, and you deserved better."

"Mom, please, I don't want to discuss anything else. Just help me."

"No, I will not, and good luck." My mother hung up on me and I began to cry. Suddenly the lights came back on and Damien was calling. He said he paid them and made an arrangement on our back bill.

Damien came in and tried to have a one-on-one with me, but there wasn't anything that he could say that would make up for cheating and not paying our bills. I told him to leave me alone and sleep in the guest room.

At three a.m., my mother's voice awoke me: "Despair, poverty, and misery. It's downhill from here . . ." kept repeating in my head. I tried to turn her voice off, but what if she was right? What if it got worse? This isn't how I was raised. Damien had grown up poor, but I hadn't. My mother made sure we didn't have to juggle bills or dodge shut-off notices.

I walked down the hall to the guest room. It reeked of cheap alcohol. Damien's body was hanging halfway off the bed and throw-up was splattered on the floor. At the moment right there, I knew I didn't have a choice. I had to leave him. I wasn't being callous or selfish. I had to protect myself. It's called self-preservation. He didn't even know where we were going to move to. And I was certain that I would not be there to witness the bank kick him out. As my decision became clearer, I felt a sense of relief take over. No more bruised ego to try to repair, no more hard times, and no more cheating husband. I deserved better.

I packed and left him a note explaining why I'd left him. I got in my car and left my old life behind. I waited until I was in Virginia before I called my mother.

"Mom, I should be home in another three hours or so."

"You are coming home? Are you alone?"

"Yes, I left Damien."

CHAPTER 25

Shanice

"No, don't hit me! Don't hit me! I wasn't talking to any man, he is just a guy I went to school with!" It was my mother crying. She was asking for my help and her boyfriend was standing over her. We were back in the apartment I grew up in. He saw me and told me to go back to bed. I was a grown woman and instead of listening to him, I picked up a shoe and started bashing him in his head. He was bleeding from everywhere, his eyes and his ears. As he bled, I took my mother's hand, and we rushed out of the apartment to a motorcycle and rode off. Then I woke up. I had just had another dream about my mother. Her coming home caused so much uneasiness. All these years later I was still carrying so much guilt. I felt guilty for not being there to protect her the night she killed her boyfriend. A few days earlier she had finally left him and we were staying with Aunt Rhonda. We were safe and it felt like everything was going to be okay, but one day while I was at school she went back to get some more of our clothes. She thought he was at work, but he wasn't. He attacked her for the final time and left in a body bag. I guess she couldn't take him hitting her anymore. She pled guilty to murder and went straight from the county jail to prison.

Aunt Rhonda and I wrote her, but she would never respond and she refused visits. I prayed that her spirit wasn't broken and that she would be able to handle life after prison.

I had everything ready for her. Just as he said he would, Deuce helped me get a house. He paid the rent for the year, and his agent was going to help me build my credit so I could buy my own house.

The four-bedroom house Deuce rented was in the suburbs of Philadelphia. It was in a good, quiet area, but also accessible by bus since my mom and aunt didn't drive. Raven could come over and have her own room. I felt like a real adult because I decorated the house all by myself. I wanted my mom to be able to come home and relax. I contacted her parole officer and gave him my address. They had to come and inspect my house before she came home. I let Aunt Rhonda move in, and she tried her hardest to say that she wasn't coming unless Ayana and Courtney came, too. I shut that down immediately. I was not about to have Courtney in my house. Once Aunt Rhonda saw the house, she changed her tune and asked if Ayana would be able to spend the night. I told her I didn't have a problem with that.

Courtney brought her over to move the last of her things in. "This is nice, Shani. My mom was so happy. She said she thought she was going to die in that apartment, and that your mom thought she was going to die in jail."

"What?"

"No, she told my mom that. For all of us to be together again is just great."

"Yeah. It is. And tomorrow we pick her up?"

We waited outside the prison gates. I don't know who cried more, my mom, Aunt Rhonda, or me. When Trisha walked toward me, I bawled like a baby. She looked like the same lady I remembered, but just older with gray hair. I did something I never thought I would be able to do again—I got to hug my mom. She held me and I held her and we sobbed. She broke away from the hug and said, "My baby girl is all grown up. Look at you. You are beautiful."

"She is just like you, Trisha," Aunt Rhonda said as she went and hugged her sister and took her one plastic bag. We all got in the car and rode away from that horrible place that had held my mother for two decades. My mom sat in the front of the car in silence, and her eyes drifted as we traveled down the mountainside highway.

"Trish, what do you want to eat?" Aunt Rhonda asked.

"McDonalds. I've been dreaming about McDonalds."

"That should be easy. There's one at every rest stop." At the McDonalds, she devoured two Quarter Pounders with cheese, French fries, and two large Cokes.

She needed new clothes, so we stopped at the mall on our way home. My mom looked around and seemed like she was scared.

"Are you okay, Mom?"

She looked around and then spoke. "It seems like everyone is walking so fast and on their phone and everything is just so busy."

"Yeah, that's true."

"Things are so different. I have to take a class and catch up and learn how to use the phone."

"It's easy to use a cell phone. You'll get the hang of it. Let's get you one right now."

"I can get one right from the store?"

"Yes."

Trish was amazed by her new phone, but she was really in love with her new house and room. She was so thankful for her own space. I had to tell her to stop thanking me.

After her parole officer left, my mom ate again and took a long bath, came out, and fell onto the bed. I placed the covers over her and watched her sleep. I remembered when I was a little girl. After she got beat up, I would be her lookout as she rested. When he would come in the house, I would wake her.

Aunt Rhonda walked in and gave me a hug.

"Shanice, get some rest. You did a good job. She's home, and she's happy. I'll make us a big breakfast in the morning."

The next morning Aunt Rhonda was peeling potatoes at the table with Trisha. I took the moment to ask my mom the one question I hadn't asked her that I wanted to know most.

"Mom, how come you didn't call or write me? Why would you shut down all contact with the family?"

"I didn't want to hold anyone up with their life. I prayed for you every day. I prayed for Rhonda and Courtney, and I hoped one day I would see you again." She brought tears to my eyes. I was mad at her for years. I didn't pray for her because she left me. I was angry that she went back to him. I was mad because I didn't have any family. I didn't know if my dad was dead or he was still walking the street.

"It was hard for me to deal with life. You have to understand that I killed the man I loved, my daughter's father, and my abuser."

"He was my dad?"

"Yes."

"Where is the rest of our family?"

"We don't have any family. Just me and Rhonda. Our mother dropped us off at the foster home when we were three and four. I didn't answer your letters, but I got every one. I was mad at myself, for being there. I wanted better for you, and then I let you down and couldn't face you. I was your mother and it was my job to raise you and I failed you."

"I didn't feel that way. I just wanted to talk and see you."

"I did fail you. That's why you have to get your daughter back. Rhonda told me she lives with her grandmom. She has to grow up with you. We have to break the cycle. I will get me a job, and so will Rhonda. We were talking, and you don't have to take care of us. I want you to take care of her."

"Mom, you just got home. Don't worry about Raven. She's doing real good with her grandmom and granddad. She goes to a private school and I see her a lot. I travel too much for her to live with me. I can't make sure she does her homework and gets up for school from another city, while I'm out here trying to make money."

"All the money in the world can't buy you any time back. Trust me, I know. You have to get your daughter."

"Mom, I'll think about it. You have to get adjusted to being back out here. And I'll handle the rest."

CHAPTER 26

Monique

London was great, but who knew I would return home to some foolishness? I knew something was up when Carl picked me up from the airport. I wasn't expecting him. He appeared to be angry and he wasn't happy to see all my extra luggage.

"What are you doing here?"

"Kadir called me. He was upset and asked me to drive down. He didn't think you would make it back in time for tomorrow."

"Of course I would make it."

"Well, I'm happy you did. You know this is all new to him. You have to give the boy a break."

"I do and I am."

"Plus, there is something at the house I don't think you are going to like."

"Like what?"

"Kadir has a friend at the house."

"Friend? What friend? I'm gone for a few days, and Kadir has a friend? Does this friend have kids? Is she a stripper? Is she a stripper with kids?"

"No, she seems nice. Her name is Abigail."

"What? Aba-who? I never met a black girl named Abigail."

"She is not black."

"Oh, hell no!"

"Mo, give her a chance. You haven't even met her yet. She seems like a nice girl. She works, has one son and her own apartment."

"She has a child? He definitely can't date her."

"You had a kid when I met you."

"But you weren't rich. He got every girl I've been warning him about in one."

I wasn't a racist, but I don't want any girl—especially not a white one—trying to take half my son's money. They are raised to go to the highest bidder, and I'm just not having it. Not at all. I stomped into the house to find Kadir and his playmate in my kitchen. He was sitting at my table, and she was cooking on my stove. She had the nerve to be wearing one of my son's wifebeaters.

"Ka, this must be your mother. I'm Abigail. My friends call me Abby." She extended her hand out to me. I just stared her up and down. Then she asked Carl if he would like dinner.

"No, he would not," I answered for him. "Why are you walking around my house with a t-shirt on?"

"Oh, I didn't have anything else to wear. My dress is in the washer."

I turned to my son and screamed, "Kadir Latif Hall, explain this shit to me!" Kadir followed me into the living room, and I asked him what was going on.

"Nothing. We are chilling and she is making me something to eat."

I walked back into the kitchen and said, "Abigail, sweetie, get your stuff and please leave my house."

Kadir came behind me and said, "Mom, this is my house. She's my friend."

"If it's a problem, I will leave. It's cool, Kadir. I'm going to just go."

"Yeah, that's a good idea. Do that."

"Mom, you can't do that. You can't make her leave," Kadir protested.

"She's going to get the fuck up out my house," I said as Kadir ran after Abigail, and Carl looked over at me like I was in trouble.

"What? I didn't do anything wrong."

"Monique, he is going to do the opposite of what you tell him to do."

"I don't care, Carl."

Half listening to him, I called for Kadir to come back and let the girl leave. She pulled off and Kadir came back in the house angry.

"Ka, have a seat. Let's talk about this."

"I'll stand."

"Where did you meet that girl?"

"At the mall."

"Don't you know she saw you coming? I'm not being mean, Ka, but tell me why you need a girl with a kid? You can have any girl you want. All people see when they look at you is a check. I keep telling you that you have a target on your back that everyone is trying to hit."

"But she's not like that. We were talking since we met and she hasn't asked me for anything."

"She hasn't asked you for anything yet! It's all right to meet people and date pretty girls, but date the kind that have something going on for themselves, too."

"But the thing is I'm grown and I can do whatever I want."

"That's true, but make sure you do the right thing. You have the charity event tomorrow. Why don't you prepare for that?"

The next afternoon I was ready to go to Kadir's first official team event. It was a charity event to help Hemby's Children's Hospital. Carl drove with me to the event. He had tried to lecture me last night, but I locked my bedroom door and I think he slept in the guest room.

"So I see you bought more of the same type of clothes in Europe. Mo, seriously, you have to start dressing a little better."

"What? Carl, shut up."

"No, it is not just me saying something anymore. You are representing your son. This is his first team event, and you are wearing a booty dress."

Kadir was suited up and played with patients from the hospital. I walked around the Time Warner Arena. I saw a few heads turn as I walked by in my little black dress, but that was expected. I looked good. What I didn't expect was the giggling. It was two women hating. "She's a groupie, and she needs to take that dress off. The club is not open yet." They said a few other things that I didn't appreciate. I knew I was supposed to be a professional, but the Philly girl in me had to let them know I heard what they said.

Luckily, Carl didn't see me arguing with the other women. He would have said, "See, I told you." I calmed myself down and had a seat on the other side of the court.

When everything was over, Carl went to the restroom and I looked for Kadir. Instead of finding him, someone found me. I felt a hand grab my waist. I knew it was him without turning around. His cologne was still so distinctive. I turned to see Dele. I hadn't thought about his six foot seven, fine, chocolate self since I left London. Well, I thought about him the entire flight home, but I wasn't sure if the feelings were mutual.

"Hey. How you been?" he asked, as he attempted to place a kiss on my cheek, but I swerved in the other direction.

"I'm great," I answered, as if I never saw his beautiful body naked. I smiled and looked around, making sure no one was picking up on our familiar interaction.

"So, is that Kadir's dad?"

"Yeah, but he is only here for this event."

"Okay, so when can I see you again?"

"I don't know."

"I've been thinking about you since you left my hotel room. I need to see you again. I'm going to text you tonight and you are going to come and meet me."

His accent made me weak. Instead of saying "no" or "I can't, it's wrong, you are my son's teammate," I replied, "Okay." I walked away from him before things seemed too obvious.

After the charity game, Kadir had a date. He had met the sister of one of the sick kids. I met her briefly and so far, so good. She was cute, black, and in college. I approved of anybody as long as it meant that trailer park girl wasn't ever coming back over again.

Carl dropped me off at the house and I couldn't wait to get to my date with my Dele. I could tell he was trying to hang around, but I told him I was sleepy from my trip and wanted to catch up on rest.

"Thanks for coming, Carl. If you get sleepy, pull over. Have a good evening," I said, rushing out of the car.

"All right. Call me if you need me. I'll be up driving. I can stay if you want me to."

"No, I'm okay. Good night."

I ran upstairs and searched inside of my closet. I wasn't sure what I wanted to wear. Yes, I looked young—but I had to make sure I didn't look like I was trying to be young. Seeing a younger man was already playing tricks on my mind. If I was going out with Carl, I'd feel confident in a t-shirt and jeans. Now, I was sitting here debating if I looked old—or worse, like someone's old-ass auntie that thinks she still has it, but doesn't. I had so many new dresses, but nothing seemed perfect. I settled on a black skirt, heels, and a blue low-cut blouse. Once I was dressed and in the car, I dialed him.

"Where do you want to meet me?"

"At the Capital Grille."

I arrived first so that I could get us a table in the back. He walked in with flowers and I was in love all over again.

"Monique, are you hiding?"

"Yes, I am."

"I love your honesty and your sunglasses at night. But why are we hiding?"

"You know why I can't be seen with you."

"I'm not that famous. People only know I play basketball because of my height. They never know my name or what team I play for."

"I can't take any chances."

"If it will make you feel better, we can take our food to go."

"Yeah, let's do that."

We took our food to go and headed to his beautiful bachelor loft in downtown Charlotte. He poured wine and offered me some of his lobster macaroni and cheese.

"I've missed you; have you missed me?"

"I don't know. Maybe."

"So, why are you here? If you are not sure if you missed me or not . . ."

I couldn't answer that question. I wasn't sure, but I did find him very interesting, and I couldn't lie and say I didn't want a repeat of London.

"I just thought we would be friends."

"What kind of friends? I think I want to be more than friends."

He sat me on his lap and he kissed me. My phone rang. When I looked at the screen and saw it was Carl, I didn't answer. And when Kadir called right after him, I didn't answer, either.

Another night with Dele felt right, but I knew that it wasn't. It was the next morning and I wished I had someone to confide in. I was so confused. And felt so guilt-ridden. On one hand, I wasn't hurting anyone because we were two consenting adults. On the other hand, he was just off-limits because he was my son's teammate. There must be a rule somewhere that mothers shouldn't fuck their son's coworkers. Still, it would've been great to dial up CeCe and get her opinion. I just couldn't risk anyone finding out. I looked over at Dele. He was still asleep. I took that as my opportunity to sneak out. I jumped up, got dressed, and walked out of his apartment. I thought I was quiet, but Dele caught me at the elevator.

"Why did you leave without saying good-bye again? I wanted to make you breakfast."

"I have to go. And, well, I don't know how all of this will work out. I will call you later." I pushed the elevator down. He leaned and kissed me on the lips and asked me to stay once more. "No, I really have to go."

CHAPTER 27

Zakiya

I pulled out Jabrilah's nightclothes and gave them to my new part-time nanny, Octavia. She was a forty-five-year-old mother of two. She became a nanny after her youngest son went away to college last year. She was referred by an agency and had been working on a trial basis for two weeks. So far she was okay, but no one would be able to replace Lena.

"Octavia, I'm going to be going out for a few hours. You can give Jabrilah a bath and a bottle, and she should be ready for bed."

"Okay, we will be fine. Have a good time."

I took advantage of Octavia's presence by attending Dawn's girls' night in. I'd enjoyed myself at her daughter Jaylen's Doc McStuffins birthday party. She was such a good mom, and her children were sweet and well-mannered. Our husbands were out of town, and this was going to be the first time I could meet all the other wives.

Dawn's home was a huge house in a gated community. I came into her living room and her housekeeper handed me a peach Bellini. I took a sip and spoke to all the other wives and girlfriends. They were staring at their phones and oblivious to my existence. No one bothered to introduce themselves. They were white, black, and Asian. Dawn introduced each woman and told me who she was married to and what position her man played. The young pregnant white one was Cara, who looked to be about twenty; the black one, Aniqua, was pretty, but she looked a little tired; and the older Asian woman, Jessica, had to be in her thirties. "Hey everybody. This is Jabril Smith's wife. The trade." I squinted my eyes and she corrected herself. "I mean, the guard that we just got from OKC."

My introduction was returned with weak "hellos" and a "nice to meet you." They silently assessed my ring, shoes, and bag. After a subtle evaluation, they returned to their previously interrupted conversations.

"Did you see my new car? It's an 'I'm very sorry. It will never happen again.' present," Jessica said. She was pretty, but she did too much contouring to her face. She almost looked like a drag queen.

"I have a couple of those," Aniqua chimed in.

"Well, this is an 'I don't know that girl, she is lying' ring." Cara laughed as she extended her ring finger, displaying a clear princess-cut diamond.

"Let me see. Wow, that is a sparkler," Dawn said.

"Ring so bright I can't see the past." Jessica laughed.

They all started laughing.

"So how about you? Any big gifts after a cheatathon?" the woman named Jessica asked me.

"Nope," I said and smiled. I was not talking about my man with these women I had just met.

"So he has never cheated before? Don't answer that question. I know he has, they all do on the road. I know you just got married, but nothing changes after the wedding but your last name and what you're entitled to when you get a divorce," Dawn said.

"I don't agree with that," I responded. "There have to be some good marriages in the league. I don't believe all men cheat. Some couples are happily married."

"True, I'm very happy. Happy with my furs, Giuseppes, Louboutins, and my summer house." Jessica laughed.

"She's right. I said fuck it a long time ago. I let my husband's girlfriends spend the night, right down the hall. I know where he is and I know he is safe. And I rest easy. Every once in a while if I want to get my pussy ate and let my husband watch, I'll knock on the door. Sometimes, I'll suck on a tittie or two, but I'm not doing anything else. But the point is, my husband knows I will ride for him. And it's no other chick that can take my place. That's why we are happy," Dawn said proudly.

That was a little too much information for me. I felt like I was talking to Nichelle and Christie again. Straight from the gate, they were talking about cheating, sex, sharing groupie stories, talking about how somebody from another team could get it, whose man wasn't shit, and a bunch of other things I wasn't prepared to hear. I didn't join in on the conversation, I just listened.

With every story, Dawn became more unrecognizable. She wasn't the cool chick from the game who took up for me or the great hands-on mom. She became one of them, a shallow, materialistic type that I could do without.

Aniqua excused herself to the restroom. As soon as she left, her friends started talking about her.

"When she comes back, tell her she needs to go shopping. I'm tired of seeing those sweat pants. She comes out of the house all the time with no makeup." Cara sighed.

"Yes, I'm like, girl get a stylist and someone to beat your face." Jessica laughed.

"How is your husband a millionaire, but you're raggedy? We all have kids, but damn, comb your hair, bitch," Dawn agreed. I couldn't believe they were talking about their friend like that. Aniqua came out of the bathroom and Dawn asked her if she was okay.

"Yeah, I just had another procedure a few days ago."

"You were pregnant again? You better get on some birth control or make him use a condom."

She coughed and then said, "He doesn't like condoms."

"He better start liking them. You can't be having abortions every month. Well, I was at the abortion clinic recently, too, but not for me. I had to take Thaddeus's little jump-off. I told her, girl, you don't have time for a baby and Thaddeus don't want any more kids. Soon as she got rid of it we dropped her ass and never called her again. You not having no baby by my husband." Again all the woman laughed like what she was saying was normal and funny.

Dawn stood up and commanded everyone's attention: "So let me tell y'all how I had to check that rookie's mom and they had to call security. Her ratchet ass tried to come for us. First of all, she had on cheap-ass shoes with a white sticker on the bottom. And her outfit was basic as hell. Carrying a Louis Vuitton bag like it was her first Louis bag. So I said something and she heard me and tried to get loud. She got in Zakiya's face and I stopped her and told her I said it."

"Are you serious? Where were we?" Cara asked.

"I don't know where y'all were, but when she came over I was like, no, bitch. We don't do that shit here. You look a mess. You need to go change. My husband is the captain, which makes me the co-captain. And she was like, I'm Kadir Hall's mom. And I was like, and? You're not a wife or girlfriend. Go have several seats. Why are you even here? Zakiya, tell them about the mom."

"Yeah, she was crazy . . ." I said uncomfortably, looking down at my drink. I didn't want to participate in any part of this conversation.

"So, I was like, bitch, this is my city, we run this house, and I don't approve of the way you are representing us. I told her she better not come to any more games that way." Dawn was exaggerating how and what she said to the rookie's mom. She did get with her, but it went down a lot different than she was claiming. I decided I didn't like her anymore. And I really didn't like her annoying, ignorant friends. I was uncomfortable.

"I'll be back," I said as I guzzled down the last of my drink. I had every intention of going to her restroom, but her front door looked more appealing. I didn't say good-bye, I just left.

The next thing I knew, I was in my car. I turned on my radio and looked at the time on the dash. I hoped Jabrilah was still up. I would rather spend time with my daughter than be with negative women like that. On the ride home, I checked in on Lisa.

"Hey, little sis. Me and the boys will be down the week after next."

"Okay. That's great. We can drive down to Disney World. I can't wait until you come. It's so hard to have a real conversation with real people."

"What are you talking about, Zakiya?"

"I don't know, Lisa, I just don't like these other players' wives. They are all the same. All they talk about is their expensive shallow lives. There is more to life than games, make-up, and shoes."

My sister began laughing hysterically. "This is coming from the person whose daughter has a better shoe collection than most adults."

"That's true, but there's a difference. I know what's important. And I don't ask Jabril for these things, he just buys them. I would much rather have a regular life."

"So, everyone is striving for extraordinary, and you are longing for regular. You are crazy, and you do not make any sense, Kiya." My sister continued to laugh at me.

"I know what I'm talking about. Lisa, I need more. Something more."

"Good night, girl. I'll talk to you soon."

I said, "Good night" and ended the call. I placed the phone down and realized the car in front of me had suddenly pushed his brakes. I tried to push on my brakes, but it was too late. The car in front of me crashed into the one in front of it. I was seconds from joining the pile-up. I tried to avoid the wreckage in front of me by steering the car away from the accident. I veered out of the way, but the car behind me tried to move out of the way, too. I turned left, he turned right, but still lost control. The car behind me came cruising sideways right toward me. There wasn't enough time to move. I prepared for impact. "Oh, God. Please help me, please help me. Don't let me die," I prayed aloud as the car slammed into the side of my car. The force of the car hitting mine flung me into the passenger-side window. I hit my head, my car cruised a few feet, and then slowly stopped on its own.

Moments later, I was in a daze. I heard sirens and saw smoke coming from all the other cars. I was shaking. People were running up to my car banging on the window asking me if I was okay. I looked up and tried to speak, but I couldn't answer them because I was still in shock.

I was transported to the hospital. I heard cries and felt panic all around me. There were hurt people everywhere. I was in a hospital bed and had come around and realized I was okay. The nurse told me I was brought in for observation, but that I didn't have one bruise on me. I knew I had been saved. I knew God had answered my call. I called Jabril and my sister. Jabril was ready to come home, but I told him not to. He didn't have to because—unbelievably—I didn't have a scratch on me and felt fine. I was released from the hospital.

The next morning, I felt the need to be near the house of the Lord. God saved me from the accident, and I had to thank him. I looked online for a church and I found the Faith Tabernacle Baptist Church. They had three services, and I planned on making their eleven o'clock program.

I drove thirty minutes to the megachurch nestled in the middle of a big baseball-size field. I walked in and immediately felt at home. The women were beautifully dressed in dresses of all different colors, and the men were in nice-fitting suits. The choir was singing melodically, swaying back and forth to "God in Me" by Mary Mary. When they were done singing, the pastor began speaking. He was young and vibrant and so was his wife. He preached about having a purpose and being the person God wants you to be. His words reached me and I knew it was meant for me to be there.

After the service, the First Lady Elise spoke and asked for volunteers to feed the homeless. I walked up to an older, round woman in her forties who was taking names, and told her I wanted to sign up to volunteer.

"I would like to volunteer."

"Welcome! What's your name, sweetie?"

"Zakiya Smith."

"Well, sign up right here. We will be meeting at our sister church, Rockclave Baptist. It's kind of a bad neighborhood, so make sure to leave your good jewelry and bags at home. We will contact you with the time and date."

"Okay, thank you."

Excited about the service, I came home, prepared dinner, and waited for Jabril to come home. Jabrilah played on the floor with her toys making a big mess. Jabril rushed in the door and hugged me. "Kiya, are you okay?"

"Yes, I'm fine. God saved me."

"He sure did. You're lucky."

"I know. I went to church today. So how's everything going? Are you adjusting now?"

"It's okay. I'm still getting to know their system. Everyone is hype over the rookie, Kadir Hall."

"Is he any good?"

"Yeah. He's good, but a little cocky, and the assistant coach acts like he's his fan and wants to be his friend. He is sucking up to him already."

"Well, you know who you are and what you can contribute, Jabril. And once you prove yourself . . ."

"When the season starts, I just hope I'm not on the bench, Kiya. It's like ego aside, I can watch the game from home."

"You won't be, Bril."

"I hope not. I can't be on the bench. I've never been on the bench."

"You won't be on the bench. All we have to do is pray. Speaking of prayer, you have to go with me. The pastor at the church is young. He's funny and hip. It's really nice."

"Well, pray I can get some minutes on the court."

"I will."

I fed and bathed Jabrilah. Once I put her to sleep I walked into our bedroom and smelled weed coming from the bathroom.

I opened the door and saw Jabril puffing on a blunt. "Why are you smoking, Jabril? What is wrong with you?"

"I need something to relax me, Kiya."

"I don't care. Our daughter is asleep, and she can smell that mess! It can get into her system."

"Chill, Kiya! I'm stressed the fuck out for real. You don't know what I'm going through."

"And when you stressed out, you don't smoke. You ask God to help you."

"Really, Zakiya? You go to church one time and now you want to preach? Man, close the door. I don't smoke all the time and if I want to chill, let me chill out."

"Whatever, Jabril."

CHAPTER 28

Shanice

I never realized how much I missed my mom until I got her back. She, Raven, and I had been having girls' time going to the movies, bowling, and we took Raven to her first concert in the park. Slowly, it was becoming more normal. I loved having her and my aunt home to cook and clean. Ms. Valerie has been letting me get Raven more. I even got her during the school week. Since I had help now from Aunt Rhonda and Mom, it made everything so easy.

"Mom-mom Trisha, don't be sad. I'll be back," Raven said as we walked toward the door.

"Okay. Little Raven, when you come back over, you have to show your mom-mom more phone stuff. I might forget."

"No, Mom-mom Trisha, you have to remember everything I already showed you. Practice makes perfect." We both laughed at Raven's young wisdom. My daughter was so smart for her age, and I knew that—unlike me—she was going to college and would grow up to be something big, like a lawyer or something.

Once we were in the car, I told Raven to put on her seat belt.

"Mom, my friends live with their mom. And their moms go to work like you, but they come home every day. Why don't you come home every day? And why don't I live with you?"

"Because I have a different type of job, Raven."

"And, Mommy, all these years, why I never saw Mommom Trisha?"

"Because she lived somewhere else."

"Oh. I have so many mom-moms, and a dad, and a pop-pop!"

"That's because you are special." I tried to change the subject. I was starting to feel guilty about having my daughter live with her grandmom, and I would have to make a change soon.

After dropping Raven off at school, I came back home and saw Courtney on the sofa showing my mom old pictures of us.

"Hey, Shani. I'm here to pick my mom up. Don't worry, I'm not staying."

"Okay."

"My boyfriend's in the car. Come meet him." I didn't care about her boyfriend or her, but I walked outside and waved. He looked young and broke, which meant he was perfect for Courtney. I wasn't sure why Courtney didn't get the hint that I didn't fuck with her like that yet. She knew I could hold a grudge forever. When we were kids, if someone stepped on my shoe by accident, I would hate them for years. So she had to know I would never forgive her.

Once Aunt Rhonda left with Courtney, my mom began to question me about the shade that I had thrown at my cousin.

"Why are you so mean to her?"

"She went on the radio discussing my business."

"I understand, but everyone should get a second chance. She comes in here and just about kisses your ass to be your friend."

"Mom, please don't ask me about Courtney. I don't mess with her and that's it." I was still getting to know my mother, and she was still getting to know me. I didn't have time to explain anything to Trisha. I had to pack and go see Deuce. Then right after seeing him I had to meet up with the producers for the show. It would be the first time the cameras from *Eye Candy Queens: The Come-up* would be following me. Before I left for a party I was hosting in Dallas, I had to go spend some time with my teddy bear, Deuce. I had grown to be very "in like" with Deuce. He was a gift-giver, and I had accepted everything except his big old belly. I tried to tell him to go to the gym, but he just might need to get some weight-loss surgery instead. I didn't know. I could see past it because it doesn't stand in the way of anything. The first time we had sex, I was frightened. I thought he was going to pull out this little dick and I was going to have to fake like I could feel it, but I was surprisingly wrong. He put it down. To my surprise, underneath that stomach, he was packing and ate pussy like a pro. Deuce and I were supposed to meet for dinner, but he said something had come up with Don Santos's overseas tour dates. He asked me to meet him at his office.

When I arrived, I spoke to Ms. Patricia at the front desk and walked into his corner office. As soon as I walked through his door, he grabbed my waist and a handful of my ass. "What's up, beautiful?" He kissed me and began to apologize.

"Sorry, I'm behind schedule. Don's manager didn't get one of the DJs his passport and visa, so I'm trying to see what I can do. It's not my job, but I want the best stage show possible."

"It's okay because you already know you have to make this up to me."

"I'm already ahead of you. I brought you something for your trip to Dallas."

"You did? You know how I love gifts. What's in the boxes?"

In the corner were two big white boxes with huge red bows. I opened them to see a three-piece classic Louis Vuitton luggage set.

"Thank you, Deuce," I said, hugging him tightly.

"You're welcome. Did you miss me?"

"Yes."

"How much?" He walked behind me, kissed my shoulder. I pulled off my jeans and took down my thong. He then bit my neck and breasts and played with my pussy. He stopped right before I was ready to cum and locked the door. When he came back to his desk I licked his bald head and sucked on his chest. I cupped and massaged his balls until his dick was fully hard. I grabbed my breasts and played with them and spread my legs wide open and waited in anticipation for his dick to enter. He reached into his duffel bag and fumbled for a condom. He slid the condom on and penetrated my walls until he couldn't take anymore. He came in a loud convulsion. He was out of breath, but I was fulfilled. I slid off the table and fixed my clothes. He tried to gather his thoughts.

"See? I told you I missed you."

"Ah, Shanice. Girl, what am I going to do with you?"

"What are you talking about?"

"I'm talking about I don't like you leaving me. Don't give my pussy away or be in anyone's face. I'm not joking." He grabbed my face and gave me a sloppy kiss again.

"I'm not. When you met me, I didn't, did I?"

"No, but I know these dudes try you every night."

"Deuce, I know. I got it."

"Honestly, I'm tired of all your hosting and traveling."

"It's my job, Deuce."

"I know. I'm not going to stand in your way of getting money, but we are going to have to make some adjustments. I need you here with me, not flying all around the country."

"Deuce, I'm going and coming right back. You know we're filming for the show."

"I know, I'm proud of you. Have a safe trip and look inside of your suitcase when you get home."

"Okay." I kissed his face and reassured him that when I returned, he would get some love and attention.

"And I got you that luggage because I'm going to Dubai in a few weeks, and you are going with me."

"I love how you never ask me. You just tell where I'm going."

"You do like being told what to do. That's my job. But I'll ask you anyway: Shanice, will you accompany me to Dubai? Also, I want you to be my main chick, then you won't have to do all that traveling . . ."

"Main chick. I better be your only chick." I laughed. "I'll give you an answer to both when I return. I promise. As soon as I get back from Dallas."

"No, I need my baby here with me tonight. Your flight doesn't leave until the afternoon. Stay with me."

"Okay, Deuce." I wanted to say yes, but I didn't want to rush into a relationship with him. We had only known each other for a couple of months and I wasn't sure he was the one. Yes, he was buying me gifts, but so did every guy with money. I still wanted to keep my options open.

CHAPTER 29

Shanice

I made it home just in time to pack. Courtney was sitting in the living room with Aunt Rhonda and my mom. I came and gave everyone a hug—except for Courtney.

"Where you going now?" Aunt Rhonda asked.

"To Dallas. I have to pack."

Courtney volunteered to help me and followed me up the steps. I threw my new luggage on the bed. I only needed one bag. I was only staying for one night. I looked on my phone, and it was ninety degrees there. I packed nothing but a dress and a pair of shorts and t-shirt for the airport.

"You stay with nice shit. This suitcase cost like four thousand by itself. What do you want me to pack?" She opened the suitcase and a stack of hundreds fell out.

"Shani, did you know that was in there?"

"Yeah, uhm, thanks." I really wanted to tell her to just get out of my way. "You know what? You can grab my flat irons."

She came back in with my hair products and flat irons. Then she went right back to being nosy Courtney.

"So who gave you all that money? You still mess with that guy Jabril?" Her saying Jabril's name stirred something in me. I hadn't been thinking about him lately, and I wanted to keep it that way.

"No. I been stop dealing with him. Stop asking me shit. And why should I tell you anything anyway? What, do want to run and tell my business again?"

"Shani, I'm not like that anymore. I got your back. I'm sorry. I'm real sorry. How long are you going to hold on to the past? We're family, and you have to let it go."

"I'll think about it." I have to admit, having family around actually felt good. I thought that maybe I could forgive Courtney.

I texted my teddy bear from the airport. I had plenty of time to text because my flight was delayed due to a thunderstorm. By the time I made it to Dallas, there wasn't enough time to go to the hotel. I had to change into my sexy dress and do my makeup in the airport bathroom. It was muggy, and all my curls had dropped. Then I got a message that the camera crew was stuck in New York and they wouldn't be filming tonight. At that point, I didn't care about the party anymore. I was going to get to the club, say hey, pick up my check, and leave.

Club Standard was halfway empty and it was 12:30. I already knew I was going to dip out by one. For some reason, I wasn't feeling the scene. I never thought that clubbing would get old, but after a while, it does.

The promoter, Kyle, tried to apologize for the low turnout. He had no idea how happy I was. I was even thinking about seeing if I could get on an earlier flight.

"No problem."

"Yeah, but give it another half hour or so and it will get good. I'm going to need you to announce this birthday. This NBA player that just signed with the Hornets."

"The Charlotte Hornets?" *That is the team Jabril plays for*, I thought. "Did they have a game tonight?"

"Yeah, it's the end of the Elite League, and this is their after party. So when they get here, the club will fill up."

I wondered if Jabril was coming tonight. I excused myself and went to the bathroom. In that moment, I understood the expression "if you stay ready, you don't have to get ready." I looked a mess and if Jabril was going to be in this club, he couldn't see me like this. I applied lipstick, retouched my foundation, and fixed my hair as best I could.

I drank four shots of Pineapple Cîroc and then waited. Just like Kyle said, the club became packed as I saw the team walk in one by one. The first guy wasn't Jabril, and neither was the second guy . . . or the fifth . . . or sixth . . . or seventh. I was hype for nothing. I got another shot. Then, in the back behind security, I saw my baby. I don't know what held me back. I wanted to run up to him, kiss him, and wrap my legs around him. It was the first time I saw him in living color in almost two years.

My excitement quickly turned into anger. Why had he avoided me? Why hadn't he ever checked on me? Didn't I mean something to him? I needed my questions answered, and I needed to know now.

I didn't care that we were in a crowded club with loud music blasting. I was going to finally have that one-on-one conversation with him. I deserved that, and he owed me. If he said to leave him alone and not to contact him again, I would do that. But I knew that he wouldn't. I knew he had to care about me. He could have treated me like all the others, but he didn't.

I approached the area he was seated in. I stood in front of him and said, "Jabril." He glanced at me, trying to make out who had called him in the dark club. It took him a few minutes to process who I was. He stood up and gave me a friendly hug.

"What are you doing here?"

"I'm in town. I'm hosting this party tonight."

"Cool. Good seeing you," he said, and then walked away to a VIP area where the rest of his team was posted up.

I couldn't think anymore. It had to be fate. Out of all the

clubs, in all the cities, on all the nights, and they asked me to host this one. I was going to say something else to him when Kyle pulled me to the stage and asked me to announce that the team was in the building. I stepped onto the stage, said something fast, and dropped the microphone. I left the stage and walked to the area where Jabril was.

"Can I talk to you, Jabril?"

He pulled out his phone and said, "Give me your number."

"No, I want to talk to you right now!"

He looked around at the guys he was with. "This isn't really a good time." I wasn't taking no for an answer. He followed me to an area in the back of the club. It wasn't exactly the place I wanted to have a heart-to-heart, but it would have to do.

"Why haven't you called me? I called and texted you so many times."

"I don't know. I been changed my number," he said, looking around to see who was tuned in to our discussion.

I looked directly in his eyes, and I couldn't tell if he still loved me or not. I didn't have anything to lose. I had to tell him how I really felt.

"Jabril, I never stopped thinking about you. You've been on my mind. I need you. Seeing you tonight is a confirmation that my feelings haven't changed. I miss you. I love you, and no one has ever made me feel the way you did. Do you miss me? Do you love me?"

"I did, but, you know, I'm happily married now . . ."

"Yeah. I know, but we were still good friends. We had some good times, right? I just want to be there for you."

"Shanice, I was feeling you back then, but after everything that went down, I changed. I can't go back down that path. I can't afford it. And I don't need any drama in my life."

"What does that mean? I took that case for you. I never brought you drama."

"It means I am doing everything the right way now. I only

have a drink every now and then. Not really smoking. Since I've been married, I don't cheat. So I doubt that I can be that type of friend to you again."

"I understand. Well, maybe I can just call you from time to time."

"We can do that, but I can't give you anything else." He inserted his new area code and number in my phone and I felt victorious. I didn't get to take him back to my hotel room, but I had his number and that was a start.

CHAPTER 30

Adrienne

If I was going to stay in L.A., I had to look the part. My plan was to go and beat on every door in Hollywood. Which meant I needed to get my hair done and buy a few things to enhance my wardrobe. I Googled African-American hair salons, and Envoy Salon and Spa came up. I clicked on their web page and it was a beautiful salon, but could they do hair? I didn't have any money to waste. Then I read a news article on their site that dubbed them the "Stylists to the Stars" and that made my decision easy. I never knew who I could network with under the dryer.

Walking into the salon, I knew I had made the right decision. There were beautiful women waiting to be serviced, and even the stylist's hair was done to perfection. They were wearing full makeup and heels.

"Do you have any open appointments today?" I asked the receptionist.

"Yes, Chike is taking one more, I think. What are you getting?"

"A wash and curl."

Chike approached the counter with masculine facial hair and a straight blond bob weave. He had a shape that would make any woman jealous. He looked at his schedule for the rest of the day and said that he would take me.

"Hello, beautiful. I love your color but not them split ends, girl."

"I know. It's a mess. That's why I'm here."

"Yes, child, just in time, too." He laughed and turned me over to the shampoo girl. I had my hair washed and blow-dried, and then I sat in his chair.

"You are so pretty. So what do you do? Are you an actress?"

"I'm a script writer."

"Have you sold anything yet?"

"No, but I'm in the process."

"Uhm-hum," he said sarcastically.

I couldn't help but laugh. "I know everyone here is an actress, a model, or a movie director. But I am going to sell my script. I am. But right now, I'm just trying to make it out here."

"Make it how? Like a job?"

"I guess. Why, do you know someone that is hiring?"

"My other client is looking for a personal assistant. You seem like you would get along with her. Plus she knows a lot of people in the industry. She was just talking about being an actress. I forgot her ex-husband's name, but you probably heard of him."

"Really? Do you know how much the salary would be?" I asked, trying not to sound too interested.

"I'm not sure, but I know it would pay really good. I heard her talking about it earlier. I have to say she is a strange woman, but I'm sure someone like you can handle her."

Chike made me feel like a new woman. He gave my hair a new life with textured curls and he added a few tracks. He called his client who was hiring, and she said to give me her information.

I called Morgan Coleman and she gave me a phone interview. She seemed to be pleasant over the phone, and asked if I could meet up with her that day.

Her house was in the Hollywood Hills; the farther I drove, the farther the city was below and behind me. The GPS declared that I had arrived at my destination in front of a beautiful mansion sitting alone on top of a hill.

I hoped I was hired, because it looked like she could afford to pay me well. I rang the bell and knocked a few times. A teenage girl answered the door.

"May I help you?"

"Yes, I'm here for Morgan Coleman."

"Mom, your new assistant is here," she yelled out and told me to come in.

I followed her to a beautiful woman with a head full of black, shoulder-length curls, sitting in a black bikini, soaking up the sun. She sat up and threw a turquoise cover-up over her olive tone skin. I had a seat at a table next to the pool. She offered me a drink. I declined, and she said, "Let me get right to the point. My ex-husband is the comedian RJ Coleman. Do you know him?"

"Yes."

"Of course you do. We were married for seventeen years, but we've been separated for a year and a half. And that bastard already has a baby and is about to marry this little non-English-speaking bitch. But that's another story. How are you? Can you work the weekends?"

"I'm fine. Yes, I can."

"So, as I was saying, he left me for a red beans and rice *chica*."

Her daughter, who pretended that she wasn't listening to our conversation, took off her pink Beats by Dre headphones and said, "Mom, she was born here. She can speak English very well. She went to Stanford. And she's not Spanish, she is Mexican."

"It's all the same. No one asked you anything, Alexandria.

Don't disrespect your mother. Okay? Don't take up for the bilingual bitch that took your father away."

"I didn't disrespect you, Mom, but she didn't take Daddy away. I asked her when they met. She said it was at the Image Awards, and that was after he had moved out."

Morgan turned her attention back to me, shook her head, and said, "Ungrateful teenagers. I'm the one who was here with them when her father was filming movies all around the world. He hasn't been to any of her games or report card conferences. He probably doesn't even know her birthday."

"That's because he is working. He does know when my birthday is. He calls me every year at midnight. And his work is the reason we have everything we have. We get to live in this big house and have nice things," Alexandria shot back.

"I'm the reason you have everything that you have. Not him."

"You are being angry again, Mom. And we went to counseling. You said it was okay if I had an opinion and you wouldn't hold it against me."

She thought about it for a moment. "I did say that, but I also know that your father ain't shit. If he was something, he would be here with your mother. He hurt me and you want to tell me how great he is. He ain't shit. He's nothing."

"Okay, Mom. He ain't shit." Alexandria sighed aloud.

"Don't cuss in my house."

"Okay, I won't cuss if you take your medicine. Please. You're making my head hurt."

I felt like I was in the middle of a scene in a movie. Morgan ordered her daughter into the house.

"Don't worry, you won't have to deal with her. My last personal assistant quit. He was the third one in three months. He was a little weird. Anyway, I need someone to make my phone calls, schedule my meetings, and remind me to pay my bills. I need someone to practically live with me. Actually, if you could live with me, I could pay you extra. I have a guest house in the back."

We walked around her sprawling home. Each room was the size of an apartment. It was enough space for several families and their pets. On the mantel, I noticed she still had family and wedding pictures up of her and RJ. I stopped and looked at them. With great pride and a smile she gave me details about each picture. "This is when RJ hosted the BET Awards the first time. That's us at the Grammys. And of course, that's the president with us at the annual White House Christmas party."

"That painting is very nice," I said, admiring a big, colorful painting on the wall.

"Thank you. I got that in France. I loved it there."

She gave me a full tour of the house and three hours later, we were talking like old friends. I couldn't believe I had just met her and I was blessed with this opportunity. I hoped she would hire me.

"I get a very good vibe from you, Adrienne. I think you would make a great assistant. I can pay you a thousand per week. When can you start?"

"Tomorrow?"

"Really? That soon? Great. I'll show you to where you will be staying."

In a matter of seventy-two hours, my life had changed. I had a job that paid well, somewhere to live, and I definitely would be able to get my script sold, get Asia back, and who knows what else.

I went back to the hotel, checked out, and gathered all my things and settled in the guesthouse, which was like a small apartment with a private kitchen. I called my mother and told her about my new position.

She didn't seem pleased. All she could say was, "Adrienne, when will you learn?"

CHAPTER 31

Monique

Reading his texts every morning made me smile.
Good Morning Beautiful! Look what happens when I think of you.

His text was accompanied with a picture of his hand grasping ten inches of hard, plump chocolate. Just seeing his naked, perfect body made my entire body warm. Damn, I couldn't wait to see him again. I turned the phone sideways to get a better view. We had been seeing each other consistently for months.

Dele was so intelligent and worldly. He taught me something new all the time. He was ten years younger, but so much wiser. Honestly, he was the more mature person in our relationship. When I was with him, he concentrated on me. I've never had a man run to the other side of the car to open my door, make my tea in the morning, and massage my body until I fell asleep. He was kind and had a great personality. Then there was his smile, that body, and his sexy accent. He always smelled so good and our sex was amazing. Then, to top it all off, he was rich and wanted to be in a serious relationship. It wasn't a lie that he didn't date a lot because, in his eyes, most American women were unintelligent gold diggers that he couldn't relate to.

I texted back.

Can't wait to see him again!!!

"Mom, what are you smiling about?" Kadir asked as he entered the kitchen.

"Oh, nothing." I exited out of the text.

He put two honey buns in the microwave.

"Now, you don't need all those sweets. There's food in there. You need to get some real food in your system for the road."

"I'm eating those and some cereal." He pulled up a chair and poured a bowl of cereal.

I wanted to ask him about who he was dating and what was going on with him. "So are you seeing anyone now?"

"I got a few girls. But I'm not bringing none of them over here."

"Good, because I don't want to meet them. Just make sure you use a condom, maybe even two. And bring your own because there's plenty of girls trying to get a million-dollar baby up in them."

"Mom, can you stop. I'm eating. Nobody wants to talk about sex with their mom," he said, and put his hands over his ears.

"It's the truth. When these girls see you, they see a winning lottery ticket."

"I know who likes me for me and who doesn't. Like Abigail, you didn't give her a chance, but she's real cool. Out of all of them, she's the one I'm feeling the most."

"I don't like her. Find someone a little darker, with no kids, and who is in college so she can help you with your businesses."

"I don't need that. I just need a chick who looks good on my arm. We can hire people to do everything else."

"I'm not going to say anything else. Just watch out for her and all the little groupies like her, Kadir."

"Mom, you talked to my dad?'

"I have, but we are not getting back together."

"I didn't say get back together. He asked me about you. Maybe go to the movies and have dinner with him. He misses you, Mom. You should go to Philly. I don't want you in this big house all alone."

"No, Aunt CeCe is coming here. Kadir, your dad and I have been having problems for years, and now we both have the chance to be happy. I don't want you worried about me. I'm okay. I want you to concentrate on yourself. You have a lot of people to prove yourself to."

The transition for Kadir from college to the NBA had not been great. Everyone said it was a faster game, and they were right. The NBA's fast-paced twelve-minute quarter means you have to shoot the ball whenever you get a chance. Kadir still had a way to go in order to build up his endurance to keep up. Also, the shot clock is only twenty-four seconds in the NBA, and those seconds had caught up with Kadir a couple of times. Luckily, it was still the preseason, and that gave Ka some time to get himself together. In Phoenix, he suffered a slight panic attack and needed to call me when he arrived at the arena. One of the Phoenix Suns fans knew his name and called him a weak player that needed to go back to the playground. He missed a few free throws that night, which cost his team the game and he got beat up on Twitter. Everyone has an opinion.

He celebrated his twenty-first birthday on the road without me. I thought I was being a great mom when I sent him a bunch of fruit baskets, flowers, and gifts to his hotel with balloons. He said not to ever do it again because I was embarrassing him. Kadir was worth millions of dollars now and he had the skills, but at home he was my man-child that needed reassuring.

"Does this look right, Ma?" Kadir asked about his navy suit.

"It does, but fix your tie. I packed everything together. Your socks are tucked in your underwear with your t-shirts. I'll drive you down to the arena. Remember, Kadir, you need to be everywhere thirty minutes early. So hurry up."

"Mom, I have something to talk to you about."

"I'm listening." I thought he was going to ask me about Dele. He got up and handed me his cell phone and showed me an e-mail.

"This guy reached out to me and says that he is related to me. And that he and my grandmother want to meet me. Am I related to the Hendersons from Twenty-third Street, in North Philly? That's where my dad is from, right?"

I felt better the e-mail wasn't about me. "Yes, your dad was a Henderson, but . . ." I said as I previewed the e-mail.

"The guy's name is Isiah. He said he's my cousin, and I have a brother that looks like my twin named Phillip, and we both look like our dad. My dad is his uncle, and they all want to meet me. And that they're all are so proud of me."

"Kadir, are you fucking serious? Haven't I told you that people would be trying to get to you now that you are famous? Carl's your dad, that's who raised you. Don't be a dumbass. Those people don't know you. Where were they when you needed a ride to school or some sneakers? Don't respond to any more e-mails."

"Mom, I know, but I looked at the picture he sent me and my brother does looks just like me."

"That's not your brother. Stop saying that dumb shit. I raised you better than to be this fucking dumb." My words were harsh and I didn't care. Kadir didn't speak to me the rest of the ride to the airport.

"I'm sorry for cussing at you. It is my job to protect you. You have all the family you need."

"Mom, come on. I'm grown now. And I can make my own decisions. I want to meet them."

"No, you will not."

"I am and there isn't anything you can do about it." He got out of the car and walked toward his teammate. I wanted to get out of the car and say something to him. Then I saw Dele. He almost looked as if he was going to try to say something, but I pulled off before he could.

CHAPTER 32

Zakiya

When I started going to church, my life began to have so much joy. I dedicated my time to tithing and reading my bible. My favorite scripture is James 1:22: "Do not merely listen to the word, and so deceive yourselves. Do what it says."

Jabril says I'm going through a phase, but finding the Lord is not a phase. God wanted to get my attention and I wasn't listening. That's why I got in that car accident and walked away, because God was showing mercy on my life and trying to wake me. I was up now and there was no going back to sleep. I was trying to convince Jabril to go with me, but he either wasn't awake in time or was on the road. I stayed for both the morning and afternoon services. I loved my new pastor, Richard, and his wife, Elise. They are in their early forties and started the church in their house with only fifteen people and now it has grown to a congregation of twelve hundred.

Dawn reached out to me a few times and I was courteous, but always unavailable to meet her. When I went to home games, I brought Octavia and Jabrilah and sat on the side of the away team. Jabril wanted us to be cool because Dawn's husband was the captain of the team and he was trying to be on, but I didn't budge. I was in a better spiritual space, and I didn't want anything to ruin it.

One night, I was going to volunteer with the outreach ministry, along with some of the sisters at our sister church. I was very friendly with a young mother named Talisha and her mother, Theresa.

When I arrived to Rockclave Baptist Church, there were at least five hundred people in line. Some young, old, families, singles, white, black, and other.

"We're almost out of macaroni and cheese, and how much longer before the pan is warm, and we need more collard greens!" Talisha yelled out.

"They're almost ready and Sister Theresa said she will be here in another thirty-five minutes with the desserts. I told her to bake her pies last night," First Lady Elise said.

"We can tell them to come back for dessert," Talisha responded.

Noticing they needed assistance, I jumped right aboard the tight, hot food truck. I washed my hands, put on my apron, and began serving.

I was put on string beans and was the last in line. I gave extra helpings and offered a prayer with a few of the people. I was so moved and so humbled by the experience. It was the best feeling to be helping other people.

When we were finally done, Sister Theresa finally brought her pies. We cut them up and gave out the dessert. We fed every person—even seconds. With each platter, we gave them invitations to come to our church.

"Praise God, we did it! Would you like something to eat?" Talisha asked.

"No, I will eat when I go home. This was great," I responded.

"It was. Now, well, on to the next thing! The praise team needs new dresses and shoes for their performance. I'm asking the entire outreach ministry to donate. I'm about to ask everyone for fifty dollars. Do you think that is too much?"

"How much do you need all together?"

"Total it's about five hundred dollars. Maybe if all the sisters here tonight give thirty or forty dollars, we will have enough."

"Five hundred? I have that. I can give it to you now."

"You can? Just like that? Wow! God bless you!"

"Yes, no problem."

Talisha shouted, "Ladies! Sister Zakiya just donated the money to the praise dancers!" Everyone came over to me and hugged and thanked me. I felt uncomfortable, but I was happy that I could help.

"I will see everyone in church!" First Lady Elise said and then came over and hugged me and thanked me for my help.

I was exhausted by the time I got home, but I felt so fulfilled. Fellowship and giving back was what my life had been missing. Jabril was sitting on the sofa changing channels and eating pizza.

With his mouth full of pizza, he started talking. "No dinner, no love, huh? I got to come home to no wife, no dinner, and a nanny playing with my daughter."

"Where is Jabrilah? I'm sorry. I got caught up."

"I put her to bed. Where have you been? I've been calling you."

How did I forget my man was on his way home?

"I didn't get any calls from you."

I reached into my bag and saw that I did have several missed calls.

"Bril, I'm sorry, baby. I forgot you were going to be here."

"Zakiya, I'm only here for a few days. I'm standing at the airport looking crazy. I'm getting scared wondering where my wife is. Did she get in another accident? Is she safe?"

"I really forgot. I was feeding the homeless with a few sisters from the church."

"Feed me. I'm hungry."

I approached my husband. I kissed him and hugged him.

"No, don't try to kiss me." He turned his face away. I was tired, but I missed my man. He pushed me away. "And you smell like fried chicken. I'm hungry, and you are teasing me."

"I don't know how I forgot about you."

"No, I'm only joking. You really like this church and these church people. I might have to go with you."

"You should. There's a service tomorrow."

"I'll go, but right now I need my wifey to smell like flowers—or something peachy. Just not like fried chicken. Meet me in the shower."

I felt so proud to walk into church with my family and sit. The usher sat us in the third row. Pastor Richard spoke about timing and being patient about waiting for God to hear our calls. He told us to never stop calling because God always picks up. I looked over and saw that Jabril was into it. I grabbed his hand and prayed.

After the service, Pastor Richard and First Lady Elise came over to us. Before I could introduce the pastor to Jabril, he shouted out his name.

"Well, well! We have our very own celebrity! Honey, did you know this is the Charlotte Hornets' newest addition, Jabril Smith?"

"You know him?" I asked.

"Yeah, I'm a huge Hornets fan. But I followed you in Oklahoma."

"Really?" Jabril asked, smiling appreciating that the reverend was a fan.

"Yes, sir. I have to make it to a game."

"I can get you tickets."

Pastor Richard and Jabril began to talk like old friends and First Lady Elise pulled me to the side and said, "Thank you for helping us out last night and giving to the praise team. Also, I want you to come to my home for bible study."

"I would love to. What should I bring?"

"You don't have to bring a thing, just your bible."

"Okay, I'll be there."

Church was a success. Jabril thanked me for bringing him and said he would be coming out as often as he could. He even said he talked with the pastors about starting a youth basketball clinic. Everything was coming along, and I felt blessed.

CHAPTER 33

Shanice

It had been three weeks and I decided to call Deuce. I hadn't been getting with him and I knew I needed to reach out. When he answered, I blurted out, "Hey, baby! What's up?"

"The question is, what's up with you? Where have you been? You don't text me back and never return my phone calls. And you're asking what's up. You're funny as hell, Ms. Amore."

"Deuce, I'm sorry. I've been doing so much. I've been caught up with my daughter, my mom, and doing all these auditions and hostings . . ."

"Shani, look. I bullshit for a living. You ain't got to lie to me. I'm good. I'm not fighting a chick to be there so I can take care of her. You didn't get back to me about the trip or our conversation, but it's cool. I got to go."

"It's not like that. Can I see you tonight?"

"I don't know about that. I'm in the studio with Santos. I'm going to be at it all night."

"Well, I can come to the studio."

"Yeah, all right."

Most of what I told Deuce was the truth. I really was busy

with Trisha and Raven, but what I didn't tell him was that I was being consumed by Jabril. We were texting a lot, and just knowing that I could reach out to him felt wonderful. It felt like old times, like we were picking up right where we left off. He mostly texted about his daughter and how he really wasn't feeling his new team, and I sent him pictures of me and talked about my life. It was casual, but friendly.

I took the two-hour car ride to New York. I had to show my baby Deuce that I still cared. On the ride up, I was supposed to be thinking about what I was going to say to him . . . but my thoughts were on Jabril and how I could get him away from his wife. I was desperate. Deuce was what I needed, and Jabril was what I wanted. How could I get Jabril back? How could I get him to see that I was the one? I thought about what I'd do if I "accidentally" ran into him again. Then maybe we could pick up where we left off.

In the studio, Deuce was behind the board and Santos was in the booth. There were a couple of guys sitting around with red cups and smoking and a few girls that looked like they were trying to meet their next sponsor. One girl looked like she might have thought she was there for Deuce.

I walked over to him and said, "Hey, baby."

Deuce looked up and gave me a stern look like I was in trouble. He nodded and replied, "What's up?"

The girl smirked and then began giggling with her friends.

"What's up? What is that supposed to mean?" I asked.

"Yeah. What's up? What's going on? What do you want?"

"What's wrong with you? Why you talking to me like this? Can I talk to you outside in private?"

"Give me a minute." I walked into the hallway and waited for him. I didn't appreciate him trying to play me in front of people.

"You got five minutes."

"I got five minutes? What the hell is wrong with you? I just drove two hours to spend some time with you, and all you can say is 'What's up?' And who are those bitches in the studio?"

"You haven't called or texted me in three weeks and you want to know why I'm mad and ask me about some bitches. They are not with me. Santos brought them. What does it matter? You don't want me."

"I do want you."

I could tell he was serious. His eyes were almost watery. "No, you don't. You're playing with me. I had to go to Dubai by myself. Everybody was out there with their wives and fiancées, and I was in that beautiful place by myself."

"Deuce, I said I would let you know. I never said I was going to go definitely. And we are not together, so why are you putting that type of pressure on me?"

"That's the problem. I want more with you. When I think about my future, I think about you. I constantly find myself holding back. You're in your twenties. I'm thirty-seven. I don't want to play games no more. I slept with a bunch of chicks. I'm tired. I'm ready to settle down. I'm not thinking about no groupie girls. I want a wife, a house, and kids in the near future. So if that's not what you want, then we are going to have to leave each other alone."

"Deuce . . . so you're saying you don't want to see me anymore?"

"I do, but I want you to want what I want."

"Can we work on it first?"

"No. I want to be working toward something or not to see you at all."

I thought about what he was saying. I wanted to be with Deuce, but I knew I couldn't give him my all, because my heart still belonged to Jabril.

CHAPTER 34

Tiffany

The last months had been so relaxing. Being back with my mother and stepfather was so much better than being with Damien. I felt at peace. No one was knocking on the door unexpectedly, and I didn't have to slum it at a job or endure being broke.

I awoke to the sun shining in my room. I felt alive and refreshed until I looked at my phone and saw dozens of texts from Damien. He'd been calling and texting daily since I left him. I was going to have to change my number and hire a divorce lawyer. In between Damien's texts, I read messages from my sister-in-law, Liz, asking me to lunch. So I gave her a call.

"Hey, Liz, I would love to go to lunch and see you and my nephew."

"Great, but I have to warn you. I'm so fat. I didn't lose all this baby weight yet. How about right after the baby's doctor appointment, around one o'clock? Let's meet at Mattie's Diner on Carson Street."

"Sounds good."

Liz came in balancing the baby's car seat on her right arm, an overstuffed baby bag on her left arm, and my newborn nephew was in between the chaos. I stood up to assist, but she had already set everything down. My nephew was wrapped in a blue blanket, and she placed him on her lap and rocked him as she ordered two glasses of wine.

I smiled at her. "How did you learn how to do all of this so fast?"

"I don't have any choice. Learning on the job."

"He is so adorable. You look great! You said you were fat."

"Compared to my weight before I had the baby, I am. I was one twenty-two, now I'm one forty. All I do is sit home with the baby. I'm tired of this already. I want to go back to work, but your brother doesn't want his baby in day care. So, how's everything? What are your plans?"

"I don't know yet, Liz. Damien didn't tell me he was going broke. Right before I left, there were people knocking on the door demanding that we pay them. It was insanity. I wanted to stay. I really did. I even got a job. But I had a conversation with my mom that made so much sense. She said my life would never return to normal being married to him. I had to leave him."

"I totally get it. Your brother makes a great living. If he woke up one day and said we are broke, I would kill him. Money is the top reason for divorce."

"I know. I tried, Liz. It was hard. So hard. And now that I have had time to think, I know I'm not going back. I have to figure out something."

"You're going to get yourself together. You know Charles's friend Edward?"

"I do."

"Well, we kind of explained everything to him, and he said he will handle your divorce. Now, does he have enough to pay you alimony?"

"No, he has nothing, He lost everything."

"Wow, well, the good thing is that you don't have any children together."

"Yes, and right before everything happened, we were thinking about it. Starting all over is so hard. I wanted kids and a great life."

"And you are going to get it. Just not with him."

CHAPTER 35

Adrienne

What had my life become? I was picking up Morgan's Starbucks and dry cleaning, paying her bills, and making reservations, all while getting little to no respect. I was a "yes" woman. I had to be. I realized disagreeing with my boss only led to her trying to convince me why she was right. Being a personal assistant was so humbling, but I needed the money. I had to do what I had to do.

After a month of working for Morgan, I knew she didn't need a live-in assistant. She needed a stylist, a therapist, an alarm clock, a workout partner, and a best friend. She insisted that all her beverages be room temperature and that no one speak to her before she did her makeup. I couldn't complain because she was paying me. Because I was on her payroll, I could put up with her quirky habits.

I was able to send my lawyer his retainer fee. I FaceTimed a lot with Asia, and DeCarious was being less of an asshole. He offered to fly Asia to Philly one weekend, and I told him that I wouldn't be in town. I hadn't told him I moved to L.A. because it was none of his business.

I was in the process of cleaning out and color organizing

Morgan's massive closet. Her toss pile was two times the size of her keep pile. Her closet was easily the size of a boutique. It was surrounded by walls and walls of shoes. It was completely unorganized with accessories, shoe boxes, and bags lying all over.

"What about this?" I asked, raising a red Valentino dress with its price tag still attached.

"You can throw that in the trash. No, I'll keep it. No, it's trash. What do you think? It's trash, right? That dress is from two seasons ago. I could never wear it."

"Do you want to sell any of this stuff on ebay?"

"Ebay? No, that's for poor people. I don't have to sell anything. Just give it away."

"Okay. If you say so."

Some parts of Morgan's life I envied. She traveled the world and had everything anyone could ever dream of. Her ex-husband made her life more than comfortable, and it would be that way for the rest of her life. His movies had grossed more than five hundred million dollars, and her divorce entitled her to a percentage of it. However, she was more than a little strange and very difficult to work for. But as soon as I got that script in the right person's hands, I knew it would be worth it.

I stood up and grabbed another bag of clothes. I pulled out a pair of white shorts that had slits along the butt and back pocket.

"What about these?" I snickered, holding them up.

"Let me see. Wow, my shorts with the cut-outs. I haven't worn these in years. I wonder if I can still fit into them . . ." She held the pants up to her waist and turned. "Even if they do fit, I don't have anyone to wear them for. My pussy probably got cobwebs on it. But it's still tight."

"I don't want to hear that, Morgan," I said, almost choking with laughter.

"What did I say wrong, it is tight! My mother taught me

how to pull my pussy in, since I was twelve. Squeeze that pussy in or let it go and get sloppy."

"You mean do kegels? Please stop, Morgan." I was used to Morgan's random sex talk, but this conversation was too much for me.

"I didn't know what they were called back then. I just know my mother said keep it tight, and you will always have a man."

"Your mom did *not* tell you that . . ."

"She did. How do you think I got RJ? I fucked and sucked him so good, I couldn't get him to leave me alone. And of course I'm beautiful and smart, but my cooch caught him and I reeled him with everything else. Ah, the good old days. My mother didn't give me a lot of advice, but the advice she did give me worked. You know my mother was a whore, right?"

I couldn't help but burst into laughter.

"No, seriously. I was born in a whorehouse. My mother didn't even know I was up in her. She went to the hospital because her stomach was hurting her. She was shocked as hell when I came out and I was taken straight out of her arms to a foster home. I was in foster care until I was six, and then she came and got me. She didn't know who my dad was, but it was definitely one of the men she was tricking. I can be anything. Half white, Indian, or Mexican . . ."

I was speechless.

"You're laughing, but you look like you got some swirl going on in you, too. Adrienne, what's your background?"

"I'm black. My mother is white and my dad is black. I know him, but he didn't have any involvement in my life."

"I knew we had a connection. We both have daddy issues."

She was somewhat right, but I didn't want to relate.

"That's why I picked the best father I thought I could for my child. RJ was a good man—until about two years ago.

Once upon a time, I couldn't pay him to leave my side. When I had Alexandria, he slept in the hospital bed with me. He would go on the road, do his shows, film his movies, and then he'd rush home. He would practice in the mirror with me. I helped him come up with his catchphrase 'You know know.' I'm the one who told him to get t-shirts made and sweatshirts with all his sayings on it, and now this little chihuahua is living my life. And he treats me like his enemy, like we were never in love." She began to cry, and I tried to comfort her.

"Morgan, you will find someone like that again. Or maybe he will come back."

She stopped crying and then became so angry she began to throw things. "I hoped and prayed he would come back home and he hasn't, and now I don't care. I don't want him back, and I don't like any of these weird men in L.A. Most of these men out here are gay or only like blondes. If it was up to me, I would go home to Detroit, but my custody agreement requires me to keep residency in Los Angeles."

I understood her pain, but I was certain she was crazy after that rant.

"Tina," Morgan called.

Ms. Tina, her personal chef and housekeeper, came running upstairs.

"Yes, Mrs. Coleman."

"I'm hungry. I want a turkey and cheese on rye. Cut off the corners. I want mustard on it, and make sure all of the meat is folded neatly facing left on my sandwich."

"Yes, ma'am."

"Do you want her to fix you anything, Adrienne?"

"No, I'm okay."

Tina walked back down the stairs to prepare spoiled-rotten Morgan's food.

"Oh, Adrienne, I didn't get my invitation for the CGA Gala. Contact them immediately." Morgan's phone was sitting right beside her, but it made her feel important to have someone else making her phone calls for her.

"Okay." I called the number written on the slip of paper she handed me. "Good afternoon. I'm Morgan Coleman's assistant and she hasn't received her invitation for your annual gala . . ."

"Let me check," the voice on the other end said.

She placed me on hold and then returned back to the call. "Yes. Unfortunately, her ex-husband has reserved his table. He is the guest speaker, and we didn't want a conflict of interest. However, she is still welcome to donate. Take care."

"Okay. Thank you." I hung up from the call, and Morgan was looking directly in my face.

"So, what did they say?"

"It is a conflict of interest because your ex-husband is their guest speaker this year."

"See? I told you. He wants to ruin me. He owns everything and everybody. I hate him."

CHAPTER 36

Monique

"Dele, I'm not hiding you. It is just a certain level of respect I have to have for my son. I'm single. I can do whatever I want . . . but that's my child. He's not going to be able to understand that his mommy is having sex with his teammate . . ."

"You will have to tell him. I'm not going to tolerate all of this hiding for much longer. Monique, I want to be with you."

"No, I am not telling him anything. First of all, I didn't know London was going to turn into all of this."

"Well, it has. Now what are you going to do? Are you going to keep hiding me and leaving me in the middle of the night? Or will you allow me to present you to the world as my woman?"

"I don't know what to say. Yeah, you want to be with me right now. This week, on Thursday, maybe even in three months . . . but who's to say that you will want to be with me in two years? This is new, it's temporary; my relationship with Kadir is forever."

"I am temporary? Really?" Dele shot out of the bed and cursed in French—something he always did when he was upset. He looked sexy when he was upset. It actually turned me on. I let him vent. He waved his hand at me dismissively and walked into his bathroom. I heard the shower turn on, and I wanted to get in with him. Instead, I started to get dressed, because I had to beat Kadir home. I was a grown woman who couldn't even spend the night with her lover. I didn't have a choice, because he was already suspicious of my late nights and early mornings.

Before I was fully dressed, a calmer Dele emerged from the bathroom with an extra wide mint-green towel wrapped around his waist. He sat next to me on the bed and pulled me into his arms. His body was still warm and damp from the shower. I couldn't lie to myself. I was falling in love with Dele, too. I just didn't know what to do about it.

"I just don't like hiding, Monique. It is not right. We have nothing to be ashamed of."

"Put yourself in his shoes, Dele. How would you feel if your teammate was dating your mother?"

"My mother is much older and still married to my father, so it would not happen. Our situation is very different."

I shook my head at him. No matter how many times I explained it to him, he did not get it. I was frustrated and ready to leave until he held me down on the bed and pulled my pants down and snatched my panties off. He pushed his thick moist tongue along and inside of every crease and opening of my pussy.

"Take your hands off of me," I demanded. "Let me up, Dele. Stop. We have to talk about this."

"Don't tell me what to do. There is nothing to discuss. It's mine. You're mine, and I'm not hiding anymore." I tried to sit up. But he cupped my butt cheeks with his hands and forced me back down. I could not resist him anymore. I grabbed his head then the pillow to muffle my scream of ecstasy.

After, I released into his mouth. He flipped me over and plowed himself into my juicy pussy. I think he tried to fuck me into submission. Honestly, it almost may have worked, but I knew I had to go home no matter what.

Kadir's car wasn't in the driveway, but Carl's was. I walked into my house, and I saw boxes and a bunch of his clothes. I ran up the steps, walked into my bedroom, and saw he was stretched out in my bed, asleep.

I shook him and shouted, "Carl, get up! What are you doing here?"

He jumped up. I hadn't meant to startle him, but he needed to get up out of my bed.

"I wanted to talk to you. I've been thinking a lot about us." I hoped he couldn't smell the scent of another man on me.

"Have you?"

"Mo, you were right. I should be enjoying life. I was at my job earlier today listening to people complaining about bills and their kids. Then I started thinking to myself. I don't have those problems. My son is great, and I'm blessed. I called Kadir and he told me he wanted me to be down here with y'all and to just to quit and go fish every day and take vacations. The truth is, we don't know when we're going to go, so we should live every day like it's our last. That's why I want to move back in. I love you and want to work it out with you."

"You do?" I asked, surprised. "I don't know, Carl."

I was trying to find the right words. How was I going to tell him that I didn't want to be with him anymore?

"I think you should stay in Philly. I mean, if you want to come down here and visit, you can. But you said we should take a break and I agreed. Now you can't just come back and say you want me."

"I do want you."

"Well, I want you to sleep in the guest room."

"What's up with you, Mo? What, have you met someone else already?"

"No, but I don't want to rush back into anything. I need my space. Everything you said was right. We aren't a couple anymore. You can stay here, but I'm going to bed."

*   *   *

The next morning CeCe called me. I was halfway asleep, but I still answered the phone, only to hear CeCe say, "I talked to Carl. He's upset. He called me and my mom this morning. And he said you won't take him back."

"What? He broke up with me. Why is he calling y'all?"

"My mom is upset and wants you two to be together and finally get married."

"I'll call Mom Laura later. What did he say?"

"That he quit his job to be with you and Kadir, and you told him to go back to Philly."

"CeCe, it's too late."

"Too late? What's going on? Why?"

I detected a bit of anger in CeCe's voice.

"It's my turn to live my life. Cee, I'm thirty-eight years old, and I have been tied down for more than half of my life. Carl said he wants to live in Philly and he wanted us to be apart. I didn't want that, but I agreed. Now, I come home and all his stuff is in my house. What type of craziness is this?"

"Not too long ago, you wanted him there . . . but now you don't. So, who is he? Or is it a she?"

"CeCe, stop playing. It's not funny . . ."

"I'm serious, you are dealing with someone. It's obvious. You're never home and you don't return my calls. You have plans, but can't tell me who it is with. Now Carl quit his job and you don't want him to stay. Tell me who it is."

"I can't."

"So there is someone else."

"Maybe."

"Tell me."

"I can't, Cee. I'll talk to you soon."

CHAPTER 37

Adrienne

Morgan Coleman is Queen Cray. One moment, she was happy. Next, she was crying. Alexandria knew her routine. She would go into her room until Mommy got better and took her medicine. Tina makes her the food she wants, cleans, and does it all by tiptoeing around the house and walking under the radar. If Tina puts a little too much seasoning on her chicken or adds eight ice cubes instead of seven, Morgan will go off and cuss her out for days. I felt sorry for them.

On this particular day, Morgan got up yelling, saying, "Fuck my life!" because she chipped her nail and her trainer cancelled on her.

I picked up my phone immediately to find her another trainer who would come to the house. But then Alexandria came into her mother's room and ruined the day even more.

"Mom, I want to go Dad's wedding."

And then it all made sense. Morgan was going psycho because her ex was getting married.

"You want to go to what? How dare you want to be present for that snake and dog's wedding?"

"I already told him I was coming."

"Alexandria. Call him back right now and tell him you are not coming."

"But Mom, I'm in the wedding. And he's on his way."

"You really want me to go crazy, right? Do you want to push me over the edge? He left me, and now you want to do the same damn thing? Leave if you want to go."

"Mom, I'm not leaving you," she said.

"You are, but it is okay. He is trying to take you from me. I know he is."

"I'm coming back. I'm going to go to the wedding and then come right back. Why do you want me to choose? Why can't I love you and him?"

"Why would you want to love a no-good motherfucker. He doesn't love you. If he loved you, he wouldn't have left your mother. He would respect your mother."

"He has respect for you."

"We don't need him. It's us against the world. Not just your dad. Everybody. I'm asking you not to leave me. Please."

Her guilt trip wasn't effective on her daughter.

Alexandria huffed as she left the room. "I can't wait until I turn eighteen."

"What did you say?" Morgan asked as she followed Alexandria down the hall.

"Nothing."

Alexandria called her father and put the call on speaker. "Hello, Daddy. Mommy said I can't come. Sorry."

He started saying something, but Morgan instructed her to hang up on him, and she did.

"Adrienne, call and book us a trip to Hawaii. I want five-star everything. My travel agent's number is in my phone. Alexandria, we will go shopping when we get there."

I went downstairs and dialed the travel agent. She was so excited when I said I wanted to book a trip for Morgan Coleman. After I gave her Morgan's credit card number, I walked down the steps only to see the infamous RJ Coleman in the flesh. He was the star of some funny movies, in which he always played a nice guy. The man who was standing in front of me was angry and considerably shorter in person. I had been waiting to casually run into him and slip him my script under different circumstances, but this wasn't the time to slip him anything.

"Who are you?"

Before I could answer, Morgan came down the steps with her robe on.

"Didn't I tell you? You are not allowed in my home."

"I pay for this shit. I'll come in if I want to. Where is my daughter, and who is this?'

"That's my assistant."

"You don't have a job, so why do you need an assistant? And why did you tell my daughter she couldn't come to my wedding?"

"Because she is getting ready to go on vacation!" Morgan screamed. "So leave!"

"I'm here, and I'm taking my daughter with me."

"Mom, can I please go with my dad?" Alexandria asked from the top of the steps.

"No, because he will take you around that bitch and her bastard baby."

"Alexandria, come here, baby, come give Daddy a hug. Sorry you have to go through this."

Alexandria ran past her mom to go and hug her father.

"You need to stop this dumb shit, Morgan. You are putting her through too much."

"That's you. I hate your ass. I hate you. Get the hell out of my house."

She ran down the steps and snatched her daughter away from RJ. He was pulling her in one direction, and she pulled her in another.

"Stop, Mom! Stop it," she cried. "I love you, and I love

Daddy. I'm going, Mom, but that doesn't mean I don't love you."

"I'll bring her back on Sunday."

Morgan ran up the stairs and began to cry. I didn't know what to say; not only had the love of her life moved on, but her daughter had accepted the woman he did it with.

Hours later all I heard my name being screamed by Morgan. I entered her room and she was slumped on the sofa. "Dial Alexandria's number. I need to check on my child. I know she really doesn't want to be at that wedding." I dialed Alexandria's cell phone and when she answered, I placed the phone up to Morgan's ear.

"Hey, how's everything? I wanted to apologize." She paused and then continued and said, "Is Grandmom Julia there? . . . And Uncle Fred? . . . Oh, tell them I said hello . . . So, where is everyone staying? . . . A private mansion? . . . Oh, is the wedding there, too? . . . Malibu? That's nice . . . The Bel-Air Bay Club? . . . I love you, Alexandria. Have fun. I will see you when you come home . . ." She hung up wearing a sneaky grin and immediately made another call. She put the caller on speaker and I heard a woman answer, "TMZ tips." Morgan told the gossip site the exact locations of RJ's wedding. Then she was happy for about a minute and then began crying,

"It is not fair. He's an idiot. He's marrying that woman and when he dies, he's going to leave everything to her. And you know what happens to the first wife who was there from the beginning? We end up with nothing. That bitch will lock his own mother and father out of his house and leave my daughter penniless. That's when everyone will say I was right. That she was nothing but a gold digger. And that's what always happens. You notice that." I looked at her tearstained face and agreed with her, and then decided it would probably be best to leave her alone with her thoughts. There was nothing I could say that would make her feel any better in that moment.

I knew Morgan was tired and had a lot on her mind, but she hadn't called my phone in a couple of hours, and that was very strange. I walked over to the main house from the guest house and it was eerily silent.

"Hey, Ms. Tina. Has Morgan been up?"

"No, do you want me to wake her?"

"Yeah, let's check on her." I hoped she hadn't gone over the edge and swallowed an entire bottle of pills. The last thing I wanted to do was find her dead. I was scared to enter her room. Tina knocked three times and the door opened a little. I entered and shouted, "Morgan!"

"Yes?" Morgan answered. She was sitting up curling her hair and smiling.

"I knocked and you didn't answer."

"Oh, yeah. Sorry. I was on the phone."

"Are you okay?" I asked.

"You know, earlier was really difficult. It's been the worst day of my life, actually. Yeah . . . but I'm over that. You know, it is just time for me to stop living in RJ's shadow. It is time for me to declare to the world who I am. The last seventeen years I have been Mrs. RJ Coleman. I want to be Morgan Tucker again. Morgan Tucker was a motherfucker. Morgan Coleman? That bitch is weak, and well, that's why I can't be her anymore."

"Oh, okay," I said, nodding along with Morgan's insanity.

"So I am going to announce to the world that I am Morgan Tucker. I want to have a celebration. I have a whole list, and I'm getting a team together to help change my life and let the world see me. I am my own star. I want to have a party in honor of me changing my last name from RJ's back to my own. He can have it back. I'm going to make it on my own, and he will be so jealous."

Of course, Morgan was delusional. I highly doubted her ex would be jealous, but I followed her directions and began to plan her name change party.

"You know, because he can have his last name back, I don't want that shit. Fuck that last name, she can have that shit." She paused and then said, "Do you ever hear that?"

"Hear what?" I asked.

"No, leave me alone."

I looked over at Tina she shook her head, crossed her heart, and mumbled something in Spanish.

"Who do you want to leave you alone, Morgan?"

"That voice. Don't you hear it?" She stood up and said, "Stop laughing at me. I don't care that he got married. I don't give a fuck." Then she swung at the air.

I was scared. Morgan was crazy, but she had never talked about hearing voices before.

"Morgan, are you okay? Maybe you need to get some more rest."

"I don't feel so good. I might have taken too much medicine. Help me get dressed. I think I want to go to the hospital. I don't feel right, like something is wrong in my head."

I helped her put on a t-shirt, jeans, and her sneakers and then walked her to the car.

I took her to the hospital, but they transferred her to the Psychiatric Center at Century City Hospital. I signed her in and we had a seat. She was in and out of consciousness. She had to sign paperwork saying that they could discuss her medical history with me. It was a responsibility that I really didn't want.

I waited with her, and I became afraid watching all the other crazy people around us. Some were talking to themselves, others staring into space. Interestingly enough, Morgan would fit right in.

Morgan's name was called, and we were sent into a room. A male doctor came in, examined her, and questioned her about her symptoms. He told me he was going to keep her for a seventy-two-hour evaluation.

"Okay, make sure she changes into this gown and she has to remove her shoelaces."

The moment he left the room, Morgan stood up and demanded I take her home.

"I can't take you home. The doctor wants to treat you."

"You have to. I'm not staying here." She paced the room. "Did you hear what he said? He said he wants to take my shoelaces. Why do they want my shoelaces? What the fuck are they going to do with my shoelaces? I got to get out of here now."

"No, I think it is a good idea if you stay."

"But I'm not giving them my shoelaces."

"You have to."

"No, I don't have to do shit. I'm leaving."

"Morgan, you can't leave. You said your head is hurting and you're hearing voices. He's going to help with that. Just give me your shoes and I will give them back to you as soon as you get out."

"Okay, I'll stay, but as soon as I call, come get me."

"I will."

CHAPTER 38

Tiffany

How many times do you have to be ignored before you get the message that the other party is not going to respond to you? I asked myself this question as I stared down at my cell phone. Damien had yet to give up so I had no choice but to answer his call.

"What do you want?"

"Tiff. Tiffany. When are you coming home?"

"I'm not."

"So just like that we're done? You're never coming back?"

I sighed and tried to make it as easy as possible, but there is no easy way to leave a marriage.

"No, I'm not coming back. I will send the divorce papers once I get a draft."

"You left me, and you are going to stick me up, too? Good luck with that. I don't have any money left to give you."

"I wasn't with you for any money, Damien. I tried to stay with you. You were cheating. You were drunk. You are depressed."

"Funny. When I had money I could drink, cheat, and you didn't say anything to me."

"Good-bye, Damien."

"So, this is all my fault? Tiffany, please come home. You are my wife. I need you here. I swear I can make a comeback, but I can't do it alone. I need you. We can get through this together."

"Oh, no, we won't. I'm not supposed to have to slave at a job. You call that taking care of me? You embarrassed me in front of the world, and you were still cheating. All of this was preventable."

"How could I prevent an injury?" All of a sudden, I heard a weeping noise come from the other end of the call.

"Are you crying? You are a man. Men don't cry."

"Please come back home, Tiffany. Please. It's been so hard without you."

"No, leave me alone. Take care of yourself. Stop it! Damien, stop calling me. I want to make this as easy as possible."

"So, that's it? I lost everything. My job, my money, and now you are going to walk out on me, too?"

I ended the call and saw my mother standing in the doorway.

"Was that Damien again?"

"Yes, it was."

"I am very proud of you. Take the time you need, but don't allow grass to grow under your feet while getting husband number two."

"I'm not sure I'm ready to be married again, Mother."

"Okay, understandable. But it will be a little sad if you don't bounce right back. You are too pretty of a girl to end up a cat lady with no husband or children."

"I will bounce right back, and I won't let myself go."

CHAPTER 39

Adrienne

"Good morning, this is Angela Ramirez, a nurse at the Psychiatric Center of Century City Hospital. You are the contact person for Morgan Coleman?"

"Yes, I am."

"She is being released at eight and she will need to be picked up."

I pulled my phone away from my ear to see what time it was. It was almost seven. I sleepily told her I was on my way.

I didn't know what to expect when I picked up Morgan. Who was going to come out of the seventy-two-hour hold? Would it be the nice lady, crazy lady, or just a manic mess? Better yet, maybe she invented someone new while she was in there.

When I got in front of the facility, she was already waiting for me. She jumped in, took her hoodie off, and said, "I'm so hungry. Let's get something to eat."

I turned onto the highway and handed back her cell phone.

"Did my baby call?"

"I'm not sure," I answered. No one had called her, but I

didn't want her to have a relapse if I didn't say the right thing.

We went through the Burger King drive-thru, stopped at the Rite Aid, and got her prescription filled. Then she told me that the doctor had told her that she experienced some mental stress brought on by RJ getting married, and if she took her medicine she would be able to cope better.

Once we were home, she showered and changed her clothes. So far, she seemed like the nice, calm Morgan.

"That medicine they gave me is working. I feel a lot better. Thank you for taking me. Now I am ready to finish planning my party. Here, I want this. Look. This is who Morgan Tucker was. I want my hair done just like this. The makeup, everything."

The picture was of a thinner, younger, happier Morgan with box braids, a cropped shirt with her abs exposed, and a smile.

"This picture is right before I met him. I want to be her again. It is more than a name-changing party. It is a reinvention party. I am going to pursue my dream as an actress. That revelation came to me when I was away."

She handed me a folded piece of paper.

"Here, I wrote down my guest list. I want everyone to wear white and I'm going to wear a stand-out color, like gold, red, or purple, because I'm a star and there is no one else like me."

Morgan's name change party was only weeks away. She hired a publicist named Terrance, who worked for Halle Berry in the nineties. She also hired a party planner, who hired a decorator and caterer. The party was easily costing around a hundred thousand dollars. Morgan didn't even blink. I just hoped there would be someone in attendance I could slip my script to.

We were on our way to meet her wardrobe stylist, Roosevelt, at the Shoppes at Beverly. He came from the back of his studio door, twirling, with two assistants.

"So what are you doing? What's the look you are going for, M?" She pulled out her picture and they were not impressed.

"This is okay, but I thought you wanted a fiercer look. We can put the box braids back in, but I want to reinvent you. Why don't you become my painting and let me paint you."

"Okay."

"I have some looks I want you to try on." He pulled out an off-white pant suit, sheer blue dress, and a silver mini dress. Everything she tried on was hideous, but that didn't stop him and his team from applauding and screaming, "Yes, honey. Work, boo. You're giving me life."

Morgan turned to me and asked my opinion: "Adrienne, what do you think?"

"They're okay dresses . . ."

Roosevelt looked at me with his jaw dropped, like how could I disagree with him and his staff.

"What else do you have?"

He rolled his eyes at me and said he would pull a few more things. I walked back to the dressing room. This time, he pulled a black dress with a long slit up the side, a pink halter mini, and a gray, ankle-length pant suit. She tried on the black dress and turned side to side in the mirror."

"Do you like this one?"

"Yes, it's very feminine and elegant. Sexy but classy and it will stand out since your guests are wearing all white."

"You think so? I guess . . ."

"Yeah." This was my perfect opportunity to tell her that *Poetic Justice* braids weren't going to achieve the glamorous look that she wanted. "I think you should get the black dress. And I also I think you should wear your hair out and get Chike to give you curls for your reinvention party."

"All right. Well, I can't decide which one I want. I'll just buy them all. I'll get a chance to wear all of them eventually. I mean, I am going to be walking red carpets solo now."

When we arrived home, Alexandria was there. She ran up to Morgan, hugged her, and said, "Mommy, I missed you!"

"I missed you, too. How was the wedding?" she quizzed.

"Mom, somehow the paparazzi found out where Daddy's wedding was. Daddy was so mad. He fired all of his security team. He thinks one of them leaked the information."

"Wow, that's a shame. How was everything else?"

"It was nice, but mostly they argued because Daddy made her sign a prenup right before the wedding. I think you are right. It might not last."

"Well, hopefully it will." Morgan cracked a grin at me, and I just turned my head.

The day had arrived, and everything was in order for Morgan's party. The setting was perfect by the pool. Her vision had come together. The DJ was spinning old-school and current hip-hop and the table across from him was an assortment of Asian cuisine. Long tables were set for her guests. The tables were adorned with white tablecloths and mirror tops with cascading light pink and hot pink flowers.

Everyone was in all white, so when Morgan entered the party, she truly made an entrance: a drama queen in a pink halter dress. Her hair and makeup were on point and she looked stunning as she worked the room by double kissing and air kissing her guests. I saw her take two drinks in fifteen minutes. I was concerned, but I didn't want to say anything. She had been taking her medicine and it had been working well.

The party was filled with a bunch of D-list celebrities and their lesser-known friends. We used every contact she had left. They mostly were people who were hoping their picture would end up on a blog.

After all her guests had arrived, Morgan stood in front of the pool with a lit candle and a big picture of her and RJ. She grabbed the microphone and gave a speech. "Thank you all for coming. A lot of you know me as being the wife of a certain person who will remain nameless, but I wanted to let you all know she is gone. No more Mrs. Coleman. Tonight I am going home. I'm Morgan Tucker, motherfuckers," she screamed, then set her wedding picture on fire. She looked like a madwoman in front of the flame. Then she threw the picture into the pool. Everyone applauded and she worked the room some more.

She ran over to me excitedly and whispered, "He's here. Oh, my God. He came. That's Warren Michael Joseph. Terrance invited him, but I didn't think he would show up. How do I look?" She pointed to a handsome man with an athletic build in a nice fitted white suit.

"You look fine. Who is he?"

"He's my future costar and hopefully husband number two. He is retired from the NFL and in the new movie with Gabrielle Union, *Crossing Hearts*. Go up to him and tell him I want to meet him."

I walked over to the handsome brown-skinned man wearing a tailored suit and illuminating smile. "Hi, I'm Morgan Coleman—I mean, Morgan Tucker's assistant. She would like to meet you and asked if you would be able to meet to discuss her acting."

"Give her my card and tell her to call me. I might know of a role that she can audition for."

I took his card and instantly knew that I would be contacting him, too.

I took his information down and then gave his card to Morgan and told her he said to call him.

I wasn't sure how successful Morgan's name change party would be. She was hoping that it would tell the world she was Morgan Tucker. In actuality, I don't think anyone really cared.

CHAPTER 40

Monique

I missed being in Philly. The people and the hustle and bustle of the city. The stores on every corner, buses riding past, the smell of cheesesteaks and the taste of soft pretzels. It had been months since I had been home. I missed being Monique from Seventeenth and Erie Avenue. The Monique who didn't receive calls asking for money or game tickets. The Monique who could see her son just by knocking on his bedroom door or going to his practice. She didn't have to check his schedule or plan a date with him. I was grateful, but still missed my baby boy.

I was back in Philly to visit CeCe and Mom Laura and also to make things right with my mom. Dele had been encouraging me to talk to her. He was so family-oriented. His mother called every morning, and he always FaceTimed with his brothers. They were such a close unit and they were all over the world. He didn't understand how my mom was in the same country and I didn't even speak to her. And although I didn't want to admit it, he was right: no matter what she did, I was her child and it was my duty to take care of her.

I came to her house and banged on her white screen door.

"Mom, it's me." She looked through the blinds and then opened the door. She let me in and took a seat on her brown love seat. I sat across from her on the gray recliner she had had since I was ten.

"What brings you to walk among the common people?"

"I wanted to talk to you."

"About what?"

"Well, I wanted to come and check on you and also tell you that I'm paying off your house and buying you a car. And taking care of any other bills you have."

"That's very kind of you, but that's okay. See, money don't make me. It might make you. But not me. I don't need your money."

"Mom, I just want to help."

"Then help yourself to the door. My grandson already paid my mortgage off and bought his grandmother a car and set me up a bank account."

"He did. That's good, but I still . . . That's not the only reason I came here. I want to talk to you. Mom, I'm sorry, I haven't been the easiest to deal with. But ever since I had Kadir, you've treated me like I was your biggest disappointment."

She sighed and then said, "I was disappointed. I wanted so much more for you. I worked two jobs so that you could go to Catholic school and to keep you away from neighborhood boys. But you still managed to get pregnant. So when you had that baby, I just thought, I can't sugar-coat anything. I have to prepare her for the real world and make her raise that baby on her own. Yeah, I was hard on you, but I thought I was making you strong. And it worked out. Look what happened, you raised a good boy, be proud of yourself. Kadir calls me all the time. He even got me cable so I can watch his games."

She got up from the sofa and came over to me and gave me a hug. "We got years to make up for. Just be better than me. Don't be so hard on him."

"I will."

I felt so much better that my mom and I were going to be okay. I felt a weight ease off my back. I decided to surprise CeCe at her job. She was an office manager for a doctor's office. She was on a call when I arrived at her office. I smiled at her and she signaled to me to give her one minute.

"What's going on? What are you doing here?"

"I came home to help my mom. My friend and I were talking about family and I felt like I had to help her, but Kadir already has been helping her. Plus, I wanted to see you and Mom Laura."

"That was nice of him."

"It was, but he is supposed to run everything by me."

"Hold that thought. Let me get my coat and clock out. I'll be right out."

We could go eat and drink anywhere in the city but we still ended up at Copas, a small Philly favorite with finger food and great margaritas. We got a table by the window and ordered two double mango margaritas with sugar rims.

"So what's going on here?'

"Nothing much. What's up with you? Are you going to reveal who your mysterious boo is?"

"No."

"I can't believe you are going to keep a secret from me! I've been your friend for how long?"

"Next conversation."

"I'll remember that. Anyway, things are cool. Faheem is doing real good. I'm chilling and working. What's going on with Kadir?"

"He's fine, but keeping Kadir focused is a full-time job. His biological father's people tried to hit him up, and this little girl named Abigail, who has gold digger written all over her, is after him."

"Yeah, we have to protect our boys."

CeCe and I had been through everything together, including her marriage and divorce. After another two double margaritas and her begging me to reveal who my boo was, I finally caved and told her.

"Cee, it's the guy from London."

She put her hand over her mouth. "Hold up, the African guy that plays on Kadir's team?"

"Yes, him. I've been seeing him ever since we met that night. That night you fell asleep, I met up with him." I waited to see how she was going to respond to my scandal.

"So you think this is cute. I'm shocked. Have you lost your motherfucking mind?"

"CeCe, I know you are not judging."

"Yes, I'm judging you. My brother, who has done everything for you, doesn't matter now because you're dealing with some young basketball player."

"Of course he matters. I just want to be happy."

"Does Kadir know about this?"

"No, not yet."

"Oh, my God. You have got to be the one to tell Kadir. Mo, you know I ride with you. But this isn't right. Carl has been nothing but loyal to you and Kadir. And you, you are wrong. This is some fucked-up shit."

"How am I wrong? He's grown and I'm grown. We are both single, consenting adults."

"Don't you know you are just the girl of the moment? What would make you think he would want to be with a woman almost forty, when he could have someone younger?"

"I didn't start dating Dele until after Carl and I broke up, so that's one. Two, age doesn't matter with us. Three, the only person I have to make happy is myself. And four, me and Carl have outgrown each other. He left me. I didn't leave him. It wasn't enough anymore."

"Funny, he was enough all these years, and now that you have money, he's not."

"It's never been enough, I've always wanted more. I tried to make it work with him."

"Sure you did. I can't believe you."

"Grandma Cee, I can't believe you are being this damn judgmental."

"Yeah, I'm judging, but I know that D is good." She gave me a half smile.

"Girl, it is! It's everything, but it's more than the sex. He is just an all-around good guy."

"Well, tell Kadir before someone else does."

Right then my screen lit up and I saw Dele's number on my phone. "We just spoke him up."

"Tell him I said hi."

"Hey, babe, what's up? Oh, and CeCe says hi."

"You told her about us?" he asked excitedly.

"Yes, and I made up with my mom. How are you?"

"I'm good, but listen, Monique, I'm calling to tell you to have a conversation with Kadir. I've been in the league for five years, and I have never seen a player so hated."

"What did he do?"

"His attitude is disgusting. He's making demands and being rude. And he's not talking to people who aren't wealthy like him. He's being very flashy and that is not okay. He had a few good games. But he said it's his team and laughed about one of the guys not having any time on the court and said he would buy him some time and a new car."

"Oh, did he? I'm going to talk to him. Thanks for telling me, baby. I'll see you as soon as you get back." I ended the call and sighed. "My son has lost his mind."

"What did he say?" CeCe asked.

"He said Kadir is being a cocky asshole. I'm going to call him now and straighten this all out."

I dialed Kadir on his cell. He answered with the music playing loudly in the background.

"Yo, Ma."

"Kadir, are you for real? Do you like the life you're living? Keep the dumb shit up and you will lose it all and be playing overseas or in the D-League somewhere if you don't get your shit together."

"What's wrong? What are you talking about, Mom?"

"I'm talking about don't get a big head. I better not hear again that the Hornets is your team. There are thirty teams and thirteen spots on each team and you better be thankful, Kadir, that you have one of them, because there are millions of boys that want to be where you're at."

"Oh, you're talking about me arguing with Smith. He was talking trash about me and I said something back. I told him to talk to me when he gets off the bench. How you know about that anyway?"

"Don't worry about it. Do better."

CHAPTER 41

Adrienne

I came to L.A. with a mission and it was time to get back to it. Plus, it was time for me to leave the nest of Mrs. Coleman aka Ms. Tucker and find my own way. She was on and off her meds and I couldn't take much more.

My goal was to try to schedule meetings. The first person on my list was Warren Michael Joseph. I whipped out the contact information I had taken and decided to give him a call.

"Good morning. This is Adrienne Sheppard. I met you the other night at Morgan Tucker's party."

"Yes, I remember. Is this her beautiful assistant?"

I was caught off guard. "It is. I'm calling because I have a script that I wrote that you may be interested in. I wanted to meet up with you to discuss it."

"I'm available today. We can meet for coffee at two at Espresso House."

"Yes, I'll see you then."

I didn't know what to wear. I was so excited. I wanted to look sexy, but I wanted Mr. Joseph to know I meant business.

I settled on something in between, a low-cut gray minidress with black pumps and a black blazer.

I grabbed a table outside in the courtyard overlooking the street. I ordered a spinach salad and raspberry tea.

"Sorry, I was running a little behind," he said, walking in.

"No problem." The waitress took his order and I let him get settled in before I started my pitch.

"So it's good to see you again. Are you from here?"

"No, originally from Philly, but I lived in Atlanta, and Miami also."

"What brings you to L.A.?" he asked.

"The same thing as everyone else. I'm trying to make something happen. I have a script that I wrote, and I am trying to sell it." I didn't have any time to sugar-coat my intentions. He was either interested on not. "I think you would be interested in it. It's called *Falcon Hall Boys*."

"What's it about?"

"It's about five guys who all lived in the same dorm hall in college, Falcon Hall. They make a vow to each other that they will all graduate college no matter what. Their family, the streets, and other things try to keep them from reaching their goal of graduating. They pull each other up and become brothers along the way."

"Sounds interesting. Did you write it?"

"Yeah, my ex-boyfriend told me about his experiences in college and I got the idea."

"I'm impressed. I thought you were going to try to sell me on a story about girlfriends trying to get married."

"No." I felt the need to tell him that I wasn't a bum and though I was Morgan Coleman's personal assistant now, once upon a time I was successful.

"I wrote *Falcon Hall Boys* and I've done a few other things. I was a nurse and then I opened a nightclub up two years ago. I invested all my savings. It is a long story, but my ex-fiancé was doing some crazy things that I didn't know about and I lost everything. So now I'm out here rebuilding my life."

"Okay. So I would love to read your script."

"No problem. I brought it with me." I took it out of my bag. Realizing I was becoming too anxious, I thought about it and said, "Or I could e-mail it to you."

"That would be better. So you do everything, club owner, natural beauty, script writer, and a nurse. What can't you do?"

"I'm just a regular girl trying to making it happen. Oh, and I have a five-year-old daughter. She's in Atlanta with her father."

"You are far from regular, but I like natural. Your teeth and boobs are yours," he said while glancing at my cleavage.

I knew I had made the right call to go sexy professional with my outfit.

"That's hard to find out here. I know you have a man back home."

"No, I've been concentrating on my work."

"Yeah, I know about that. It's hard to find a woman that can deal with my hectic schedule. I am gone for weeks at a time. My last girlfriend said she was always lonely and said the money wasn't enough and she didn't want me to rescue her. She wanted to make it on her own."

Money would be enough for me and I want to be rescued, too, I thought.

"Everyone can't deal with career-driven people. Can you?"

"I don't know; tell me a few things about yourself."

"What do you want to know? My real name is Warren Michael Joseph. I have three first names just like my father, Warren Michael Joseph, Senior. I'm really a Junior, but that was too much."

"I agree." I laughed.

"What else. I'm from Memphis. My dad's a preacher, my mom was a teacher and then she became a principal. So I couldn't go anywhere and get peace. No kids like me. I was either at the church or school. I love my dad, but me and my dad don't really get along. So I stayed busy."

"You don't have a southern accent."

"I lost it when I went to college. You remind me of my college girlfriend a little."

"I do? What happened to her?"

"She left me for my teammate. I was heartbroken."

"Damn, that's not good. I don't know if I want to remind you of her."

"No, it's cool now. It was a long time ago. I'm over it. She was a self-entitled princess. You don't seem that way. Plus, they got married and are happy."

After talking at the coffee shop for four hours, we moved our conversation to a Chinese restaurant called WP24 located on the twenty-fourth floor of the Ritz Carlton. Our business meeting was getting flirty, considering the skyline view and martinis in front of us. I would take business or pleasure, whichever one he was offering. Either would be beneficial to me.

"This is my favorite place in L.A. and the sushi is really good. I like to chill out when I can. I have two movies coming out, one next month and the other at the beginning of the year. Now that I'm retired, I'll have more time for acting, but football will always be my first love."

"What team did you play for?" I acted like I hadn't done my research.

"I played for the Carolina Panthers. I was with them for nine seasons."

"Okay, my ex-husband played for the Seahawks."

"You were married to an NFL player, too? What happened, you couldn't take the lifestyle?"

"No, we just fell out of love."

"Well, he must have been crazy to stop loving you."

After dinner, we sat poolside and took in the scenic view and talked for another two hours.

"I can't believe we've been out for eight hours."

"Good conversation, a beautiful, interesting date, and we handled a little business. I'll say time well spent. Actually, I have a confession. When you called me I was like is she asking me on a date or does she want to do business."

"I was thinking business, but I guess this has turned into a date."

"So we are on a date, so that I'm clear."

"Yeah, we are."

"Well, now we know. No blurred lines. I'm very interested in you. You are so genuine. It's hard to find that out here and I really I enjoyed your company all day."

"I enjoyed yours as well."

At the end of the night he gave me a sweet, simple, romantic but promising kiss on my lips.

To say my first date was wonderful was an understatement. I was blown away. I came back to the house on a natural high, until I spotted Morgan sitting up on the sofa. She grimaced at me then at her phone. I felt like she was my mother and she caught me coming in late.

"Where have you been?"

"Out."

Who was she talking to?

"Good night, Morgan," was all I could manage to say. Before I said something a lot less pleasant, like kiss my ass.

"Where have you been?" she asked again.

"What I do when I'm not working for you is honestly none of your business."

"Yeah, that's true, but this is my house and I don't want anyone coming in my home after two a.m. When I close my eyes I like to feel secure and know that no one is running around my property."

"A curfew? You're ridiculous, Morgan. Go to bed."

* * *

The next morning I showered and came into the main house and saw an extremely large floral arrangement with combination of white, red, and yellow roses.

"Nice flowers," I said.

"Thanks, but they're yours. I suppose you got lucky last night. Don't get sidetracked."

A text came through my phone.

I sent you flowers and you couldn't even send me a thank you?

I texted back:

Thank you. I just got up.

He texted again:

Are you free later this week for dinner?

I waited ten minutes just to make him sweat a little, then texted:

Yes.

His response was:

I'll send a car. See you Thursday.

CHAPTER 42

Zakiya

"Good afternoon, Zakiya, this is Sister Elise."
"Hi, Sister Elise. Yes, I'm coming to bible study today. I'm running a little behind. I have to bring my daughter with me, because my nanny couldn't make it."

"Okay, that's fine. I'll see you when you get here, but I was calling you for two reasons."

"Yes."

"Well, the pastor and I have been talking. And after seeing you and your gorgeous, successful husband, we think you would be perfect for our 'Blessed, Saved and Married' conference."

"I don't know. What would we have to do? My husband is out of town a lot and he doesn't do much talking."

"It's only four dates in Charlotte, Memphis, Little Rock, and Houston. We would like you to be guest speakers and talk about having God in your marriage and being a successful, happy couple. He wouldn't have to speak."

"Can I think about it? I'll need to ask Jabril. What was the second thing?'

"Do you think you will be able to contribute money to get the church a van? We are going to buy a used van. Brother Miles said it will be about twenty thousand dollars. We are going to ask the congregation on Sunday for donations. Hopefully everyone will be generous, but I wanted to get a head start on the fund. How much do you think you can give?"

"Twenty thousand dollars. Let me see. How much do you have now?"

"Two thousand."

"Uhm. I can donate five thousand. I'll write a check and bring it with me."

"Okay."

Pastor Elise had given me her address, but I wasn't sure I had the right house, because I had pulled up to a mansion. I double-checked the address and it was correct. I parked in front of a large fountain. There was a silver two-door Bentley, a yellow Ferrari, and a gold Rolls Royce Phantom all parked on an angle in front of the house.

I was greeted by a butler and maid. I saw Sister Elise and I waved to her. She came over to me and hugged me and Jabrilah.

Walking into her grand home, I marveled at the winding double staircase and the huge picture of her and Pastor Richard that hung on the hallway wall.

"What a beautiful home."

"Well, thank you. I'm sure you have seen better. Do you have the check?"

"Yes, it's right here."

"Thank you. It will help so much."

I came in and greeted all the other ladies, who ranged in age from teenager to senior citizen. I had a seat on her plush tan leather easy curved couch. I put Jabrilah and her bottle down on the sand-colored carpet and pulled out my bible. I saw Talisha and waved at her and began reading a selection in my bible.

"You understand that version? I can't get into all that thou and thee stuff. You should get you the NIV version. It is so much easier to understand," Talisha said.

"Thank you! I thought it was just me who was slow," I said laughing.

"Nope. girl." We laughed and talked until Sister Elise interrupted us.

"Get your baby and her bottle. I don't want any dirt on my carpet." I looked over to see Jabrilah was turning her bottle upside down.

"I'm sorry." I picked up my daughter and placed her on my lap.

"Okay, ladies, let's begin. We will be reading the Good Girls and Bad Girls of the Bible. It is important that we look at both. We are going to read it and analyze the text."

After our bible study, Sister Elise's maid and butler served us dinner in her extravagant dining room. The table was set with white plates with gold trim at formal place settings with name cards. I found my name and had a seat next to Sister Elise. I sat Jabrilah on my lap and began nibbling from the salad that was in front of me.

They went over some official church business.

Sister Elise stood up and said, "Okay, I know you've heard the rumors about Pastor Wyatt and his wife getting a divorce. A few women have come forward and said that they have had a sexual relationship with him. I don't believe it, but that is between him and Sister Althea. I think these women are scum for ruining his marriage, but that's my opinion. I just wanted to make you all aware of it. Any other business?" Sister Elise asked.

"Yes," an older sister name Joan said. "I want the choir to have a dress code. Sister Vanessa sings like an angel, but it is wasted, because she doesn't like wearing underwear. She wears them thongs every week."

"What does that have to do with church business?" Sister Elise responded.

"Well, it's just disgusting. Her butt just shakes up and down and back and forth when she walks. And it's distracting for the male members. How is a man not supposed to look at that?"

"Sister, I don't know, but that's not important."

"It is important, because her first baby already don't have no daddy and she don't need another one. She should wear some real underwear in the house of the Lord."

"That's true, but God does say come as you are. Anybody else have anything to add?"

"Elise, don't ignore me. Say something to these young girls. God wants you to cover your butt."

"That's enough. Changing topics, I want everyone to welcome Sister Zakiya. Both she and her husband are going to be coming to our marriage conference. Zakiya's husband plays for our Charlotte Hornets. Praise God. They are a dynamic young couple and I knew there was something special about her when we met."

I smiled at her but I was upset because I didn't like being put on the spot, and I had told her I would let her know.

For the rest of the night I enjoyed the fellowship with the other ladies. It was refreshing to be around other people who were on the same spiritual journey.

It was a Tuesday afternoon and I could think of a hundred things I'd rather do than have lunch with the Franklins.

"Hurry up! I don't want to be late."

I didn't want to go and was intentionally moving slowly. I was hoping Jabril would leave without me.

"I'm coming." I sighed as I slid my green dress over my head and put my heels on. I grabbed my earrings and entered the living room and overheard Jabril on the phone with the bank arguing.

"What's wrong?"

"There's money missing out of our account."

I had forgotten to tell him about the money I gave to the church over the last month or so.

"Oh! The money isn't missing. I donated five thousand dollars to the church, they needed a new van. And I wrote a few other checks."

"Fifteen thousand dollars' worth of giving, Zakiya? We don't know what is going to happen with this team. I'm sitting on the bench right now. What if I get cut and next season I don't get picked up? Then what? It's not like you have any money coming in."

I didn't even respond. I was going to let him get his frustration off of his chest.

"Jabril, so are you going to take everything out on me? If I spent money on clothes, it would be okay. But since I'm helping people it is a problem."

"No, there is a difference. One you have something to show for it, the other you don't. I can't deal with this dumb shit. This is why my life is out of order."

"No, it is out of order because you don't pray, and you need to stop smoking, then maybe God would bless you. And you would get more time."

"What did you say?"

"I said, Jabril, you are probably slow because of all the weed that you smoke."

"Worry about yourself, Zakiya, and stop giving out free money. They don't need our money. That pastor has a lot of donations already and a big congregation."

The mood was already wrong, but he insisted upon having a double date with the captain and his wife.

"I don't see why I have to go. I don't like his wife, she's very messy. You told me not to be too cool with everybody in Oklahoma, now you are pushing that woman on me."

"No, her husband is the leader. It's different. Zakiya, you

don't understand. I can't be on that bench. He's in the assistant coach's ear. Last night we were up by fifteen and still nothing. I'm dying, seriously."

"Fine."

We met them at Bentley's on 27, a restaurant in downtown Charlotte. My skyline view was beautiful, until Dawn came and sat next to me. She was wearing designer everything, with an inauthentic personality. She bent over to give me a hug, but I didn't bother to meet her halfway. I just leaned back and waved. They had a seat and Jabril asked could I walk him to the restroom.

"That was rude, Zakiya."

"Jabril, I told you I don't know how to be fake."

"You have to pretend. You have to do this for us. You want to spend thousands of dollars, but if I don't have a job, how are we going to survive? Play the game, Kiya."

"She was nasty to me, Jabril. She said I should let you fuck other women in our house. And she said she took Thad's mistress to the abortion clinic. What kind of wife is she? And what kind of husband is he?"

"Babe, that's them. We are us. I'm not getting anyone pregnant and I come home. Keep your opinion to yourself and just be nice."

"Fine, Jabril." I pulled away from him and walked back to the table.

I came back and told Dawn I was a little under the weather and didn't want to give her my germs. I complimented her on everything from her hair to her boots. She took it all in and by the time our double date was over, she invited us to a couple of events over the next couple of weekends. I told her we would go, but I knew we would never go anywhere with her.

CHAPTER 43

Shanice

I'd known Deuce for a few months, but I wasn't ready to be exclusive with him. I reasoned with him that I wanted to give him my all, but I just wasn't ready yet. The truth is I wanted to see what would happen with Jabril. I just kept imagining us being back together and him being mine. And I hoped that what I was about to do would bring me one step closer to realizing my dream.

I knew Jabril was playing in D.C. and I wanted to meet up with him. I was going to pretend that I had a video shoot and act like we just happened to be in the same city again. I didn't have anything to lose. And if he asked to see pictures, I already had some old pictures with me from an old photo shoot.

On my way to D.C. I sent him a text. I knew he kept his phone on before the game.

I texted:

Hey, you. What are you doing?

He responded back, **I'm at practice. How about you?**

I replied, **I'm in D.C. at a video shoot.**

He texted back, **We play the Wizards tonight. What a coincidence. Do you want to come to the game?**

I responded, **I can't I'm working, but maybe we can meet up when I'm done.**

I knew it would be late and I knew he would probably think that I was setting him up, which I was. I wanted him to feel comfortable and not under any pressure. So I quickly texted back:

Or maybe another time.

He texted:

No we can meet up. I'll text you when I'm back at the hotel.

I waited to hear from him. He sent me a text with the address where he was staying and said to meet him at a bar down the street.

I wore jeans, a t-shirt, and a blazer. I pulled my hair up in a sloppy bun and put on a little nude lip gloss. I didn't want to look like I was coming to seduce him. He was wearing a hat all the way down, a t-shirt, and loose sweatpants. I had a seat and he kept watching to see who was watching us. I could tell he was nervous that someone might see us and send a pic to a blog or his wife. He stood up and gave me a brief hug.

"You look nice and smell good," he said.

"Thank you."

"That's crazy that we in the same city at the same time."

"Yeah, my manager just called me and was like, can you do this video? It was short notice, but I just decided to do it." I laughed.

"Who's the group?"

"You never heard of them, they are local, but the pay was good."

"That's what's up. You are always working."

"Yeah, my manager has us doing a television show. I was supposed to be filming the night I ran back into you."

"Television? That's good," he said while staring down at his phone, and then he passed it to me and said, "This is my daughter, Jabrilah." I took a look at the screen and saw a pretty little girl.

"She is cute and big."

"Yeah, that's my baby girl. She acts just like me but looks like my wife. She runs after me saying Dada. Yo, I never thought I would be that dude, but my daughter can't date ever."

"That's so sweet."

"So how about you? Did you get your daughter back?"

"Sort of, and my mom came home. I'm taking care of both of them. I got us all a house."

After about an hour of talking, he said he had to go. I wanted to hold him tightly and tell him to stay with me. The meet-up confirmed one simple thing that I already knew. I still loved Jabril. And I would do anything in the world to be with him.

I got on the highway and drove all the way back home, when I got a text from him saying it was good seeing me. If he only knew what it took to see him.

I was almost near my exit when Ashley V called.

"Hey, lady."

"Hey, boo, what's going on?"

"Girl, I just want to warn you about the camera crew. When they come to your house, make sure you keep your composure. They told me they were coming at two and came at ten. I wasn't even ready. My hair was in a ponytail and I didn't have any makeup on. Even though I know how to speak on camera, I was nervous. I was stuttering and repeating myself."

"Seriously?"

"Yes, they will try to get you."

"Okay. Thanks for the heads-up. I'll make sure I'm already dressed hours before they get there. I'll call you."

"Okay, good luck."

Two days later I was back in New York and finally met with the film crew. The cameraman was a young, short white guy named Larry with brown curly hair. He was the eyes behind the oversize camera on his shoulder. He was with a young brown-skinned girl named Chamber who wore shoulder-length burgundy dreads and a nose ring. They seemed cool, but they were really business-oriented. They didn't smile and if they didn't like what I said or did, they told me to do again. Although I was just supposed to be myself and forget that the camera was following me, it was hard to forget with a micro-phone pack taped to my back and people staring at me as I walked down the street. A few people actually came over and asked what we were taping.

They got to film me at an audition for a body wash com-mercial and having lunch with Ashley V. They, however, weren't coming to my house because I lived in Philly. I was happy. I wasn't really trying to put my mom and aunt on tele-vision anyway.

By the time I got back home, I was tired and I fell asleep. I was awakened by my phone ringing. I sleepily answered.

"Hey, I'm in Philly."

I thought I was dreaming. It was Jabril.

"Are you up?"

He might as well have said, "Baby, I love you. I miss you, I need you." I sat up and squinted to see that it was only eleven.

"Yeah, I'm up."

"I called to see what you were doing."

"I was relaxing a little. What are you doing here?"

"I took a drive and next thing I knew I was here."

"Where are you staying?"

"I don't know yet. I'll probably stay downtown or I might go to my mom's house. I was seeing if maybe we could get to-gether."

We agreed to meet at Silk Nine. It was an upscale lounge. When I entered, he was already seated at the bar with two empty shot glasses in front of him. He stood up and hugged me. I sat down next to him and ordered a vodka and pine-apple juice.

"So what's up with you? What are you doing in Philly?"

He appeared to already be feeling his drink. "I don't know, I just felt like driving."

"What's wrong? You look like something is on your mind."

"Nothing, I'm just tired. Been dealing with some team stuff and a situation with my wife. She's giving all this money away to her church without telling me."

"Well that's not a bad thing."

"No, it's not, but when it's fifteen thousand dollars in a couple of months."

"To the church? Yeah, that's a lot of money."

"And she's not really getting along with my teammate's wife. She doesn't want to be a team player and it is making me so mad. We went out with my teammate and his wife. They are the couple that you want to be cool with. If you're cool with them off the court, then you're cool with them on the court. Then when he has the ball, he'll pass it to me and I can get some numbers on the board. If I get them points, I stay on the team. But that's not going to happen if my wife is being a bitch."

"She probably has her reasons."

"Yeah, she said they were materialistic and they trash talked. But you know what, so what? Do this for me. Anyway, enough about my situation. You look nice. You always look nice. What you been up to?"

"Filming the show I'm a part of, *Eye Candy Queens: The Come-up*."

"Is it like one of them crazy shows where everybody throws drinks on each other?"

"No, it's about our work doing videos. Our hustle. That type of thing."

"You do be hustling. That's what I liked about you. We had a good thing. If I wasn't already in a relationship I would have been with you. I just had a lot going on."

With those words, I knew I was not going to be able to hold back anymore.

"I don't care what was going on, Jabril. You should have called me. I was there for you, I took a case for you. I was there for you but you just left me. Like I never meant anything to you. I know you had your situation, but what about me?"

Tears were flowing down my face. I didn't mean to cry. I didn't want to scare him, but I was upset. He brought me into him. He kissed my forehead. I didn't care that people were staring.

"I'm sorry, baby. I'm real sorry. My uncle was in my ear heavy around that time. He kept saying you need a good girl that would always be in your corner no matter what. Get rid of everything on the side."

Becoming more upset, I pushed him off of me and cried. "I rided for you. I didn't put those drugs in your car."

"I know. I never found out how they got there, but it was just a crazy time. But you got the money I sent you, right?"

"I did, but that's not what we were about. I wanted to talk to you. I've missed you."

"I've missed you, too. I thought about you."

He grabbed my face and kissed me passionately. He was drunk. I knew he was having a moment of weakness. Jabril took my hand, kissed it and then looked in my eyes.

"I'm sorry. I was wrong. I should have called and checked on you. Let me make it up to you."

We ended up at the Loews hotel. The moment I waited for was finally happening. I couldn't believe it. My baby was kissing me. We couldn't get our clothes off fast enough. His strong hands glided underneath my shirt to unhook my bra. I couldn't wait to feel him inside me. I had already forgiven him and my heart and pussy had been aching for him. He sucked my breasts through my shirt and I pushed him against the door of the room. He pulled down his pants and I turned around and I bounced my pussy up and down onto his long pole. We were finally united. He was moaning, trying to hold back from releasing. It only took a few minutes of pounding for a warm gush to run down my leg.

"It's coming out, Bril!" I screamed.

"I see it. Damn, this is some good pussy. I missed your sexy ass," he said, biting my neck roughly.

"Look how that pussy is getting wet for me. You missed me, didn't you?"

"Yes, yes, yes, Jabril." I could barely speak. Tears streamed down my face. I was so happy he was back with me. His dick felt like it was reaching my stomach, but I was overjoyed with pleasure so I didn't make him stop.

"I missed you so much," I screamed.

"You did? You missed me? Show me." He stopped mid-stroke and ordered me on my knees. "Suck it like you missed him." He shoved all his thickness in my mouth, almost choking me. I managed to breathe and began caressing his balls and sucking, kissing, all over him. He was almost coming, but he stopped himself and told me to get on the bed and get on top. I sat on top of his dick and I rode him slowly then fast. I wanted him to know I was in control. I had to make him remember why he should never leave me again.

CHAPTER 44

Adrienne

"I love you, Mommy." Her cherubic face smiled from the other side of the phone.

"I love you too, Asia." Looking at my baby through a screen made me so angry. FaceTime was okay, but I wanted my daughter with me. I'm glad I lived on the West Coast because I had contemplated killing DeCarious and his wife several times. But then I thought about it: if I killed them, then I would be in jail and Asia wouldn't have anyone. With all that said, I would just have to let the judicial process run its course.

"Asia, Mommy is going to talk to you later." I ended our FaceTime session. At least she was happy. I couldn't wait to go to court with my lawyer and get my child back. Then I would make the decision if I would stay out in Los Angeles.

Morgan had been chilling, and Talene had been paying her rent. Everything was falling into place and getting better. I was in a way better position than I had been four months ago.

Warren and I had been talking and texting on the phone for hours at a time. He seemed real cool and down to earth and our second date was today.

He didn't send a car to come get me; instead he pulled up in a blue Ferrari. Morgan watched me from the door. Before I got in the car, she screamed, "You know it is all good in the beginning. They take you out, treat you nice and then they marry you, have babies by you and leave you like you never meant anything to them."

I ignored Morgan and left her alone with her misery. That was her story, it wouldn't be mine. He opened my door and we sped off. I had dated plenty of famous men. I dated athletes before, but the difference between them and Warren was the caliber of man and athlete. Not only was he worth fifty million dollars, he was also well spoken and extremely handsome. He was someone who could walk in a room and everyone would turn their heads and be in awe. He had a good upbringing, was college educated, which made him very marketable for endorsements. I never had the full package before. A man with good looks, intelligence, and wealth.

We had dinner at a place called Spago in Beverly Hills. We pulled up and the valet took the car and cameras began flashing. I wasn't prepared to be blinded by the bright flickers of light coming from every direction. There were at least ten men with cameras. Then they started to ask Warren for an impromptu interview.

"How was it working with Gabrielle? Did Dwyane come to the set and make you nervous?"

"It was great! She is a talented actress and I was a gentleman, so no, he didn't come after me. We were only acting."

Once inside, we were escorted to a table in the back of the establishment. My eyes were trying to get adjusted to the normal lighting. Warren asked if I was okay.

"Yeah, that was just unexpected. How do you get used to this?"

"It comes with the territory. I think my star is rising, because the movie is about to come out. Before, I could walk down the street and no one knew who I was. I have guys who are football fans who would give me a head nod, but now women are running up to me to take pictures.

"My boy Edwin is the only one who believed in me. Everyone just saw another football player trying to act."

"That's good. I'm still not sure if I could get used to all of this. I like it out here, but I want to get my daughter home with me."

"Once you have her back, are you staying?"

"I haven't decided yet. I miss her like crazy and we have never been apart."

"You'll get her back. My father knows a lot of people in Atlanta. I'll call one of my uncles, he knows all the judges and attorneys. I'll ask him to go with you to your next court date."

"I have an attorney. I know the court made a mistake because he lied, but yeah I need as many people as possible to help plead my case. I have a job, took a drug test and parenting classes. I just need them to reinstate my full custody back."

Dinner was picture-perfect. Everything about Warren was perfect. I almost couldn't believe how my life kept getting better and better.

"This is all very impressive, Mr. Joseph."

"Thank you. I try I go all out when I'm trying to impress a woman that I'm really interested in."

"What happens after they are impressed?"

"We go back to my house and have passionate sex and then whatever you want from there."

"At least you are truthful, but that only happens in the movies."

He licked his lips and said, "I think it can happen in real life, too."

We left the restaurant and headed to his place. He said he had to pick up something. I knew he just wanted to get me to his house. His home was huge, but slightly smaller than Morgan's. He showed me pictures of his parents and all his awards and trophies. He asked me did I want anything else to drink. I declined, because I knew he was trying to get me to stay. I'm sure he had to have had plenty of women and I had to be different than the rest of them. Under no circumstances would I allow him to convince me to sleep with him. So I played uninterested as he left and told me he would be right back. He got what he needed from the house and then dropped me off at my door.

"Good night, Adrienne. I'll see you when?"

"Call me tomorrow."

The next morning Warren asked me out for an early brunch. However, I didn't know we would be dining at his house. He had breakfast delivered and we ate on his back deck.

"I thought we were going to a nice restaurant. I got dressed for nothing."

"We were, but I am still a little tired from last night. You shouldn't have left. I don't know why you didn't stay."

"I couldn't, but I'm here now."

"You are. So can I at least get a kiss this morning?"

"You can." He came over to my end of the table and then stood me up and leaned me back and brought me forward.

"How was that?"

"That was a cute movie kiss."

"It was? How about this? You have to close your eyes." I closed my eyes and felt his tongue in my ear, his hands on my thighs. Then his tongue was on my navel and swept both of my nipples, teasing them both and making them perk up. And then he stopped.

"How was that?"

"Very sensual, but more than a kiss, but interesting," I said, opening my eyes and shaking off the orgasmic rush. He caught me off guard and kissed me again. This time he didn't stop and removed my clothes while he was doing so.

Everything was happening so fast. He guided me into his

bedroom and slid on a condom and soon he was inside of me tearing walls down from the front. Then he stopped, flipped me over, arched my back and spread my ass across the deck. He re-entered me, took three long hard thrusts, and then went completely limp midstroke.

"What's wrong?" I asked him, kissing his neck and massaging his dick to get it revved up again.

"I don't know. I think I'm just too excited. Give me a minute, it will come back up." He left the room and walked to the bathroom. I heard him punch the wall and then water ran. He came back in and said let's chill for a while. He turned the television on and pulled me in to his side while I took a nap waiting for round two. A half an hour later I felt him turning me over. Once he was back in, he was nonstop. It was crazy. He would eat me, fuck me, then I would suck him and then we repeated the cycle for hours.

It was almost five in the afternoon when I got up and found the bed empty. My body was tender from our marathon sex session and Warren was gone. I grabbed my bag and checked my phone. I had seven missed calls from Morgan. I put my clothes and shoes on and called out for Warren. I stood at the top of the steps when I noticed his friend Edwin was downstairs with another woman. They all looked up at the top of the staircase.

"You're finally up," Warren said. They all laughed. I didn't. I came down the steps.

"Adrienne, they wanted to see if we want to go running with them at the canyon."

"I didn't bring any workout clothes."

"No problem, we can call over to the cycle shop and I'll have them send some over. Tell Edwin your sizes."

"No, I need to go home and do a few things."

When I got back, Morgan was sitting on the sofa watching television. I tried to talk to her but she kept looking straight at the television.

"About time you returned."

"What's the emergency, Morgan?"

"I haven't decided yet. Did you check my e-mail? Has any-body contacted you about interviews for me?"

"No, not yet."

"Oh, and by the way, be proud of yourself. You made it to the blogs as a mystery woman."

"I did?" She showed me her phone and I saw a picture of Warren and me entering the restaurant.

"He must like you. Fancy dinner and he let the cameras capture your date."

"I guess."

"Since you've been slobbing knobs with my next costar, see if you can get me a part in his next movie." I could take her last comment personally or I could keep collecting my check. I didn't feel like being her on-call slave anymore, but I would play along with her until I didn't have to anymore.

CHAPTER 45

Monique

"Go, Kadir! Go, son! Yes!" I yelled as my son caught the rebound and took it down the court. When everyone thought he was going to the basket, he passed it to Thaddeus Franklin and he slam-dunked on the Pacers. They were about to secure their tenth win in a row!

Carl came to town for the game and he finally stopped talking about us getting back together. He said he had met someone and I was happy for him. Although Kadir was grown, we could learn to be friends and co-parents. And little Ms. Trailer Park, Abigail, was at the game, too. She spoke to me, but she was scared to say anything else. I tried to be nice to her since it seemed Kadir really liked her.

"So how's your son?" I asked.

"He's fine, but I'm trying to potty train him. So I won't have to buy anymore Pampers."

"I remember I made Kadir sit on the potty the entire weekend, until he went. And I never bought another diaper."

"I might have to try that," she said, and we continued to make small talk the rest of the game.

Once the game was over, everyone was congratulating the

team on their win. News cameras and reporters rushed the floor to discuss the victory. Kadir was out of breath and his face was covered with perspiration, but the reporters were still sticking microphones in his face. He was able to share the stage with Thaddeus Franklin and be a star in his own right.

"Hey, our guys won, right?" Thaddeus Franklin's wife said. I ignored her. I never forgot her comments from the charity event and I wasn't interested in being her friend.

Dele was signing autographs, but then he walked over with Kadir. I was beyond nervous; my hands were trembling.

"Mom, Dad, this is my teammate Dele." I extended my hand out to shake his. "He looks out for me. He helps me cool down when I get too hype."

"He does? That's nice."

"Nice to meet you, Mom," Dele said, then Dele shook Carl's hand as well. He knew he was making me nervous, but he didn't care.

After all the interviews were over, Kadir came out of the locker room, took my hand and said, "Mom, I want you to meet somebody."

"Who?"

"This is my brother Phillip."

I did see Kadir in his face. But knowing that didn't stop me from being upset with Kadir for pushing this child on me.

"I don't want to meet him."

"That's mean, Monique. He can hear you," Carl butted in.

"I don't care. I'm surprised you are cosigning this foolishness, Carl. Kadir, you can be a fool if you want to. I already warned you. You're already sneaking around to help your grandmother out. I don't care, fly all of them down here and when they rob you blind, don't come running to me."

"I am and I will. And I already went to Philly and met my family. I have money, Mom, so what's the problem? I look out for you, so why can't I look out for them? They say I look just like my dad."

"Your dad's name is Carl, Kadir. That's who raised you. Them Henderson folks are greedy people that just want a free ride."

"Mom, give him a chance. Please, for me? I want to take us all to dinner like a family."

I met Kadir, his long-lost brother Phil, Abigail, and Carl for dinner at Del Frisco's. I was already angry about all of this, but my night went from bad to worse when I spotted Dele sitting three tables away with a beautiful young woman. She had light brown skin and had natural, long honey blond curly 'fro. She was wearing a body-hugging taupe-colored dress that made her almost appear to be nude. She couldn't be any more than twenty-three. They were laughing and smiling at each other. I wanted to go over there and choke him, but I couldn't. I had to play it cool, but he would have to explain this ish to me. How was I supposed to enjoy my meal?

"Mom, are you all right? You look like you might be getting sick," Kadir asked.

"I'm tired." I glanced over at Dele's table and he smiled at me. I gave him a "fuck you" face. Meanwhile, I caught Carl catching Dele looking at me, which made me look over at Phil.

"So, Phil, what do you with yourself?"

"I'm a junior at Morehouse. I'm studying microbiology."

"Mom, he's real smart. He started college a year early on an academic scholarship."

"Oh, that's real nice. I'm impressed."

Kadir shot me a look like "I told you."

"Who is your mom, Phil?"

"Her name is Stacy, but my grandparents raised me. My mom was in the streets, back in the day."

"Oh, okay."

"But she's getting herself together now."

"That's good."

"I didn't know I had a brother. People start telling me this guy Kadir Hall looks just like me. Then my grandmother told me and my cousin that we were actually brothers. I've been an only child my whole life, so I've always wanted a brother."

"Just like me, Mom."

Kadir was right. Phil seemed to be pleasant and intelligent and he did look like my Kadir—from his height to his mannerisms. He actually might be a good influence on his younger brother.

Carl was quiet and Abigail was on her phone and my eyes wandered back over to Dele's table. He had now put his arm around the young woman. I couldn't take much more, but it got worse. Dele up and walked over to our table. My heart was in my stomach. I didn't look up.

"Hey, Kadir. I didn't know you were coming here," Dele said.

"Remember, you told me about this place. I wanted to check it out." He said nice to see everyone again and went back to his table.

I waited exactly ten minutes and then rose from the table.

"Well, it was nice meeting you, Phil. I'm not feeling well and I'm going to go home."

"We all gonna chill. Pops, you gone make sure Mom good?"

But I cut off Carl before he could say anything. "You can stay, Carl. I'm going to drive myself home. Y'all have fun."

I couldn't get out of that steakhouse fast enough. I pushed start on my car and pulled off. I called Dele's phone. I knew he was still at dinner, but I didn't care. He answered, still being smart and said, "*Bonsoir.*" Which meant good evening.

"Dele, don't fucking play with me."

"Monique, do not speak to me in that manner."

"You're lucky cussing is all I'm doing. What was that all about? Huh? Who is that girl? Why were you having dinner with her?"

"Would you have gone with me? I can answer the question for you. No, you wouldn't have wanted me to go to dinner, to celebrate my team's win. As for the young lady, she is a friend. She's my friend's cousin in town from Paris. Maybe she has a crush, I am not sure. But don't ask any questions unless you are ready."

"Ready for what?"

"Ready to be out in the open with our relationship."

"Dele, you know I can't do that."

"Then you will not question me."

I went to say something else and noticed he had disconnected the call. I had no idea what I was going to do. I loved Dele, but I couldn't hurt Kadir.

CHAPTER 46

Adrienne

"Adrienne, I need to see you before I go to New York. Let's get something to eat and then I have a day party to attend. I'll meet you at Casta on Wilshire Boulevard in an hour."

Warren had a busy schedule, but he was making time for me and I couldn't wait to see him. He'd been consistent with his time. He called me and texted and I'd spent the night several times. I knew we were only dating, but I liked him a whole lot and I knew it had the potential of being more.

I showered and pulled out a sexy aqua-colored dress. My hair was pinned up and I had put a little bit of makeup on and I was on my way out of the door.

Morgan came behind me in the mirror. That crazed look had returned. "Where are you going? I need you to go over my lines with me. I have an audition on Monday."

"I'll help you when I get back. And, Morgan, we have to talk about my hours. I can't be on call all the time. I need a day off. Or I can work from seven to seven or something like that," I said, applying mascara.

"No, that is not possible. Actually, you are fired. You have two weeks to move out."

"I'm fired? Okay, Morgan." I wasn't thinking about Ms. Tucker. I would handle her when I returned. I couldn't wait to see Warren. However, I was extremely disappointed when I arrived at Casta and saw that it was a group date. His entire team was there, including his agent, Edwin, his stylist, Tayman, his publicist, Simone, and her assistant. He explained that they were going over his schedule and the movie company's marketing plan. That was nice, but I was wearing a sexy outfit for nothing. I immediately asked him if I could have a word with him.

"Why did you invite me to this strategy session?"

"Oh, because I'm going out of town and I wanted to give you this before I left. Here."

"What is this?"

"The money for your script." I looked down at a check for forty thousand dollars.

"But we didn't sign anything yet."

"I have the contract at the house. This is just to option the script, but if I can get it bought, I'll put you on as one of the producers." I didn't want to cry.

"Warren, I'm glad you liked it. This is perfect—it came at the right time. Morgan just fired me and told me to be out in two weeks. This is perfect. I can get my own place now."

"Just stay at my house while I'm gone. When I get back we will find you a place."

"Okay."

I came back to the table in a better mood. I was grateful. We ordered appetizers and we were all startled by the flash of multiple cameras. The paparazzi were up at the table snapping pictures, which alerted passersby that there was someone famous seated at our table. People started coming over and asking Warren for his autograph. He signed photos and took pictures with a half a dozen people. Once the pandemonium was over, Warren had a seat and apologized.

"You shouldn't have to apologize. Don't they see that you are eating? I mean I can't understand how people can come over and interrupt your meal," his stylist Tayman said.

"It's not right, but I understand it. If I were to see Will Smith walk into this restaurant, I would have to ask him if I could get a picture. When is the next time I'm going to see Will Smith again?" I said.

"I see Will all the time. Him and Jada jog in my neighborhood," Simone stated.

"I'm talking about everyday tourists."

"I agree that makes sense. You guys are disconnected. I understand what she is saying. It's not normal to see celebrities just run by you," Warren added.

"The media is a necessary evil; you can't want it on Monday and then ask why they are following you on a Thursday. It is a part of the job," his publicist Simone said.

From lunch we all went to a day party where Warren was making an appearance. There were beautiful people drinking and dancing everywhere. It was a different experience—it felt like a club but it was the middle of the day. We were escorted to a roped-off area off of the pool area to a huge white cabana. A bottle girl brought over our drinks. I caught Edwin gazing at me a few times. And then he came over and sat next to me.

"Hey, beautiful, are you enjoying yourself? Do you want another drink?"

"No, I'm fine. I had enough."

"So are you going to be at the house while Warren is gone? I'll come and keep you company." He grabbed my hand and stroked it. I was alarmed, but I didn't want to overreact, so I let it slide. Everything was going so well, I didn't want to tell Warren his best friend was hitting on me if I wasn't absolutely sure. And then he was unmistakably flirting with me when his hand started stroking my thighs under my skirt. No one could see his hands under the table, and I didn't want to create a scene, but I had to get away from him. I stood up, but he followed me. And then he grabbed my ass.

"So what's up?"

"There is nothing up. I don't know why you just did that, but I want you to never put your hands on me again."

I found Warren and took him to the bathroom.

"Warren, you might want to have a conversation with your friend Edwin."

"Why? What did he say to you?"

"He was being all flirty and he grabbed my leg and ass!"

"Oh, that. I'll talk to him. I forgot to tell him not to bother you."

"Tell him what?"

"Not to test you. It is something we always do, just to see."

"To see what? Why are grown men playing games?"

"He has to make sure everyone is around for the right reasons."

"The right reasons? I don't play games. You better be glad I didn't smack the shit out of him."

"Calm down. I'm sorry; my friends are just very protective. You have to understand. Everyone is out here with some type of ulterior motive."

"Yeah, well, that's not me."

"I know." He called Edwin over to apologize to me, but I didn't forgive him and knew that I didn't like him.

Chapter 47

Shanice

The cameras were following me around New York City again. I stopped by April's office, then went to an audition for a national water company and landed the job. I was so excited that I had something good to talk about while they filmed me having lunch with Ashley V. Today I did forget that a camera was taping my every move. I just prayed I didn't say anything that I would regret later.

One day I was in New York and the next I was in Charlotte and I couldn't wait to get to Jabril. He went from being unsure about being with me to my full-time boo again. Yes, he was married, but so what, and with that said I ended it with Deuce. He's a nice guy, but he wasn't what I wanted. I felt a little bad, but I didn't love him. I loved Jabril. The heart wants what it wants. So I told Deuce I wasn't ready for a relationship yet and he said he understood and to get with him when I was.

That wouldn't be any time soon. I'd been spending so much time with Jabril I didn't even miss Deuce. I've been on the road with Jabril for a few games. This week he had a few days off so he wanted me to come spend some time with him in Charlotte. My flight had just landed and I was in an Uber headed to his hotel.

"Where are you?" Jabril asked.

"I'm on my way, I just got in the car. You should have picked me up."

"Nah, I started drinking already, just hurry up. I need you, Shani. I'm in room seven thirty-nine."

"All right, I'll be there."

We drove from the airport to downtown Charlotte and it took about twenty minutes. I was in the hotel lobby and my phone rang again.

"Hello."

"Are you here yet??"

"Jabril, I'm downstairs about to get in the elevator."

"Good, I need you. Hurry up." I didn't mind him calling me back-to-back like that. I was just so happy he was mine again.

I tapped on the door twice and Jabril came to the door in his boxers and a t-shirt. He pulled me into his arms and started tonguing me down as we went inside his room. He pulled back and looked me over and then squeezed me again. He pushed me on to the bed and commanded me to take off my pants.

"Can I get I get my jacket off first?"

"No."

"Jabril, I'm going to use one of your lines. 'We have all night.'"

"I know, but I've been thinking about being in that pussy all day."

"How much have you had to drink?"

"Not enough. Now get naked."

I began undressing as he slipped his boxers off and lay on the floral cover and began stroking his dick up and down.

"Come here."

I put his dick in my mouth and began licking it from side

to side, and then I slurped on his round hard tip. I took him all in, humming, sucking, and pulling on him. He was holding my face down.

"Shit, shit, shit, damn."

Just as he erupted, I released him.

He was panting and out of breath when his phone rang. Then there was a text message notification. Then his phone rang again.

But I was ready for my turn, so I pushed his dick into me, and tightened my muscles. He fucked me back, but still managed to grab his phone.

"It's my wife. She keeps calling. I got to answer." He pulled out of me and walked into the bathroom and closed the door. I pulled the covers over me and changed the channel to the E! network. I took a glance at the menu and thought about ordering something.

Once Jabril came out I attacked him this time. I wrapped my arms around him and he pushed me off and said, "I have to go somewhere tonight, but I will be back in a couple of hours."

"What? Go where? Jabril, I flew out here to be with you and now you have to leave?"

"I have to do something with my wife. I forgot about it. If I don't show up, she is going to go crazy on me."

After a few hours I awoke alone and bored. I didn't know anyone in this city and I didn't have a car and Jabril didn't leave me any money. I had my own money, but I wasn't about to spend a dime.

I took a shower and planned what I was going to wear and what we were going to do. I looked on Instagram and posted a few selfies from the hotel.

Jabril finally texted me at seven.

It's so boring, Shani. I have to make it up to you. I wish I was there lying in the bed with you.

I wish you were too!

As soon as it is over I'll be right there
Ok
I texted back. I didn't know what to do.

Later that evening, when Jabril came back, he was wearing a dark gray suit and a navy tie and shoes. He flopped on the bed and asked me to pour him a drink. He pulled some weed out and began rolling it. He lit the blunt and inhaled the smoke.

"Are you okay? You seem a little tense."

"Yeah, I'm cool, just thinking about life."

"Like what?"

"My career and my family. Just some things got to change."

"Like what?"

"I don't know. I feel tied down. Sometimes I have to ask myself do I want to be married? I got right out of college and went straight to the NBA, and then I had a girlfriend and a baby and now I'm married. Now I'm with another team where I feel useless. I didn't have a chance to have any fun. Other people have kids and baby moms but they don't live with them. I come home to mine and I don't feel like she appreciates anything. All she does is come down on me all the time and I'm sick of it."

He exhaled and continued to speak. "Don't get me wrong, I love her, she's cool, but I need her to chill sometimes. Relax, don't be all up on me. You see how we smoking. When I smoke at home, she'll be like, 'Jabril put that out. It stinks, the baby going to smell it.' Then she nags and now all she wants to do is talk about church and the bible. I get it. I love God, he loves us. But not every damn day. She's going overboard and I don't know how much more I can take. She wants me at all these events with the church people. They are nice, but I don't have time for them right now."

"I don't know what to tell you. Just have a conversation with her. But you do pay all the bills and it's your home. So you should be able to smoke in your house. She needs to make your life easy, not hard. Let you relax. It's not that difficult. You need to be able to come home to a clean house, a good meal, get some head, and then get fucked to sleep."

"Exactly. See, that's why I like your sexy ass. You get me." He picked me up and flipped me over. "Now, take your clothes off so we can finish what we started earlier."

I was happy they weren't getting along and hoped that they never worked it out, because being back with Jabril full-time is all I ever wanted.

CHAPTER 48

Zakiya

"These people paid seventy-five dollars per person to hear us speak. You better get here, because I can't be at another marriage summit without my husband," I yelled at Jabril and then I hung up the phone.

I didn't know where he was, but I was fuming mad. He agreed and then cancelled on the Married, Saved, and Blessed conference. That was okay for Arkansas but he needed to bring his lazy ass to this one. Right here in Charlotte. Pastor Richard knew his schedule and I didn't want to lie to him. Lately, Jabril had been staying out overnight, clubbing, drinking, and smoking again. And when I say something about it, he tells me I'm overreacting.

Within an hour he came home looking disheveled and was pouting. "I'm here. You signed us up for this shit, not me."

"When you were talking to Pastor Richard, you said you would do it. Now be a man of your word." He sighed and headed for the shower. He put on his suit and we drove to the church in silence. I slammed the car door and stomped into the church. Before I hit the stage I walked into the restroom and gathered my thoughts. I had to pull this off, because after this I was going to tell Sister Elise that we could not do any more events.

Once we arrived he was acting like the stellar husband he was not. He spoke to everyone on our panel and then grabbed my hand and listened to Pastor Richard intently. One deep breath and I pushed a smile on to my face. Jabril was pretending too well, which made me very angry.

When it was my turn to speak, Sister Elise introduced me as a worshiper of Jesus, great wife and mother. She had two out of three right. Everyone was cheering and then I stepped up to the podium and spoke. I gave them fifteen minutes of lies and I felt horrible about it. I told them how my husband and I prayed together and our belief in God was what kept us together.

After the panel was over, the attendees were able to come up and ask us questions. A young couple in their twenties came over and started speaking with us. "It's so good to see a happy young couple with Jesus in their life. Can we have a picture?" the husband asked.

"Thank you," I said as Jabril and I stood up and smiled for the picture.

After the couple left, a message came into Jabril's phone. I glanced over at it, but he turned his phone to the side so I couldn't see who he was texting. It was probably best that I didn't see what was on that phone, because I would have kicked his ass in the house of the Lord.

CHAPTER 49

Zakiya

All we do is argue and that can't continue. I love my husband and I have to make it work. I have to save my marriage. I came up with an idea to surprise Bril on the road. We haven't been getting along and he's acting like he used to act when he was cheating. It was a reality check. I don't want to go back to be where we were when I was pregnant and lost our first baby and was checking blogs to see who he was with and where he was at. So I had to do something.

I decided I was meeting him on the road in Orlando. It was a crazy idea and hopefully it would work. And it would as long as the front desk clerks went along with it. There were two women stationed at the desk, an older Hispanic woman and a young black woman. The older woman appeared like she would follow every procedure in the book. So I put my money on the younger one.

"Hello, my husband is checking in tonight and I arrived early. His name is Jabril Smith."

I handed her my credit card and she said, "This room is already paid for and reserved by a private company. And the rooms are not listed."

"Yes, I know there is a separate list. It's my husband's birthday and I'm trying to surprise him."

"I don't know if I will be able to do this."

"I can show you my ID and I have this for you." I slipped three crisp one-hundred-dollar bills across the counter. "I know the rules, but I'll do anything. I can get you tickets to the game."

"I don't like basketball, but I do need to pay my car note and I can give the tickets to my dad. I'm not going to check you in, but I'll make you a key and then you can take the service elevator up to that floor, because there is security."

"That's fine and thank you."

Jabril came into his hotel room and was shocked to see me. I was propped on his bed looking sexy as hell in La Perla lingerie.

"What are you doing here?"

"I wanted to surprise you."

"You must have been reading my mind, Zakiya," He dropped his bag and came over to me and I began kissing him. "I've been thinking about you and Brilah all day. I know I've been acting like an ass and I'm sorry. Everything been crazy and I have been taking it out on you."

"I know, Bril, and I'm sorry for not being more understanding. I just want to be with you and our family. I'll do whatever takes."

"And I only want you. And right now I'm thinking about making our family bigger. Brilah needs a brother." He kissed me and then looked me over again. "You look good, Kiya. Can you meet me in every city? And wear this outfit."

He picked me up and held me against the wall. He took his dick out and inserted it in me. He pushed up and I pressed down. We made love for hours. I felt sexy and loved, like his lover that he missed.

CHAPTER 50

Shanice

I missed Jabril so much. I needed to touch his skin, smell his cologne, and feel him inside me. There is only so much sexting you can do. Our schedules have been out of sync for the last few weeks and we haven't been able to see each other.

After taping two times a week for the last three weeks, I had an opening in my schedule so I decided to fly out Cleveland to see him. Our visit would be short, but at least I could spend some time with my boo. When I got to the hotel, he was watching a movie and smoking. I was happy to be with him, but I wanted to go out somewhere. I was tired of us just lying in the bed.

"Did you eat?" I asked.

"Yeah, if you are hungry, get some room service. I ordered something earlier."

"Okay." I came up to him, lovingly kissing on him, and gave him a hug and he told me to chill. Didn't he know I had been in the airport for hours and got on two planes to be with him, and he wouldn't even give me a hug?

"Come on, I'm trying to watch this movie. You know I'm

out of here in the morning. That's why I told you it didn't make sense for you to fly all the way out here."

"I know, but I missed you and wanted to see you. I wanted to please my baby." I got up and began searching for the room service menu. "We are wrapping up taping and I don't know what next week is going to look like. They said soon we have to start promoting."

"When you are doing those interviews, just make sure you don't mention my name."

"Why would I say your name?"

"You know how they start asking you who you deal with. There's a lot of drama associated with them type of shows. For your sake I hope it is worth it. And you're not on there looking crazy."

"I won't. Our producers are nice and they have been real cool."

"Come on, you are smarter than that, Shanice. Once you get on one of those shows, it is like opening a Pandora's box. I don't want anyone Googling you and somehow my name gets brought up. I don't need that. I don't think I can deal with that. We might have to fall back."

"So you are saying choose to promote the show or you. That's not even fair."

"You just have to figure out what you want to do. You know how I feel about you. I just can't have any extra attention on me. I have a wife and child and that's that."

I was speechless. He was just talking about how unhappy he was and now he's talking about his wife and kid. I was about to be on television and he wanted me to give everything up to be his number two.

"Listen, Jabril, one thing don't have anything to do with the other. I already did the show, and I want to be with you. I need to take care of my mom and daughter, and this television show and all the opportunities that come along with it can help me do it."

"All right, do the show, but I'm good," he said as he blew smoke into the air. "We still cool, though, but I'm good. I am a married man. I can't be out here all reckless."

"So what am I supposed to do? Just be hidden underground with you the rest of my life?"

"Zakiya, get out of here with that shit."

"My name is Shanice!"

"My bad. Look. You know what it is with me. I may go through things with my wife, but I'm not going to ever leave her. You gotta be able to live with that or be out."

I wanted to leave him. I hated him right now. I hated the way he was acting like he didn't have any emotions and was just plain mean.

"It's men that would love to have me on their arm and treat me right."

"The door is always open, Shanice. No one is keeping you here."

I hated when he spoke to me like he didn't care or like I didn't mean anything to him.

"Then maybe I need to leave." I got up off the bed and rolled my suitcase out the door. I didn't really want to go anywhere, but he didn't come running after me. I was confused about what had just happened. I came to spend some time with him and that upset him? I'd rather go home than be disrespected.

In the airport I texted Deuce.

I MISS YOU.

He texted back in less than a minute.

I can't tell.

I dialed his number. I felt so alone and I hoped he still wanted me because Jabril and I were over. "Babe, I'm ready now."

"Okay, when you coming to New York?"

"I'm coming tomorrow."

I felt tears coming down my face. I was done with Jabril and going back to my teddy bear.

When I made it back to Philly, I got in my car and drove straight to Deuce. He didn't ask any questions. He just took me in. I went to hug him and noticed there was less of him. He had lost weight and Jabril had lost me forever.

CHAPTER 51

Adrienne

I was looking for a place every day and there wasn't anything that was nice and affordable. I didn't want to be living in a war zone again and so Warren asked me to stay with him to save my money; plus, he liked having a live-in girlfriend. I had cashed his check and sent some money to my mom and left the rest in the bank. I decided I wasn't going to send any to Ian or his stepmom yet. I still needed to recover my entire two hundred thousand dollars before he got anything. Plus, what was he going to do? Sue me from jail? The script was registered in my name, which meant I owned it.

Warren had everything I needed—money, good looks, and star power. He had a few simple flaws, which could be worked on. He worried a lot and overanalyzed everything. I think he worked himself up sometimes so much, he couldn't concentrate when we were having sex. It's strange, he was very sensual, but sometimes he went all night and other times he came in minutes. It was most certainly not a deal breaker; those things could be fixed. I'd rather have a rich boyfriend with a fifty-fifty stroke than a broke one that could always get it up.

I couldn't wait to get to Georgia and get my Asia. Six months had passed by and I had everything the judge wanted me to have: a steady source of income and I had completed my on-line parenting classes. This time I walked into the courtroom feeling very confident. Not only did I have my attorney, but Warren hired an additional attorney and sent his uncle with me to court.

DeCarious's mouth dropped when I walked in with my legal team. Needless to say, I won. The judge granted me primary custody and I could take Asia with me to California, effective at the end of the school year. I could live with that, because I wasn't sure exactly what I would be doing or where I would be living.

I thanked my lawyer and called Warren. "Babe, I won. I'm about to pick her up from school and then I'm going to spend a few days out here."

"That's great news . . . Okay, I will. Give me a minute." He was in and out of the conversation.

"What are you doing, Warren?"

"Nothing."

I heard a female voice say, "We need to be out of here in fifteen minutes."

"Who is that in the background?"

"The publicist for the movie. I have to call you back. She needs to prep me for the red carpet. Congratulations, babe. But I got to go. I can't wait to meet Asia." He hung up before I could say good-bye.

Warren never called me back and I felt a little uneasy, so I called him back. And he didn't answer. Warren had called me every day, but since the premiere not one phone call. Not one text. What was going on? I didn't even know if he was still in New York or on his way back to L.A.

Now back in L.A., I called his phone and my call went straight to voice mail. I went to work out to get my mind off the fact that I hadn't talked to my man in two days. I felt like

I was about to lose my mind. I kept thinking about all of the beautiful, stylish New York supermodels and actresses who would love to date him. I felt a little insecure. I couldn't help it. I wanted to call him again, but instead I decided to go to Morgan's and pick up the last of my things. I could only imagine what she was going to say when I went back to retrieve my things from her house, so I decided to give her a call and let her know I was on my way.

"Hey, Morgan, I'm coming by to get my things."

"Okay. I have your last paycheck and my new assistant already packed your things."

When I first met her I was down and out, and Morgan had a life I could only dream of. Now I was standing almost on the same level as her. Granted, I didn't have the alimony and the kids yet. I knocked on her door. Morgan answered and had everything packed neatly for me in storage containers.

"Thanks, Morgan, for everything."

"Yeah, you're welcome. I hope everything goes well for you. I wish I could tell you that you have a job with me if everything doesn't work out, but I would be lying to you." She laughed at her own joke and then smiled.

"No, I won't be needing it. Thanks for the opportunity. I owe you."

"You do and I will come and collect one day. Be careful. I'm happy you found love and got a good one. He would have been nice for me, but who knows . . . RJ is getting a divorce, so anything is possible."

"It is."

I knew people who worked doubles and still managed to call their significant other. And with all the modern technology Warren couldn't find a way to communicate with me in five whole days! That was unacceptable. I was done calling him. Eventually, he would have to come home and then he would have to explain everything. I cleaned out his closet so I would have more room for my belongings.

On the sixth day Warren came in calling out my name. I purposely walked past the door and acted like I didn't see him.

"So what am I, invisible? I know you seen me just come through the door."

"Well, maybe I'm treating you like you have been treating me for the last six days. How is it possible that you can't answer your phone?"

"I was working."

"You found time to tweet and post pictures."

"Are you serious? I don't do that; you know the PR team is in charge of that. I haven't had three hours of straight sleep since I've been gone. Even on the plane they had me working. Interview after interview, radio station after radio station. Since I was in New York, they decided it would be a good idea to have me do some surprise advance screening appearances at a few theaters. I'm exhausted. I have been in nine states in three days."

"You couldn't have sent one text message? There is no excuse."

He wrapped his arms around me and said, "You know what, Adrienne. I'm sorry if I didn't answer your call. I'm so tired. Come get in the bed with me."

I pulled away from him. "No, because I don't know who else you have been sleeping with."

"Who I have been sleeping with? Whatever. Don't start acting crazy on me. There isn't anything going on. You are my lady and to prove to you and the world I'll let you walk the red carpet at the premiere here. Will that make you happy?"

"Yes, it will."

CHAPTER 52

Adrienne

It was a full-circle moment. I was staring at myself in the mirror and I couldn't believe my life. I felt like Cinderella and Warren was my Prince Charming. It was only a few months ago when I was about to go back home to Philly, but then I decided to stay in L.A. I went to the salon to get my hair done, met Chike and he told me that Morgan was hiring. Now I'm dating Warren and I'm going to the premiere of my boyfriend's movie. I snapped a picture of myself with my cell phone to send to my mom. Even she couldn't believe how much my luck had changed.

The red carpet opened at six p.m. I was nervous as we approached the Grauman's Chinese Theatre. Warren grabbed my arm and he helped me out of the limo. The carpet was much longer than it appeared on television. Fans were lined on both sides of the carpet taking pictures with their phones and screaming Warren's name. *Hollywood Daily* approached us. I stepped to the side and just smiled and kept looking away from the camera.

"Hello, Mr. Joseph. You and your date look amazing," the correspondent said.

"Thank you."

"Who is your lovely date and what is she wearing?"

"This is my girlfriend, Adrienne Sheppard. Babe, tell them what you are wearing."

I stepped in front of the camera shyly and responded, "Elie Saab."

"Very nice."

One movie premiere, a six-thousand-dollar dress, a champagne buzz, and an after party in the Hollywood Hills at the director's house. My night was going great and we were winding down at home. We had just made it to the house when Warren began to freak out.

"I hope everyone likes the movie. A few critics slammed it. They said my acting was unintentional comedy. I really want this to work."

"It will. Warren, Just relax and let me take care of you. You had a hectic night and it is time to ease your mind."

I walked downstairs and pulled out a bottle of vodka. I made him a drink and one for myself, mixing the vodka with raspberry and cranberry juice.

"Adrienne, you are the kind of woman that I need in my life."

"Do you mean that?"

"I do."

He sat on the sofa and I fell to my knees. I unzipped his pants and took out his dick and covered it with my mouth. I sucked and sucked, I pulled up and down, but he didn't have any reaction. So then I used my hands *and* my mouth, but still nothing happened. After twenty minutes, I had lost my buzz and gave up.

CHAPTER 53

Tiffany

I was feeling alone and useless back home. My stepfather tried to cheer me up. He asked if I wanted to go to the auto show with him. I knew my mother had put him up to it.

My mom peeked her head in and said, "They have great food, a silent auction, and some guys from the firm will be there. Lawyers that may ask you out on a date?"

"No, I'm okay. I think I'm staying here."

"You need to get out. You never know who you might meet."

"Mom. I haven't even filed for divorce yet. I don't care about meeting anyone. But fine, I'll go."

I reluctantly went with Wilson. I figured that at the very least I could meet someone and go out for dinner. I was glad I did my makeup and decided to straighten my hair, because there were plenty of available men there. There were a bunch of exotic and fast cars on display. That part reminded of Damien: he loved cars. I was walking past a red Porsche 911 Turbo Cabriolet when I saw Warren, my ex-boyfriend from college before Damien. What was he doing here? Oh, my God, I couldn't let him see me. I hadn't seen him in forever. I knew Warren was also in the NFL and was even in a few movies. He was the guy my mom said I should have married. He still looked so handsome and polished. He was wearing a black tailored suit with navy shoes. Although I didn't want to see him, he had already noticed me.

"What are you doing here? It's been so long."

"I'm with my stepdad—you remember him?"

"Yeah, I do. Where's your husband, Damien? How are things? I saw something in the paper about him?"

"He's fine. We are separated. I recently moved back down here. I'm starting over."

"Separated. I'm sorry to hear that. So what's next for you?"

"I don't know."

"You are still the prettiest girl at the party."

"And you still know exactly what to say."

"Yeah, you know I use to play for the Panthers and I retired last season. So I'm doing some meet-and-greets for them as well as pre-promotions for my next film."

"I saw you over the years at games when your team played the Broncos. I always wanted to say hi, but I couldn't."

"I understand. I wouldn't want my beautiful wife talking to her ex, either. Well, let me say this. I haven't seen you in ten years, but I know I can't let you get away again. You have to hang out with me for a little after this. I'll drive you home."

"Okay. We can. Let me just tell Wilson."

CHAPTER 54

Tiffany

Why hadn't I stayed with him? I kept asking myself the same question over and over while staring across the dimly lit table at Warren Michael Joseph. We went to a southern restaurant that also featured a live jazz band, not too far from the convention center. So many years had gone by, but our chemistry was still the same. We were already on our second drink, reminiscing about the past. Warren was always easygoing and a pleasure to be around. He had some other things going on in his life, but the good always outweighed the bad with us.

"Being together tonight reminds me of being back at the library studying, pulling all-nighters. You would run and get the Mountain Dews and I would bring all the Jolly Ranchers and Swedish Fish and somehow we would make it to class and pass our test."

"We sure did, with A's and B's"

"Just imagine if we would have stayed together. We probably would have a bunch of kids by now," Warren said.

"I was just thinking that. We used to have a lot of fun."

"Yeah, I remember all of that fun. Then you had to go and leave me?"

"I've wanted to apologize. I'm so sorry."

"No, it's just I didn't see it coming. One day we were the happy couple and the next day I'm walking around campus and people are saying, 'Damien stole your girl.'"

"I know. I felt so bad, but I . . ."

"I had to go check myself into one of those places for the weekend."

"Check yourself in where?"

"A mental institution. I was just dealing with a lot at the time. They had me on suicide watch. I questioned everything in my life after." He threw his drink back and then said, "I never loved anyone how I loved you. We were so close. I shared everything with you. You knew everything about me. Then you just got up and left me. That was devastating. I'm okay now. Time heals everything."

"I never knew that. I loved you, too, but, Warren, I was young and I didn't know any better."

"Yeah, we do a lot of stupid things in our youth. So now after all that, you guys are getting a divorce. Was he cheating?"

"No, I left him. We were having financial problems."

"Finances, right. I heard he was running out of money after he got hurt. I thought you two were going to be together forever."

I didn't want it to sound like I left him because he was bankrupt, so I spun the story some.

"No, we were having problems in our marriage, before the injury. So how many movies have you done?" I asked, changing the subject.

"I filmed an independent movie last year. Including that, two coming out this year. I'm up to five. I've been back and forth between here and Los Angeles. But now that I'm done playing, I'm just going to stay out there. You have to come out to the West Coast."

"We will see, but right now I have to go to the restroom.

I'll be back." I was feeling my drink. I walked into the bathroom and tried to make sure I looked good. I fluffed my hair and my phone rang. I knew it was my mother calling me to give me advice. I'm sure Wilson had told her I ran into Warren. She was probably planning my second wedding. I answered only to hear Damien crying on the other end of the telephone. I didn't have time to deal with him right now.

"So you left me with no explanation. I gave you everything, Tiffany, and you just left me."

"I didn't leave you, Damien. I left misery. You're miserable and just because you fall down, doesn't mean you have to give up. I can't talk right now."

I disconnected the call and powered my phone off. I was amused at the irony. Damien had stolen me from Warren, and now he was calling me crying while I was out with Warren. I came out of the restroom and Warren was on a call. I sat patiently until he hung up. "You were in there for a while."

"Not that long."

"So it's getting late. I thought I would be able to drive you home, but honestly I think I had one too many. Let's get you an taxi or I can get you a hotel room."

I would have preferred if he asked me to stay with him. I was enjoying spending time with him.

"It's going to be crazy driving in a car with a stranger for thirty minutes. And you don't have to get me a room."

"Well, you are welcome to stay with me and I'll get you a car in the morning."

"Then I'm staying with you."

"Let's have one more drink and toast to old friends," Warren said, holding his glass up.

"How about old friends becoming new friends?" I said as I winked at him.

"Sounds even better."

Once we were in his room, I sat on the sofa and he began talking again. And then he planted a gentle kiss on my lips. I already knew that once I was in his room, I would allow him to seduce me. I wanted to make up for ten years ago and show him I was a new woman.

We made passionate love. He was so excited and he came in minutes, but the second time we went at it, he took two hours just to release. It was rock hard and would not go down. Warren made me feel like a new woman again. I cried in his arms and told him about everything I'd been through with Damien. From him filing bankruptcy, to the lights being cut off and me having to move back home with my parents. Warren wiped away all my tears and held me. He told me not to worry anymore, that everything was going to be okay because he was back in my life.

In the morning we showered together and Warren dried me off and lotioned every part of me from my toes to my shoulders. He tucked me under the covers and then he ordered breakfast and cut up my bacon omelet and buttered my toast and fed me.

"I can feed myself."

"I know you can, but I loved taking care of you. Remember when I use to feed you Pop-Tarts straight out the microwave."

"Yes, I remember, but you can't do all this spoiling and then get on a plane and go home. When are you leaving?"

"I am going back to Los Angeles tomorrow, but I do want to see you again. Whenever you are in town, I want you to come and stay with me. I'm having a birthday party in a few weeks; maybe you can come out then? And from there we will see where this will go."

"Okay." He finished feeding me and then we began to make love again.

CHAPTER 55

Adrienne

"Warren, how is Charlotte?"

"Cold. Not too much going on here. I saw a lot of cars I liked, took some pictures, and basically made nice with some sponsors and car company reps. I had a lengthy conversation with the owner and his friends. They were asking me about possibly doing some coaching."

"Will you do it?"

"No, I don't want to coach. Not yet anyway. I can't wait to get back home to you. I miss you."

"I miss you, too."

"I don't have anything else scheduled until after my birthday. The trip was actually really good until I ran into my ex. The one from college. I felt sorry for her. She was crying about her husband going broke and financial problems. The guy she left me for."

"How sorry did you feel for her?"

"Adrienne, come on. Not that sorry. She had her chance, but she blew it ten years ago. I'll be there in the afternoon. See you then."

I couldn't wait for Warren to get home. It was nice to have access to his credit cards, cars, and money, but I missed him.

I had five hours to get ready for my man. I wanted to look super sexy. I wanted to go to Chike to get my hair done, but he didn't have any openings. So I decided I was going to take my time curling my hair and applying my makeup. I started on my makeup while the curlers warmed up. I applied my foundation and then lined my eyes with black liner. I smudged a little and then accidentally knocked my eyeliner behind the sink. I reached to pick it up and next to it was a bottle of medication. Warren's name was scratched off the bottle. I opened it and saw a yellow pill. What was he taking pills for? I took out one pill and put the rest of the pills back in the bottle. I noticed there was a small "C20" written on the pill. So I did an Internet search for "C20" and when the results came on to the screen, I covered my mouth in shock. He was taking Cialis! That explained why sometimes Warren could go all night and other times he was as soft as bread. I felt a little relieved to know that it wasn't me, but why did he need them? I thought about asking him, but I didn't want him to be ashamed.

CHAPTER 56

Tiffany

"So how was your date last night with Warren?" my stepdad, Wilson, asked.

"It was great. Just like old times. We sat and talked all night about our college days. Then he got me a hotel room, because he had to fly back to Los Angeles today. He set up a car service for me to bring me home."

"That Warren was always a great guy. That's the one your mother and I thought you were going to marry."

"Well, thank you for pulling me out of the house. I am so happy I went and we ran into one another."

I was feeling so good that I had to tell someone about my beautiful evening with Warren, so I gave Liz a call and asked her if she was free. She was, so I hopped in my car and drove over to her house.

Her house was littered everywhere with baby toys and she looked like she had been up all night.

"So what happened when you went to the auto show yesterday? Did you meet any men?"

"Yes, I did. I ran into Warren, my ex-boyfriend from college. I don't know, it was so crazy. Wilson kept asking if I wanted to go with him to the auto show and I kept turning his invitation down. But finally something told me just go and get out of the house. And as soon as I got there, I saw him. We talked all night."

"That's all that happened?"

"No, we did more than talk, but he still cares about me. I felt such a connection with him. He's doing so well. He's retired from the NFL and has been in a few movies. You may have heard of him: Warren Michael Joseph."

"Yeah, I heard of him. Your brother said he knew him, but never said how. He's real handsome."

"He was my first love. I should have married him."

"Well, it's not too late."

"I know! He's not married yet and he said whenever I'm in L.A. to come and stay with him."

"You need to go out there and visit him. You know you have to keep that momentum going."

"Then this morning look what he texted me." I pulled out my cell phone and showed her his text.

I had a really nice time with you. Call me if you need anything and I wish you could celebrate my birthday with me.

"That was so sweet."

"He invited me to his birthday party."

"So are you going?' "

"No, it is all the way in L.A."

"Okay, then you just get a flight to L.A., get a dress, and go get your man."

"But I don't have money for all of that, Liz."

"I will give you the money to do everything you need to do. I'm so excited for you. You are getting a second chance at your first love. Please let me be in your wedding."

"He did say he never stopped loving me. I'm going to do it. I'm going to L.A. to get him back."

CHAPTER 57

Monique

I was lucky to have such a patient man who was so understanding. Dele would not wait around forever. He was kind, intelligent, handsome, wealthy, and most of all he loved me. He intentionally tried to make me jealous and it worked. Seeing him with another woman brought everything into perspective. I could not keep our relationship a secret anymore. I even asked CeCe her opinion and we both agreed that I shouldn't wait any longer. And right after I told Kadir I was going to call Carl. I didn't think he would care, because Kadir said he'd been dating.

Kadir was coming home from a seven-game road trip and as soon as he got in the door, I was going to sit him down and talk to him like the grown man he always tells me he is. I called Dele to see how much time I had.

"Hey, babe, are y'all back?"

"We just landed. Are you on your way to my home?"

"I am, but first I'm going to talk to Kadir about us."

"Finally."

"Yes. Finally."

"Well, let me know how everything goes. He will under-stand, Monique. He knows I am a good guy."

"As soon as I'm done, I'm coming. I might have to live with you for a few days until he calms down."

I smoked five cigarettes and thirty minutes later I heard Kadir's keys at the front door. He walked in and placed his luggage by the door. He gave me a lackluster "Hey Mom. Have you been smoking? Is everything all right?"

"Yeah, I don't know, I just felt like a cigarette today. It's no big deal. How is everything with you? You seem sad."

He wiped his eyes and said, "I'm fine. I'm a little tired from the road and Abby caught me talking to this other girl and said she didn't want to talk to me anymore."

"Oh, I didn't know that was your girlfriend."

"She kind of was, but I was talking to a few girls that she didn't know about and now she wants nothing to do with me."

"She'll get over it. How about sending her some flowers?"

"I tried that and she sent me a picture with them in the trash." He showed me his phone with the red roses in a trashcan. I couldn't hold in my laughter.

"Mom, it's not funny."

"Yes, it is. That's something I would do. She's probably really hurt."

"Yeah. I understand. She's hurt. She said I was the only guy she introduced her son to and that she didn't have time for games."

I couldn't believe I was about to give him advice to get this girl back—a girl I didn't particularly care for. "Kadir, just tell her that you made a mistake and you want to talk to her in person. Buy her some more flowers, take her out for dinner, and get her a nice gift. And tell her how much she means to you and that y'all are young, but could work on being in a relationship."

"You think that will work?"

"It should."

"Thanks, Mom. I'm going to text her now. So how have you been? Anything going on with you?"

"No, nothing at all." I couldn't do it. He was already sad. I couldn't make him feel worse. I would have to wait to tell him about Dele and me.

CHAPTER 58

Shanice

Why be a side chick when you can be a queen? Go where you are celebrated. And guess what? My teddy bear Deuce celebrates me. He loves me unconditionally. Fuck Jabril. He doesn't care about anyone but himself. He treats me like trash. Why was I dealing with Jabril, a man whom I never will ever be able to have to myself? Zakiya and Jabrilah and everybody else will always come before me. I come in around number twelve as far as his priorities are concerned.

I've been back with Deuce for a month and he has spent all his available time with me. He holds my hand in public and introduces me as his lady. Deuce has no problem with me being on a reality show and he's been helping me start my own my clothing line, Ms. Amore.

I was staying at his condo and now I was looking for a house for us right across the bridge in Jersey. Sometimes you have to put stability over chemistry. He said we are going ring shopping next week and he is going to still give me a surprise proposal. I will marry him, buy our house, get my daughter, have my own company, have more babies, and he can drive over the bridge into New York every day for work.

"Deuce, baby, what do you want for dinner?"

"Whatever you make. You know I'm easy to please. I still can't believe you're in the kitchen."

"Be quiet."

"All right, babe. I'll be there around six."

After I made Deuce dinner, a text came in from Jabril.

WYD?

He was too lazy to type me a whole sentence and that's why I couldn't be with him.

CHAPTER 59

Tiffany

I bought a short black-and-silver optical illusion dress. All the southern eating had packed ten extra pounds on my little frame. Warren didn't seem to mind the last time I saw him, but I wanted to make sure I looked amazing this time. I was going to call him to tell him I was coming out there, but Liz convinced me to just show up as his gift.

I packed enough clothes for a week and took a cab to the airport. On the drive there, a strange number appeared on my phone. I answered, only to hear Damien again. I was upset that I had been tricked into answering his call.

"What do you want?"

"I need you back, baby girl. I'm in the process of getting everything together. I know I was wrong to have you living crazy, but I'm back. Come home."

"What are you talking about? You don't even have a place for me to live."

"I know, but I'm about to. I got some serious things in the works. I'm staying at my cousin's. Back in Brooklyn."

"Tevin in the projects?" I suddenly felt sorry for him. He

swore he never would go back to the projects. "Are you okay, Damien?"

"I'd be better if you'd come back home. And I'm not in the projects. I can explain everything to you when you come up. I'm getting us a new house next week."

"Damien, I'm not coming back. So get you a house."

"Why not? I love you and you love me. Is it about the money? The money is coming back. I promise you the money is going to come back. I have some investments that are about to pay off."

"Well, that's very good, but Damien, I have to go."

I made the wrong choice ten years ago, but I was going to make the right choice now. I needed a sure thing and that sure thing was Warren Michael Joseph. If he and I were to get married, it would make up for all the hardships I'd been through with Damien. I had to go and get the life I was supposed to have.

CHAPTER 60

Adrienne

I checked myself in the mirror ten times. Everything was flawless and yet I was still nervous. I was wearing a black-and-gold vintage Versace dress. I walked down the hall toward the steps. Then I walked back and checked the mirror once more. I don't know why I was anxious. It was probably because it was my first time being the lady of Warren's house. Tonight I would be meeting all of his friends and his parents. His father and mother were coming from Memphis and I wanted their approval.

I came down just as Morgan was walking in with a young Spanish guy on her arm. I gave her hug. "I'm glad you came."

"I'm glad I did, too. He's cute, right?"

"He is." I spoke to him and he just nodded.

"He doesn't really speak English. It's great, he can't argue with me. And he knocked all the cobwebs off."

"Oh."

"You are doing well for yourself. You know you have me to thank."

"I do."

Edwin came up to me and told me Warren was looking for me. He took me to Warren's side. Warren was in the middle of posing with his parents for a picture. After they were done, he grabbed my arm and said, "Mom, Dad, I want to introduce you to my lady, Adrienne."

"Nice to meet you." I went to shake their hands and they both looked confused.

"I thought you were dating Tiffany again?" his mother said. "I just saw her a few minutes ago. She came up to give me a hug."

"She did? She's here?"

"Yes, she's here. What is going on, Warren?" his mother asked and his father looked over at him sternly.

They walked away. Warren would have to explain to me why his parents would think he was with his college girlfriend.

"What's going on, Warren? Why is the girl who broke your heart here? And why do your parents think you two are together? Why would you invite her?"

"Because she is going through a bad divorce and I did tell her any time she was in town to come by, and I mentioned I was having a birthday party."

"So do you still have feelings for her?"

"No, she is just an old friend. Be cool, Adrienne. It is not like that at all. I promise you."

"Why are you being so nice to her?"

"I don't know. That's just me. I've always been the nice guy. I'm not going to knock someone when they are down. She's my friend. Edwin let her in. Don't be upset. Trust me, I'm not thinking about her."

He could say whatever he wanted to, but I had to personally let her know that she was only here because Warren felt sorry for her.

Edwin pointed her out to me. She was cute, probably prettier in college. She behaved just like the entitled princess he described her to be. I had my diva ways, but the difference was that I had to work for mine. I didn't have any respect for bitches whose parents handed them everything and who never had a job. I walked over to her and made it very clear to her that there wouldn't be any sparking of old flames.

Chapter 61

Tiffany

After that great night we had together I knew he would want to see me. That thought hadn't stopped me from feeling uncertain. He had invited me to his party, but what if he didn't mean it.

He definitely meant it, I reassured myself. Yet I still wasn't feeling that confident. I was starting to actually feel crazy. Like I had made the wrong choice. But it was too late, because I'd been dropped me off in front of Warren's house.

I called Liz and said, "I'm about to go in."

"You are? Go get your man, girl. Make up for lost time."

"I am. Thanks for helping me get here. There's security everywhere."

"So? He invited you."

"You're right. Wish me luck." I placed my cell in my bag.

People were stopping at the gate and I just walked through like I was already in the party.

"Ma'am, do you have an invitation or is your name on the list?" a man in a blue jacket with yellow security writing on the back asked.

"Of course I'm on the list. My name is Tiffany Holcomb. Warren and I are very good friends."

"Sure you are, but I'm going to need you to wait right here. Step to the right please while I call someone to verify you, because your name is not on this list."

"Okay."

Moments later a man came out to where we were standing.

"And you are?" he asked like if I said the wrong thing he wouldn't allow me to gain access to the house.

I looked at him and very politely said, "I'm Tiffany Holcomb, Warren's college sweetheart. Warren said he was going to put my name on the list."

"Tiffany. Yes. I heard of you. Let her in."

I thanked him and walked with him up the driveway behind him.

Once I was in the party, I made my way through the crowd with one thought on my mind, and that was to find Warren. I walked over to the bar and ordered a glass of champagne. Instead of my finding Warren, his mother tapped me on the shoulder.

"Hi, Mrs. Joseph. You still look the same."

"Tiffany, it's been so long! How are you? What a surprise. I didn't know you and my Warren were still in contact."

His father was eating, but he still managed to wave to me with a mouth full of meatballs.

"Well, we just ran into each other, but you never know. I just came to wish him a happy birthday. Where is he?"

"He's around here. Well, take care until next time."

I circulated through the crowded party looking for Warren, but he was still MIA. I decided to stand in one place. He would eventually walk past.

A woman in a fabulous black-and-gold gown came up to me and said, "I'm Adrienne Sheppard, Warren's girlfriend. And you are?"

"I'm Tiffany," I said, extending my hand out to her, confused. "Nice to meet you, Adrienne. I'm his college sweetheart and I'm here to wish him a happy birthday."

"That's very nice of you to travel so far just to say happy birthday. You could have sent a text or a card."

"That's true, but I thought him seeing me in person would make the perfect gift." Right in front of her I spotted Warren. I walked over to him and gave him a huge hug and said, "Surprise."

"Hello, Tiffany. Good seeing you." He was acting as if we hadn't just had mind-blowing sex weeks ago. He took Adrienne's hand and told me to enjoy the party. I was shocked. How was this possible? He didn't tell me anything about a girlfriend. I was becoming ill. How could he have done this to me? I kept my composure and waited until I saw Warren alone. I pulled him to the side and told him we needed to talk.

"You invited me and I came out here. And now I have to learn that you have a girlfriend. After seeing you, all those feelings from college came back and I thought we were meant to be."

He looked around and then pulled me into the bathroom to talk to me alone.

"It's good to see you, but what happened can't happen again. I had a lapse in judgment. I have someone in my life. It was a mistake. My parents are here, so please don't embarrass me."

"It wasn't a mistake. Look at me and tell me that night didn't mean anything to you. Why did you invite me here?"

"I didn't think you would come."

I didn't allow him to say anything else. I kneeled down and opened his pants and sang "Happy Birthday" to his lower region. He tried to squirm away, but I already had his dick deep in my mouth. I heard people walking back and forth past the bathroom. Someone even knocked on the door but that didn't stop me from trying to suck the life out of him. He told me to get up and stop. I was so humiliated. What was I doing? I couldn't even seduce him properly.

He stepped out of the bathroom first. I waited a few minutes, fixed my clothes, and then left.

I walked around the party and that woman Adrienne appeared next to me while I was sipping my second drink.

"It must be so nice to see each other after all this time."

"It is, since Warren always refers to me as the one who got away."

"Really? That's not what he told me. You're the one that left him in college for the guy that is now bankrupt. I'm happy that Warren is such a good man, that he would invite a friend that once betrayed him to his house." She came closer and then said, "Listen, I understand you had something special about ten years ago, but he is done strolling down memory lane with you. It is over and you can leave."

"I'll leave when I'm ready."

"You're ready now," she said, stepping closer to me.

Before the conversation could go any further, Warren's friend Edwin pulled Adrienne away from me and over to Warren. Then Warren dropped to one knee and did the unthinkable right in front of my face.

CHAPTER 62

Adrienne

I'd known Warren four months and I knew we had great chemistry and I saw a future with him, but even I was shocked when he knelt down in front of me and presented me with a canary-yellow diamond engagement ring in front of his parents, his best friend, his ex-girlfriend, and all of the attendees at his birthday party.

"Adrienne, I know it has been a whirlwind romance. And I know we are just getting started, but I know I want to spend the rest of my life with you. Will you marry me?"

It took me a few moments to process everything. I knew we liked each other and I did see a future with him, but I wasn't sure if I loved him. There was about a forty-three percent chance that I did and the other fifty-seven percent would have to catch up, because I said, "Yes!"

After he heard my answer, he picked me up and swung me around. His parents would have to like me more now because I was about to become their daughter-in-law.

Warren represented everything I needed in my life and in a man. I was so happy I hadn't lost my cool and beaten ole girl's ass. I would have missed my happily ever after.

The next morning while I was still in bed, it hadn't quite sunk in that I was engaged and my last name was about to change. I hadn't decided on Adrienne Sheppard-Joseph or Adrienne Joseph. I didn't know which one I would choose.

"So when do you want to set a date? This weekend in Vegas? In the Bahamas? Where?" Warren asked.

"We don't have to rush. I have to find a school for Asia. And you still haven't even met my mom."

"You know your mom is going to love me and Asia will go to whatever school you pick. I'll make a phone call. We need to make you a Mrs. as soon as possible. My parents want grandkids."

"Then let's set a date."

He pulled up his calendar on his phone and said, "How about April?"

"I need more than three months to plan a wedding."

"Okay, let's have a June wedding."

"June it is."

Warren was out shooting a commercial for Grub Burger and I was in the big house alone. I walked around amazed at what I had accomplished in such a short amount of time. Warren loved me unconditionally and hadn't even brought up a prenuptial agreement. I called my mother to inform her about Warren's proposal. "So when is the wedding?"

"In June. Right after Asia gets out of school."

"I'm happy you found love again. I just want you to be sure."

"I'm sure, Mom. I want you to come out in a few weeks to meet him."

CHAPTER 63

Tiffany

What would possess me to travel three thousand plus miles unannounced? I felt like a desperate dumbass. Why had I let Liz convince me that it was a good idea? I was so glad I hadn't told my mother my plans. I think she would have probably permanently disowned me.

I cannot tell anyone that Warren proposed to another woman in front of my face. Karma was a hard and swift bitch. He didn't even know I was coming; I guess he had already planned to do that. I had horrible timing.

I was back to square one, which was nowhere. I sat at the kitchen table wondering what I was going to do with my life, since winning Warren back was no longer an option. I was back home and my mother and Wilson were on their way out, but first they had to bother me and let me know how much my life sucked.

"Please put some makeup on and fix yourself up. I do not want to come downstairs and see you looking this way."

"I will after I get something to eat."

"You really shouldn't be eating anything. Your waist is expanding more and more every day."

"Be nice, Helen. There is some fruit in the pantry," Wilson joked.

"Yes, and please return Damien's calls. He has started calling Wilson at his office and I have twelve messages from him on my phone asking me to tell you to call. I don't understand why he won't leave you alone and just sign the divorce papers."

"I don't know, either, but I will ask him to stop contacting you both."

After my parents left, I gave Damien a call. "Damien, sign the divorce papers and stop calling my family. It's been months. Don't you get it, I'm not coming back."

"I understand that, but can you give me one weekend? Just one. I want to prove to you that I have changed and I'm doing better."

"No. I'm not coming ever."

"Tiffany, I have a place, just come and I'll show you. If you like it, you can stay. If you don't, you can go home."

"Leave me alone and sign my divorce papers. I'd rather live in the room I grew up in than in poverty with you."

"No, Tiff, it's all good again. I bought another house. My investment paid off like I told you it would."

"What investment?" I asked curiously. This had to be good.

"Remember, I told you people owed me money and they were going to pay me back ten times? It happened and I flipped a few houses. And I made enough to buy a new house in the next town over from our old house. I told you to be patient and things were going to start turning around, didn't I?"

"Yes, you said that."

"I put some money in your account. That's what I wanted to tell you."

"What account?"

"Your checking account. Do you see it?"

I pulled up my account on my phone and saw ten thousand dollars.

"Yeah, I see it. Thank you, Damien."

"So go shopping today. And I'm going to put more money in there later in the week. I'm going to get you a flight. What day are you coming?"

"I'll come on Friday."

I couldn't wait to go to South Park Mall. I felt like a kid who had been let off of punishment. I hadn't been shopping in so long. When my mother and Wilson returned, I was dressed and heading out the door.

"Where are you going? You seem like you are in a good mood," my mother asked.

"I am. Did you need anything? I'm going to South Park. Damien sent me money."

My mother gave me a look like she didn't approve.

"What? I can accept his gifts. That doesn't mean I'm going back to him."

"You most definitely shouldn't."

"Well, if you decide you need something, call my phone. It's been a while and I'm just happy that Damien is trying to make it up to me."

"That's impossible, but enjoy your shopping."

On my way to the mall down Interstate 77 my phone began to ring. It was Warren, but I wasn't sure if I should answer.

"Yes."

"Hey, Tiff, it's me, Warren."

"Warren? Yes, how can I help you?"

"Don't act like that, Tiffany."

"Act like what? Act like you proposed to another woman in front of my face and didn't embarrass me."

"Ha, I embarrassed you? You don't know about being embarrassed, but I can tell you about it. Embarrassed is having your girl stolen by a player on the same team and almost losing your mind and having to go to another school to save face."

I was silent.

"So this is what this is about? Huh? You wanted to get revenge. Well, you got it."

"Actually, it wasn't. When I saw you at the auto show, I was excited and old feelings came back. I was in love with you. You were supposed to be my wife. I know I was wrong. I had a girlfriend and I should have told you about her."

"A fiancée," I corrected him.

"Okay, a fiancée. I'm sorry everything happened like this. I apologize. The timing is wrong this time around. You're still married. I'm getting married."

"Yeah, the difference is your knew my situation. And I can get a divorce, because we are not together and I have nothing to hide."

"Well, I'm sorry. I didn't mean for any of this to happen this way. If you are open to us being friends, I want to be your friend. You know me. The real me, before all of this fame, and you know we had something special. Just know that I will always be in debt to you."

"I know that you have changed. You are a big movie star now and one day you will have to pay that debt. Have a pleasant day, Warren. If I ever need you, I will call you."

I ended the call. At least he had the decency to apologize.

CHAPTER 64

Tiffany

I didn't know how I would feel when I saw him. I had been so evil and nasty to Damien and yet he still was showing me kindness. I'm not sure what he expected of me, but I knew it was worth a try to see what he had going on.

Damien looked like the young champion I married when he picked me up from the airport. His hair was cut, his body had returned to an athlete's frame. He was wearing a tight gray shirt with blue jeans and boots and a black leather jacket. He kissed me on my cheek and took my bags. We walked to his new black SUV. It had the new car smell. There were three dozen red roses waiting for me in the backseat.

"My flowers are pretty, baby. Thank you."

"Anything for you. Babe, I'm so glad you are back." He wrapped his arms around me and held me firmly for an entire minute. "I've been lost without you. Wait until you see the new house. You are going to love it."

"I'm sure I will." I placed my seat belt across my body. He typed in the address and he sped out of the airport. He followed the GPS, which led us into a double garage of a modest single home. The residence wasn't the nine thousand square feet that I used to live in, but it was very nice.

"So what do you think?"

"From the outside it looks nice. How many bedrooms?"

"Just four, but at least we own it and no one can come and take it from us."

"What do you mean, we own it?"

"It was a foreclosure. I bought it in straight-up cash. We don't have any loans or a mortgage. We own it outright. My cousin put it in his name for us so no one can try to claim it. I got it for one hundred and seventy-five thousand, but it's worth way more. It needs some work, but it is ours."

New and no liens made the house beautiful. I got out of the car and Damien unlocked the front door and gave me a tour. There was a big backyard and lots of land. I followed him up the stairs into the master suite.

"This looks familiar, right?"

"You made the bedroom exactly like the old house." I wanted to cry. I couldn't believe it.

"I'm not done with your surprises." He took my hand and told me to close my eyes. "Now open them."

I opened my eyes and saw a custom-made closet with all my clothes I had left behind perfectly hung, and in the corner was a new dress, bag, and a pair of Gucci shoes. I cried right there.

"So do you like it?"

"Yes." I didn't know what to say.

"Babe, this is just the beginning. I know I put you through a lot, but I'm going to make it up to you. I promise. I told you I would take care of you. Didn't I?"

"Yes, you did. But how?"

"So what I've been doing is real estate. I flipped six houses."

"I thought the real estate market wasn't good right now," I said.

"It wasn't, but it is coming back. And me and my cousin,

we're coming in at the right time. He has his Realtor license and we are killing the game. Look at this." He showed me a bunch of pictures on his tablet. "This is one of the houses we flipped. The first one was grandkids that just wanted money immediately. They didn't research the value or anything. We offered them fifty thousand and they took it. We put in a new tub and fixed some other things and we doubled our money in a few weeks. Did I do good, baby?"

"Yes, you did very good."

"Well, can you show me some love?" He pointed to his cheek. I gave him a kiss on his cheek. "So now you have to call your mom and tell her I'm taking care of you again and she can stop calling me a loser."

"She knew you weren't a loser. You've never been a loser, Damien."

"Try on your dress."

I put the dress on. Damien zipped the back. It was a little snug.

"I gained some weight."

"That's okay. I like the extra meat. I love you, Tiffany, at any size or weight. I'll put a gym in the basement for you if you want. I just want you to come back home. I don't want you to have to worry about anything ever again. Please just never leave me again. I couldn't take not having you by my side."

He locked up the house and we walked toward the car. I noticed he was staggering.

"Why are you limping?"

"My leg has still been bothering me a little; I think I have been working out too hard and then fixing the houses. I go by and help the contractor and the workers sometimes. The faster they fix the houses, the faster we sell and get checks. I wish I knew about flipping houses when I had more money, but everything works out for a reason, right? Here, you drive. I have to make a deposit at the bank and then we'll go to the city."

I drove and he stopped at the bank. He went in and made his deposit and came back out.

By the end of the night I felt like I did when I first married Damien: like a queen. I appreciated all he did for me. I decided that I would move back in with him and work on my marriage. I was thankful that I didn't have to go back to my mother's.

CHAPTER 65

Tiffany

Damien asked me to answer some calls, organize his receipts, and call around to see if we could get cheaper building supplies. I didn't mind working for the greater good of us. After seeing how much money he was making, I was thinking about getting my real estate license. He could fix the houses and I could sell them. Win, win, and win. Now that everything was settled, I felt confident calling my mother to tell her I wasn't coming home.

"Mom, I want to talk to you about everything."

"Go ahead. So what have you been doing up there? How long are you staying?"

"This may disappoint you, but this is my life. I wanted to tell you that I am working it out with Damien. He is doing very well again. He had a few investments come in and he is flipping houses with his cousin now. He is starting small, but he showed me some of the properties."

"He's in real estate now?" she huffed.

"Yes, he is."

"He wasn't that good of a football player, so I know he

will not be a great businessman. When you are burned again don't come running to me. I'm closing the door on you."

"Fine, Mother, do what you must."

"You've been warned."

I couldn't let my mother worry me. She would come around.

Right then, Damien came in the room and told me to plan a trip for us.

"To where?"

"Somewhere hot." A horn beeped. I looked out the window.

"Who is that out in the car?"

"That's Rich. He wants me to invest in a car lot. He's going to take me to the auto auction in Fort Dix. His dad has a dealer's license. He said you can flip cars in days and make thousands of dollars. I can take that money and put it into the properties."

"Oh, I never heard you talk about him. But, baby, we don't want to invest in too much, right?"

"No, we are good for money. I'm never touching our reserve again. He leaned over to me to give me a kiss. When his shirt rose I saw a gun on his hip.

"What are you doing with a gun?"

"I'm hanging out in the city more and I don't want anyone rolling up on me and thinking it is sweet. I'm going to have to shoot them."

"But having a gun is asking for trouble."

"No, having a gun is smart. And I will only use it if I have to."

CHAPTER 66

Zakiya

Jabril and I were getting along again, until he injured his knee. He was at practice and fell during a drill. The doctor said he would be out until the end of the month. Which wasn't the end of the world, but Jabril's pessimistic behind could not see it that way. He just sat on the sofa and moped the entire day, barely talking to me or interacting with Jabrilah. She was lying on top of him since Daddy was in a bad mood.

"Do you want anything to eat, Bril?"

"No, I'm not hungry."

"Are you sure? I can make you a sandwich or order something before I go out."

"Can you leave me alone?"

"Everything will work out. It's midseason, Bril. You just have to keep a positive attitude and pray and everything will turn around."

"Zakiya, you've been saying the same shit all season. Nothing has changed."

He was depressed. I thought if he got out of the house he would feel better. But Jabril didn't want to go to All Star Weekend. He said he felt like a loser and he wasn't playing so what was the point. Instead he stayed in the house watching Netflix.

He got me a Chanel bag and flowers for Valentine's Day, but I would have preferred for him to be happy and in a good mood. Something else was bothering him, but I wasn't sure what it was. I was going to a seminar at the church and I would deal with him when I returned.

"I'm leaving. You sure you are okay? Please get up and watch Brilah; she might be hungry."

"I got you. Have a good time. Brilah, say bye, Mommy."

"Okay, I'll only be gone for a few hours."

I left and then I snuck quietly back in the house just to make sure he was up feeding Jabrilah. He was up feeding her, but he was also on the phone. I heard him say something and then I heard the name "Shanice." I knew my husband was not on the phone with his old mistress. I couldn't confront him right then, so I left and went to the church seminar.

I entered the convention center. Pastor Richard and First Lady Elise were standing on the side of the stage. Pastor Richard came up to me and greeted me.

"How is Jabril managing his injury?"

"He's healing."

"I'll pray that he heals fast. Well, the good thing is you are here and your message will be heard today about being a good woman before you become a wife."

"Thank you."

Pastor Richard was having a women's only program called "Single, Saved, and Searching." I was one of the lovely panel members. It was my job to inspire the women in the audience. I was introduced and then I began speaking.

"Good morning, ladies. I've been invited here to share my story of marriage and show you what God has in store when you put him first. Marriage is a great thing, but it is not perfect. I met my husband when I was nineteen. My husband has a job that has a lot of temptation and we have had our struggles. But in those dark times I sought and asked God for his mercy. I prayed for him to change, to be a good father and husband. And it worked. It's not magic, it's prayer. My husband became the man I asked God for. I'm living proof, keep God first in your life and he will send you the mate you're destined to be with." I went on and on saying anything and everything that sounded good and by the time my speech was over, I had a standing ovation. People were running up to the stage to meet me.

"Wow, sister, your testimony was awesome. I love to see and hear about black love. It is the best. Usually men cheat. And no disrespect, but especially a man of your husband's stature, but the fact that he remains loyal to you shows you that anything is possible if you put it in God's hand."

"It is."

Little did she know that I was a fraud. My husband was home on the sofa ignoring me and calling other women. And here I was telling women not only how to get a husband, but how to keep him. Someone needs to tell me how to do it.

I made it through the conference without bursting out in tears from anger and embarrassment. As soon as I was in the parking lot, I called Jabril, but he didn't answer.

When I got home he was gone and Jabrilah was asleep in the arms of Octavia.

"Did my husband say where he was going?"

"No, he just called me and offered me an extra hundred dollars if I came right away."

"Okay."

I was fuming mad. He got a sitter and left. Where the hell was he going?

So I looked through my phone and found the e-mail I had sent myself with the number of his whore Shanice. I had saved it just in case I ever needed it. I dialed her and as soon as she answered I screamed, "Why are you talking to my husband?"

"Who is this?"

"You know who this is, Shanice. I heard you talking to him earlier."

"Girl, bye. I don't mess with your husband. And if you are looking for your husband, you need to call his phone and not mine."

She hung up on me and I called her phone right back, but she didn't answer.

CHAPTER 67

Monique

All Star Weekend landed on Valentine's Day weekend. All our hard work had paid off and Kadir had been voted into the Rising Star Challenge game. It was the game between first- and second-year NBA players. I always watched the festivities on television and now I was there. There were so many celebrities and players from every team. I saw Shaq in the lobby of my hotel taking pictures with fans. I was excited to be going to the game. Kadir got me seats in the fourth row. Dele wasn't playing but was still going to the game. His brothers were in town with him to party.

Dele and I had a room together and I promised him that after this weekend I wouldn't delay sitting Kadir down and telling him everything.

Dele loved me and I loved him and it was time to be out in the open with our relationship. I called Kadir. I wanted to make sure he was preparing for the game and that he was nowhere close to where we were going to be.

"Kadir, where are you?"

"Abby forgave me and she flew out here. I'm at a club with her and her friends."

"Where? Which club?"

"I don't know, some club. The driver dropped us off."

"That's good. Well, I love you, son, and I'm proud of you and soon I want us to have an important conversation."

"About what?"

"I'll tell you, but right now just focus on having fun and enjoy the moment."

"I will. Mom, where are you staying?"

"I didn't check in to my hotel yet."

"Okay, well call me when you do."

Later on that night, I met up with Dele. We had a table in the corner of the VIP section of the club. We were dancing and enjoying ourselves. Our server brought over champagne and we made a toast and then Dele leaned over to kiss me. I kissed him back and we took several glasses of champagne to the head. I didn't care who saw us. I was in love and not going to hold it in another moment. I looked into his eyes. His heart and his intentions were pure when he said, "I love you, Monique."

"I love you, too, Dele."

I spent the entire night enjoying this time with my baby. We stayed on the dance floor all night dancing, kissing, and hugging. I felt so relieved that I was finally able to be a real couple with my man. Plus, in the crowded party no one knew us or even cared about who we were.

The next morning the sun was shining into our hotel room. I had a champagne and love hangover. I didn't remember much from the night before, but I knew I had an amazing time with my babe. I was snuggled on his chest, relaxed with my eyes closed. I heard him typing on his phone. I cracked my eyes open and yawned when he jolted up.

"Monique, get up. It is important."

"What is it?" I didn't like the blank expression on Dele's face. "What?" I asked him again, confused.

He showed me his cell phone screen and I read the head-
line on some gossip site: "NBA Mom Finds Love in the Club."
There were pictures of Dele and me kissing from the night before.

Who took pictures of us? I didn't think that I was that important, that anyone would recognize me with so many more
famous people around. I had twenty-three missed calls. I missed
calls from CeCe, Kadir, and Carl. The phone rang again and I
dropped it. I was too scared to speak to anyone. What was I
going to do? How could I talk to Kadir? This was his big
weekend and I was ruining it. What could I possibly say that
would explain the way I acted last night? I felt like crap. The
phone kept ringing, but I didn't answer.

"Dele, we are all over every gossip site."

"I told you, you should have said something to him."

"I don't need that right now, Dele."

I wasn't sure what to do, but it was out there now. Should
I call Kadir or just go to his hotel? I decided to call him just
to see how he sounded before I saw him in person.

"Kadir, I want to talk to you. Are you at your room?"

"Mom, you know you doing too much. Right? You out
here kissing and grinding on people in the club wearing tight
clothes like you young, but you're not. You are embarrassing. Everybody else got good moms and mines want to be a
thot. I don't want to talk to you right now. And don't come
to the game. I'll see you at home."

"Kadir, you know you can't talk to me like that. I am your
mother and you will respect me."

"What? You want me to show you some respect. How
about show yourself some first. And tell Dele when I see him
I'm going to smack him." Then he hung up on me.

I didn't go to Kadir's game, but I watched my son from the
hotel room television. His team won, but I couldn't congrat-
ulate him. I lay in the bed for the next day and a half and
Dele tried to comfort me, but there wasn't anything he could
do. I had wronged my son and I had to make it right.

CHAPTER 68

Monique

Monday morning I checked out of the hotel and went straight to the airport. My phone was still ringing. I was happy my nightmare weekend was over. I had on sunglasses for two reasons. One, to cover my eyes and the other, to hide my identity. Not that anyone really knew who I was, but just in case. I cringed every time I saw a picture of me tonguing Dele down. My phone rang again. This time it was Carl and I answered.

"Yeah, Carl."

"Monique, I don't care about what you doing or who you are doing with. But you need to be concerned about what you are doing to Kadir. You wanted to chase away everyone and say how everyone's out to get him. And look who is the one who is actually hurting him and ruining his career. He is where he's wanted to be his whole life but he can't enjoy it, because he has to fight to defend his mother."

"Kadir was in a fight?"

"Yes, you know how he feels about you. Somebody said something about you and he went off. How come he had to hear about it on the radio and gossip columns?"

"Is he okay?"

"Yeah, he's fine, but he's so angry. I've never seen him this upset."

"You're right. I'm going to talk to him. I'll sit him down and we will work it out. I'm going to call him now."

My flight was boarding and I decided it would be best to just go to the house and talk to him. As soon as I landed, I pushed my way off of the plane and drove straight to the house.

Kadir's car was already there. I took a deep breath. I was going to go in the house and reason with Kadir. I turned the lock and realized my key no longer worked. All I could do was laugh. I was locked out of my own house.

I rang the doorbell and Abigail answered; not only was she there, but so was her son.

"Kadir is mad at you. He told me not to let you in, but because you are his momma I'm going to let you in."

"Young lady, I'm really trying to be nice to you, but you need to get out of my sight ASAP and mind your business."

"Kadir is my business." She looked at me. I walked past her and saw all my belongings by the door, already in boxes.

"Kadir, your mom is down here," Abigail yelled out.

"Kadir Latif Hall!" I screamed as I stomped up the steps. "Did you lock me out of my own house?"

Kadir appeared at the top of the steps. "Yeah, I locked you out of *my* house. I pay the bills."

"You better watch your tone."

"Why should I? Mom, you on some other ish. You left my dad and now you out here thinking you young."

"I don't think anything."

"Well, whatever you want to call it. I guess you're a cougar or something. You were dealing with Dele like it is cool. I'm in the locker room and the guys are talking shit about you. How could you do this to me? He is almost my age. He's only seven years older than me. You got people coming at me on Instagram and you were a trending topic on Twitter."

"I'm sorry. I didn't mean for any of this to happen."

"Well, it did and I hope you told Dele I'm going to knock him out. That's a promise."

"You can't fight anybody else. Let's have an adult conversation. Don't I deserve to be happy, Kadir? He treats me well. And I wanted to tell you, but I didn't know how to."

"I don't want to talk to you, you got to leave. Go be with your boyfriend. You chose him over me anyway. All the people in the world and you picked him." He walked back to his room and closed his door. I knocked on the door and he told me to go away.

"Kadir, I'm not going anywhere."

"Mom, get out of my house."

I felt like kicking the door and arguing with him, but I was wrong and I knew I needed to give him his space.

CHAPTER 69

Shanice

Jabril's wife kept calling my phone. The first time she called I didn't know who she was. The second time I answered, she screamed, "You home-wrecking whore. I got rid of you once and I'll do it again. Leave my husband alone! They should have kept your whorey ass in jail and thrown away the key. Next time I'm going to make sure it's enough so that they keep you."

I knew immediately what she was talking about. She put the drugs in the car. She finally confessed. What would Jabril think if he knew his precious wife was the one who set him up?

"I'm sure your husband would love to know that you set him up and tried to ruin him, but call your man, stop calling me. I got a man."

I hung up on her. Then I cussed her out and hung up on her again when she called again.

It was Valentine's weekend and her husband wasn't home, but he wasn't with me. She better check with one of his other side chicks. I was in Atlanta with my baby about to go to the *Eye Candy Queen: The Come-up* premiere. I wasn't thinking about Jabril or his wife.

The phone began ringing again. I picked it up and screamed, "Bitch, didn't I tell you not to call my phone again?"

"Shanice, it's me," Jabril said from the other end of the phone.

"Yo, I don't know what's going on, but I know you better tell your wife to stop calling me. I don't deal with you, so I don't know why she is bothering me."

"I don't know, either, but I need to talk to you."

"That's not going to happen. You had your chance to talk to me. Leave me alone and go work it out with your wife. I'm busy. And just so you know, your wife did it. She was the one who put the drugs in the car. Your sweet Zakiya almost ruined your career." I felt vindicated. I had no more time to put into Jabril because my baby was waiting in the other room.

Deuce came into the hotel bedroom. "Babe, what's going on?"

"Nothing."

"I thought I heard you yelling."

"No."

"You almost ready?"

I saw multiple text messages appear in my phone. I turned off my ringer and continued to get dressed. I gave my boo a kiss and we headed to the party.

Our show premiere party was at Prive in Atlanta, Georgia. The ATL was showing us love. Stars from other reality shows were also at the club to see our show. Deuce had on all black with black shoes and I was wearing a black-and-white dress with a slit that stopped right before it reached my hip. My new stylist, Pearsa, had been dressing the fuck out of me. I could not wait to get my clothing line, Ms. Amore, off the ground with her help. We were going to be dressing everyone.

The club was filled with rows and rows of chairs. The entire *Eye Candy Queen* crew was there. I saw Ashley V. She gave me a hug. "I see you still with Deuce. He lost so much weight, he looks good."

"Thanks. Yes, we've been hanging in there. What have you been up to?"

"I'm filming a movie in May."

"I'm so excited for you."

"Yes, I'm retiring. No more music videos."

"I know what you mean. I have a few more dates on my schedule and then I'm going to start concentrating on my dress line, Ms. Amore."

"Okay! You have to send me a dress."

"I will. Good seeing you. Let me find my seat."

I had invited Courtney, my mom, and Aunt Rhonda. I couldn't wait to see how I looked on camera.

"Are you nervous?" Deuce asked.

"A little. I just hope the days they were following me I wasn't talking too fast. And I seem like I have some smarts."

The lights in the club dimmed and I saw my face on television. It wasn't like a music video, because I was talking. I grabbed Deuce's side. Then I turned back around and watched myself. It wasn't bad; it was actually good.

The rest of the night people were coming over to me and complimenting me. So far the star was definitely Ashley V, and I was okay with that. As long as people knew who I was and I got some screen time I could play a supporting role.

Deuce went to get us drinks. I was enjoying my moment when I heard a voice say, "Nice work. I guess you're glad you didn't listen to me."

I turned around and saw Jabril. I was speechless. I never thought I would see him. How did he know about this party?

"What are you doing here? How did you even know where I was going to be?"

"Everything is on the Gram, but forget that, I need to talk to you. I was wrong, Shanice."

I was holding a smile together, but I was so aggravated. "This is not the time. I'm with someone else now."

"I see. You dealing with old out of shape dudes now?"

"Don't worry about him. I never have to wonder if he wants me or doesn't. And he's not married."

"You know I loved you, I just asked you to understand my situation."

"He doesn't have a situation. And I'm not dealing with yours anymore. Good-bye."

"All right, Shanice. If that's the way you want it."

"I do. Jabril, you are not going to make me feel bad about being with someone who wants to be with me." He yanked my arm just as Deuce was walking back over with our drinks. Deuce came over and said, "Babe, who is this?"

"A friend of mine. He was just saying what's up and leaving."

Deuce put the drinks down and went to shake Jabril's hand.

"Nah, I'm not a friend, this is my girl and I'm talking to her," he said and snatched my hand.

"Jabril, we are not together! Leave me alone." I yanked away from him. Whatever he was on must have made him think he could take Deuce. He swung on Deuce and Deuce punched him straight in the middle of his face. Jabril's entire body slammed into a table. I saw everyone looking and the camera caught everything. I kneeled down and saw Jabril's face was beginning to swell and his nose was shooting blood.

"Let's go, Shanice." Deuce shouted at me. I was torn. For two seconds I thought about staying with Jabril and making sure he was okay, but he had never chosen me. I was embarrassed and I knew the cops were on the way. I gathered my family and followed my man out of the club.

Chapter 70

Monique

"Monique, get to Philly," Mom Laura cried.
"What's wrong?"

"Faheem was just walking to the store. He was in the wrong place at the wrong time. And he's been shot."

"Mom Laura, what? Where is CeCe?"

"She's at the hospital. He was shot four times in the leg and chest and right now it is not looking good. They're taking him into surgery."

"We are on our way up there."

I couldn't believe this was happening. Faheem was a good boy in college and now he was fighting for his life. I called Kadir and Abigail and had to ask her to speak to my son. She seemed annoyed. She had no idea that if she said anything slightly out of the way that I was going to smack her when I saw her.

"What, Mom?"

"Kadir, get dressed, we have to get to Philly."

"What's wrong?"

"Faheem was shot. He is in surgery and we need to be there when he gets out."

"What, Ma? No!" He broke down and began crying. I heard Abigail trying to console him.

"I'll be there shortly." I had been staying at Dele's house until I found a place of my own. He wanted to come with me for support, but I knew that wasn't a good idea. I threw enough clothes to last a week in my bag and drove to pick up my son. Faheem had to hang on. I had to get to Philly to be with Carl, CeCe, and Mom Laura. I thought about the worst and began crying, but I was hoping for the best.

CHAPTER 71

Zakiya

How many tears can you cry before you run out? My life was falling apart. I had no control over it. When things go wrong, I usually consult my sister, but the last few days it has been God only. I looked at Jabrilah sleeping and became instantly upset. She deserved to have a family. She loved her daddy and needed to be with him. I wanted my daughter to have her father, but I wanted to be happy, too. I didn't know how I was going to be able to make both happen.

I went to sleep in prayer and prayed for my family, and when I awoke Jabril was on the sofa sleeping. I saw his body form under the covers. I was thankful he was home. We were going to make it.

I made him breakfast and took it to him. And then he lifted the covers off his head.

"What's wrong with your face and eye?"

"Some guy tried to rob me last night."

"Did you call the cops?"

"No, because I didn't want it to make the news."

I believed him. I really believed him until I saw a half dozen screen shots that my sister had sent me of Jabril fighting in a club. Jabril had driven all the way to Atlanta last night to fight over a video hoe?

I snatched the covers completely off of him. "Jabril, you have lost your damn mind. You were fighting over your mistress last night. How is that supposed to make me feel?"

"Zakiya, I don't want to hear your mouth. You weren't there, you don't know what happened."

"The evidence is in front of me. I know you have a black eye."

"Look I'm not talking about this anymore. Yeah, I had a little scuffle last night, but when I left the club this guy robbed me and knocked me out. He took my wallet."

"The same wallet that's sitting by your keys, you liar?" I asked, pointing to his wallet on the table. "What am I, a fool? Do you think I'm going to stay here? You weren't in a fight with anybody else. Look around. You are self-destructing. I'll leave before I see you destroy yourself."

"Believe what you want. If you leave, Zakiya, stay gone. Matter of fact, you don't have to leave. I'll leave." He jumped off the sofa, grabbed his coat, and walked toward the door.

"Where are you going?"

"Does it matter?"

"Yes, it does matter. Fuck it, you know what? It doesn't matter anymore. I'm done. Go to your dirty stripper whore."

"She's not a stripper."

"So now you are defending that dirty, trashy bitch?" I picked up his plate of food and threw it at him. He ducked and yanked the door open and slammed it closed. After he left I cried. I got on my knees and prayed. I didn't know what else I could do. I asked God for strength and to protect my family and to turn my Jabril back to the man I used to know. I wanted the man who begged to be with me, the one who wanted to be my husband and wanted me to have his children.

CHAPTER 72

Tiffany

I was packing my bags for the trip I had booked for us when I heard a noise coming from downstairs. Damien was here sooner than expected. Our flight left Newark International at five, but we wanted to beat the turnpike traffic. We wanted to give ourselves time to get through security and grab lunch before our flight.

"You're here early."

He came up the steps out of breath holding two suitcases with money falling and hanging out of them.

"Where did you get all that money? What the hell is going on, Damien?"

"We will talk about it later, but I need you to hide it."

"For what?" I stood still for a moment, then he started pulling out guns from under the mattress. Then he gathered more money from the back of the closet and handed it to me and told me to hide it.

"Why?"

"Just do what I tell you to do. Put it in the bathroom. Put it somewhere and fast. We have to go."

I followed behind him, when we were both stopped in our

tracks by the sound of multiple cars pulling into our driveway. Then a loud banging noise came after that. I looked out
the window and there were several police cars outside.

"What's going on?"

"My investment and business opportunities are here."

A voice on a bullhorn said, "Damien Holcomb, come out
with your hands up."

"What the hell is going on, Damien? Tell me. Why are the
police at the door?"

"Because I robbed some banks."

"Banks?" I screamed and covered my mouth.

"We have to hide this money."

I didn't want my prints to be on the money and I didn't
want to be a part of any robbery.

"Damien, you have to turn yourself in. This is insane."

I began walking down the steps. He cocked his gun and
said, "I'm not going to jail."

"You can't shoot at the police. What are you thinking?"

"Come here." He closed the door and the shades.

"They are not going to go away. Let me go to the door and
talk to them."

"No, come here," he shouted. At that very moment I didn't
know if I was a hostage or a conspirator.

"Oh, my God! This is going to be on the news and my
mom will find out." *She told me not to go back to him. I
should have listened to her. Why didn't I listen?* I thought.

"Damien, what are you planning to do?"

"We will just wait for them to come in."

"Then they will come in shooting."

"We don't have a choice. You are here with me, until death
do us part. Right?"

"Huh?"

"This is your fault anyway. You were the reason I started
robbing banks in the first place. I was sitting back in the projects after having millions. Who can ever say they touched a
million dollars? People work they whole life and may never

accumulate that type of wealth. I had fifty of them and they are all gone. I saw cats from my old neighborhood wondering why I was back on the block. They said, 'Dame, I know you got a stash somewhere. It is not possible to spend that kind of money.' They don't know, do they? How much goes to taxes, what's eaten up by agents and lawyer's fees. Then you treat yourself to a few things and the rest goes to a greedy-ass wife that you can never say no to."

"Don't you try to blame this on me. It is not my fault. I didn't put a gun in your hand. I didn't say go rob banks."

"Be quiet. You didn't complain when I called you and told you I was rich again, did you? You came right home." His words were interrupted by a noise coming from downstairs. It sounded like the police were in. Thank God. Damien went to check where the noise was coming from and I knew this was my opportunity to run. I had about five seconds. I ran toward the window and began trying to lift it. The window wouldn't open, three men pointed their guns toward me. I raised my hands and silently screamed help to them. One reached out his hand and told me to jump.

Damien was coming toward me with his gun raised and an angry look on his face. I rushed toward the window. I crashed through it. I felt the glass pecking my face and I saw the man's arms open. I also felt my ankle being grabbed. I kicked away and felt my body land on the top of the waiting man. We were far from safe because Damien began shooting at all of us. Other cops came toward us and rounds of bullets were shot into the house. Damien continued to shoot back until there was silence. I knew the silence meant that he was shot and my life as I knew it was over.

CHAPTER 73

Tiffany

A plastic cup of water and a bandage to my left arm was all the medical treatment I received. I couldn't call my mother. She would bail me out of jail, drive me to a dirt country road, and strangle me herself. I held my head on my palms. I had a massive headache. I should have stayed in Charlotte. I should have known better. The truth is I didn't know what he was doing, but all the evidence told another story.

They brought me into a small dark green room with no windows and sat me down at a table with two older black detectives. One asked if I wanted coffee, the other offered me a cigarette.

"How many banks did you and your husband rob?"

"I didn't rob any banks. And I didn't know he was robbing banks."

"Are you sure about that? Your husband was penniless and broke and then out of nowhere he had hundreds of thousands of dollars. That didn't seem a little strange to you?"

"No, because he said he had investments and people owed him money and he was flipping houses. He took me to one."

"Where were the houses he took you to?"

"In Brooklyn, somewhere near the high school he went to."

"You were about to skip town with all the money you stole."

"No, I said we were on our way on vacation. I didn't rob any banks."

"I'm going to ask you again. You don't know anything about the bank robberies? Have you ever gone to the bank with him?"

"No, I haven't."

"Are you sure? We have someone driving a getaway car that looks a lot like you."

He held a blurry gray picture of me and Damien coming out of the bank parking lot. "Is this you?"

I took a look at the picture. It was me driving. "That's me but—"

"But you said you never went to the bank with him."

"This is when I first came back. I didn't know what was going on. He stopped at the bank after he picked me up from the airport." The detectives were having a hard time believing me; I knew the truth and I still thought it sounded unbelievable.

"I didn't rob any banks. Ask my husband. He will tell you. I'm innocent."

"We did ask him. He's not talking. So right now you are looking at about ten to fifteen years for armed robbery."

"I didn't do it. I need a lawyer. A phone call, something," I shouted angrily as I became more and more frustrated.

"If you testify against him, we can give you less time. But if you don't, you will face the same amount of time as he does. So what's it going to be? We will give you some time to think it over."

With my one phone call I called the only person who could get me out.

"Warren, I need your help. I've been arrested. I'm in the Bergen County jail. You know you owe me this. And you know why you must come through for me."

"I'll get you out."

CHAPTER 74

Adrienne

" Chike, how should I wear my hair? These engagement pictures are going to be on every blog and entertainment website."

He looked at me in the mirror, holding my hair and then bringing it back up.

"That's true, but I don't want you to just have curls. I want to give you an old Hollywood glamorous look."

Chike's shampoo girl came into the studio reading her phone.

"Chike, these football players are out here losing their mind."

Chike and I asked at the same time, "Why are you saying that?"

"Look at this. Some football player was robbing banks!"

I looked down and read that it was Tiffany and her husband. I wondered if Warren knew about all of this. I stood up out of the chair and went to call Warren. His phone just rang and rang,

Chike came over to me with his phone and said, "I think

your fiancé already knows. Look who bailed little Ms. Bank Robber out of jail. Your fiancé."

It was on all the websites. I Googled her name and I saw it for myself: Warren walking out of the police station with her.

"Let me see." I couldn't believe Warren would help her. He said she was a horrible spoiled gold digger, but yet he bailed her out of jail. I was furious.

"Girl, I know you are upset. But I wouldn't even bother your man about that bullshit. He probably is just being a good friend. You know he don't want a felon for a woman, and you have a wedding to plan. And engagement pictures to be worried about."

Everything Chike was saying was accurate, but I still needed to tell Warren off. How dare he rescue this chick again? He was supposed to be in New York on business, not bailing out his ex.

"I'll be back." I stormed out of the salon. Warren finally decided to answer his phone and I didn't allow him to get a full hello out before I screamed, "Why did you bail that bitch out of jail?"

"That Tiffany situation is nothing. I'm on my way to do a radio interview. I'll be home in a few days."

I called his phone for an hour straight and he never answered. He ignored my twenty text messages, too! I was fuming mad. A few days! Did he really think I would be here waiting to have a conversation with him? I looked through my e-mails to see his schedule. He would be doing *The Today Show* and *The Breakfast Club* tomorrow in New York City and I would be right there when he was done with his interviews.

He said there wasn't anything to their relationship, that she was an old flame that he felt bad for. And I was dumb enough to believe him. He thinks that I'm stupid since he's still dealing with that bitch.

One part of me said forget him, go shopping, but the other

part was not about to marry a man who was publicly being seen with another woman. I booked an overnight flight to New York.

My flight left at twelve a.m. Instead of sleeping my five hours, I thought about how I was going to confront him and beat her ass.

I entered the Marker Hotel and all I could think about was if he stupid enough to have this bitch in his room. Could he be that dumb? I didn't know who I was going to hit first, him or her. One way or the other, I would know the truth.

I started to knock on the door, because who was I fooling; I wasn't going to leave him. I needed his money and I wanted to marry him. More than anything, I wanted to prove more to him that I wasn't crazy. The voices or the other side of the door belonged to a male and a female. I turned around and walked back to the elevator. Then something came over me. I just had to know the truth. I pounded on the door.

"Who is it?" a voice asked.

"Housekeeping," I said in my best Mexican accent.

Tiffany opened the door naked just like I expected and I screamed, "You no good motherfucker. You bailed this bitch out of jail and now you are getting your money's worth out of her. Warren, I'm going to kick this bitch's ass and then you are next."

I dragged her by her hair through the suite and into the bedroom. More shocking than seeing her naked was seeing Edwin naked sleeping next to Warren, who was knocked out. They looked like drunken lovers who must've fallen asleep during the middle of an act. Even though I was seeing it with my own eyes, I still couldn't believe it. Tears rolled down my face. I was speechless. What the hell was I supposed to do? Run, scream, or fight? I stood in place completely in shock. I still had Tiffany by her hair. I stood quiet for a moment and then I started screaming and hitting everyone—that bitch, Edwin, and Warren. Punches awoke them both.

"How could you do this to me? You are not only fucking

her, you are fucking him, too. What the hell is wrong with you? You disgusting pervert."

His eyes met mine. He spoke and either he couldn't get words out or I couldn't hear him. I didn't move. I began to hyperventilate. He grabbed my arm. Edwin jumped up and threw on his clothes. My scream was so loud the hotel security came up to the floor and was in the room.

"Does she have asthma?" I heard one of them ask.

"Yes, she is having an attack."

I couldn't correct him, and he ought to have been happy because I would have told the security guards what type of man he was.

"Adrienne. Adrienne." I heard him call my name and then I blacked out.

When I came to, Edwin and Tiffany were gone and I went right back into beast mode. "You wanted me to be your beard, huh? That was what the rush to get married was all about? To protect your secret? If you are with me on red carpets, no one will ask if you are gay? How could you do this to me? Are you fucking crazy? I don't want to marry you. Now it all makes sense. That's why your dick don't stay hard for me, because I don't have the right equipment. Sorry, I don't have a dick. And all the pill-popping you do. Your Cialis. Yeah, I knew about it."

"Adrienne, you don't have to be nasty. I still love you and care about you. It's just a few things I didn't tell you about myself. I apologize."

"So you can say sorry and that is just going to make everything okay?"

"Listen, once you are calm I would like to talk to you about everything. I do love you, and being my wife will guarantee you a great life for the rest of your life. I will be discreet in the future. I can't help it. Sometimes I want to be with a man and other times with a woman. It's something I've known since I was a child. I always liked girls, but there's a part of me that also likes boys. I never understood it."

"If you don't understand it, how the hell would I? What? Do you think I am some desperate, needy bitch? I don't need you. What would make you think I would be okay with this?"

I ran out of his hotel. Who was I going to tell that the man I was about to marry, the very rich man who wanted to marry me without a prenup, likes to have sex with other men? I wanted to go home to L.A., but three thousand miles was too far of a drive. I had to stay somewhere. I went to my real home in Philly. My phone was flooded with missed calls and texts from Warren. I answered his calls and he said, "Come back, I need to talk to you."

"No, stop calling me. What do you want?"

"I need to make sure—"

"Make sure what? That I won't say anything? Please, me outing you is the least of your worries."

Damn, I thought I had it all figured out. I was about to marry a successful retired NFL player who was also on his way to becoming an A-list actor. Now I was back at square one again. Maybe my mom was right. She said you can't run from one dream to the next. Everything was catching up to me. Every lie, every scheme, and every person I hurt. It came down on me all at once.

CHAPTER 75

Adrienne

I was back in Los Angeles to get all of my belongings. While I was in town, I agreed to meet Warren in a public place. He didn't even know I was thinking about his safety when I chose to meet him at Mr. Chow's. He sat down and took off his sunglasses.

"You begged me to talk to you. So now that I'm here, talk!" I demanded.

"There is so much I want to say to you right now." He went to grab my arm.

"Please don't touch me."

"All right, what do you want to know?"

"What the fuck do you mean? I want to know why. Did you really call me here for this shit? What is there to talk about? You are gay. Everything has been a lie. The end."

"I'm not gay."

"Oh, I'm sorry you like men, which means you don't want me. I should have listened to Morgan. She told me to watch all you Hollyweird men, that all of you were dick suckers. And I thought she was crazy. She was right."

He grabbed my arm. "Don't be disrespectful. I'm still the

same man. Nothing has changed. I didn't know how to tell you any of this."

"You didn't tell me this. I had to catch you."

"I really hoped you could forgive me and we could move forward."

"There is nothing you can say that will make me forgive you."

"I understand that. But hear me out. There is a lot more to all of this."

"Look, you lied to me and pretended I was the one you needed. When the reality is you don't even like women. I don't see why you went through with all of this in the first place. It's a new day and time, you don't have to hide anymore. People won't condemn you." I stood up and told him to enjoy his day. "I'll give you your car back and move all my belongings out by the end of the week."

"Don't leave." He snatched my arm and forcefully made me sit. Now I was upset. I'd chosen a table in the back. No one was paying attention; no one could see that I was being held against my will.

"You wanted to know. I'll tell you. I was molested, okay. I was molested as a little boy. My dad's friend used to come and get me and he touched me. So you would think that would make me not want to be with a man because he stole my innocence. I hated him. I was so mad and angry. That's why I don't get along with my dad, because I couldn't understand why he didn't know what was going on. He was too busy fucking all of his women and preaching that he wasn't aware that his only son was getting abused by his best friend.

"To make up for it I made myself busy. If I had something to do at school I didn't have to go with my dad and I wouldn't see Mr. Gregory. I went to school and did the best I could. I wanted to be the best at everything. I didn't want anyone to see that I might be a little different. So not only did I play football as a star running back, I was also on the debate team. I wanted to be an attorney. I wanted to be everything except gay. And now that I'm an adult, I don't know what happened. I just want someone to love me." The tears that shot down his cheeks were real. He was crying and in so much pain.

"Warren, you don't have to marry me. Be who you are. I'm upset because I think you should have told me."

"But I don't only like men. I like women, too! I'm attracted to both. I know it can be confusing."

"But it is a different world now."

"That's true for white boys and lesbians. All that happy-to-be-gay, coming-out-the-closet waving-a-rainbow flag doesn't apply to a black football player from the south. It's not worth it. My dad is a pastor at one of the biggest churches in Memphis. So how do you think his son coming out as gay would affect his life? Huh?

"I'm sorry you had to find out all of this this way. It's not fair and I know it's hard for you to accept. But know I want you. Not only do I want you, I need you. I can't have any of this come out. I just can't. I just signed a multi-movie contract with Parx Pictures. They have signed me as an all-American guy, a football player. I know people choose to come out and live their truth, but that's not what I want to do. And besides all of that, my mother and father can never know about his. I don't want to disappoint them. I can't disappoint them."

"So instead of coming out, your solution is to try to hide behind a relationship with me. What exactly are you asking? You want me to enter into a sexless marriage?"

"No, I'm not asking you that at all."

"Well, I'm not having sex with you anymore."

"I'm not asking for sex. Everything else can be worked out. But I will make it worth your while. I'll still make your movie, make you a producer, and give you one million dollars at our wedding and an additional million for every year we stay married."

"I can't do it. I don't know what to tell you. You want me to be your fake wife."

"No, I want you to be my real wife. You will marry me and you and your daughter will be well taken care of. I can give you whatever you want."

"Two million dollars and you are going to make me the co-executive producer on the movie."

"Fine. I'm going to give it to the VP at Parx. Just please do this."

"How can I be sure of all of this?"

"I'll put it writing. You'll sign a confidentiality agreement and I'll have the money transferred into your account. I will take care of you. My feelings for you have not changed. I need you, Adrienne. I have too much invested."

Two million dollars to live a lie. I needed the money, but I wasn't sure I could do it.

CHAPTER 76

Zakiya

The definition of faith is the substance of things hoped for, the evidence of things not seen. I have faith in God, but my faith in people is down to none. Everyone around me has disappointed me.

What I began to realize is my church family was just as shady as the worldly basketball wives I was trying to stay away from. There were babies born out of wedlock, cheating, affairs, backstabbing, gambling, and stealing. People were still concerned with who has money and who doesn't. The only difference really is Jesus, being anointed, and walking with God was thrown in the conversation.

I knew God wasn't only in the church. He was inside every crack and crevice of everything and everybody. And knowing that, I had been praying and praying, hoping God would speak to me. I picked up the phone. I had to speak to somebody. I felt defeated.

"Sister Talisha, it's me, Zakiya." I paused and then I couldn't hold back the tears as I cried.

"Zakiya, are you okay? Whatever it is, give it to God."

"I know, I'm trying. I'm trying. I've been reading my bible all day and praying and . . ."

"What's wrong?"

"I can't take it anymore. I prayed and I prayed. I prayed hard and my husband still isn't faithful. He still drinks and smokes. What can I do? Do I stay and continue or do I leave?" I waited for her answer. At the moment, I was afraid that she would share that I had a sham marriage to the other church-women. But I just knew that she had a relationship with God and that she couldn't possibly tell me to read a part in the bible or a passage that would fix everything.

She didn't ask me any more questions. She just went straight into prayer mode.

"Lord, we believe in you. Father God, you are the best, we know that you are present every day and that we don't walk alone. It is you who walks besides us holds our hands and guides our steps. I'm asking you to please help Zakiya, please help her husband and family through any hardship they are going through. Please strengthen her through this storm and bless her life with your love."

"Thank you for the prayer, because I feel like I'm losing my faith."

"Don't say that. You must always have faith."

"No, I do feel this way. I don't understand it. I've been helping people, praying, giving to charity. How can this whore win my husband? Why hasn't God answered my prayer?"

"He will, be patient."

"When? When is he going to do the right thing? When? When? When? I need help now. Right now. Because I don't know what else to do but leave him. I'm going to divorce my husband."

"God is perfect, man is not. If in your heart you feel like you have done everything you could have done, then remove yourself from the situation."

I stopped crying momentarily and asked, "Do you think I am making the right decision?"

"That's between you and the Lord. Let God lead your steps. Whatever you need to do I am here for you."

I muttered a "Yes," in between sobs. I knew what I had to do.

CHAPTER 77

Shanice

I should have hung up the moment I heard his voice. He wasn't my problem anymore. Whatever was going on with his life, he needed to deal with it on his own. All those thoughts were in my head, but deep down there was a place in my heart for him. He was still my baby.

"Jabril, you ruined my party. You started a fight and now you want me to care."

"She's gone and she took my daughter and left the keys, her ring, and divorce papers. I need you here with me. Shanice, please come here. I need you." The sucker in me felt sorry for Jabril, but I had my own business I needed to handle.

"I can't come. I have an appearance tonight in Maryland. And they paid me half of my money already."

"I'll pay it back."

"It's seven thousand dollars."

"I don't care. I'll give you the money to refund them."

"I can't, Jabril. I'm sorry." I felt horrible for Jabril, but what did he expect. His wife should have left him. He never was home and when he was home, he was asleep and his mind and his thoughts were elsewhere.

Courtney came into my room. She was so excited I was allowing her to travel with me.

"Shani, what time are we leaving?"

"I don't know yet. I might have to go to North Carolina. Jabril's wife left him."

I could tell Courtney wanted to say something, but she didn't want to be back on my bad side.

"If you love him, go. He does love you. He came and took that ass whupping for you."

We both laughed. "Deuce did fuck him up." I sat on the bed. "I'm so confused. Just because she left him, does that mean I should go back to him? I do still love him, but I have Deuce."

"It won't hurt to just go check on him."

"I can check on him. Make sure he's cool. He's going to pay me the money the promoter already paid me, so I can pay the promoter back. Don't worry, I'm going to still give you the money I promised you."

"You don't have to."

"No, Courtney. I'm going to give you your money. I have to figure out how I am going to get out of this club date without upsetting the promoter and April. Then I can't let Deuce find out."

"Just say you're sick."

I had Courtney take a picture of me looking sick and posted it onto my Instagram. I called April and told her. She told me she would handle everything for me and to send her the money in the bank.

Charlotte was ten hours away from Philadelphia. I could have flown, but I drove and talked Jabril off the cliff the entire ride. So why was he on the phone when I got there ordering flowers for her?

"I'm confused; what do you need me here for if you begging her to come back? I have a man and I don't have to put up with this."

"Calm down, Shani. It's not like that. I just don't want her to take me for everything I have."

"Well, tell me how it is."

"I love you, Shanice, but I love her, too, but me and her are never going to work. We are just two different types of people and I want to be with you."

I waited years for Jabril to tell me he loved me. And now that he finally had, I didn't know what I was going to do.

CHAPTER 78

Monique

6 months later

Praying over my nephew's bed every night for two weeks brought me back to reality. My reality is family first. Faheem survived being shot, but will walk with a limp for the rest of his life.

I was so shaken up by Faheem getting shot that I had to fix my relationship with Kadir immediately. Nothing in my life was more important than him.

I moved Mom Laura and CeCe to North Carolina with me. I didn't want any of my family in the city anymore. I even asked my mom to move down, but she said she was okay.

Faheem is going to school down here, too. He transferred to North Carolina A&T.

I put all my energy into Kadir and his career. He's been on the cover of *Slam* magazine and he's been named one to watch by ESPN writers. I want Kadir Hall to be a brand, get endorsements, have a legacy, and be able to enjoy his wealth. We've put ourselves on a budget and are not spending as much. With that said, I couldn't make my son look bad any-more, so I ended my relationship with Dele. I'm Kadir's mom and he is my son, but we share the same last name and I rep-resent him, so Dele had to go. It wasn't easy, but I did what was necessary. Dele told me I was making a horrible decision, but I couldn't think about me—I had to put Kadir's interest first. I think about Dele from time to time. I still love him, but Kadir didn't approve, so it couldn't be. No matter what happens, it's me and Kadir against the world. It has been Monique and Kadir since he was born. And no one will ever come between us. No one, not even Abigail, who is finally gone for good. Kadir is dating a nice girl who is a sophomore at Howard University, studying biology. She wants to be a pediatrician. He met her All Star Weekend; her name is Laila. At least something good happened that weekend. I like Laila and I'm trying not to get too attached to her, but hopefully one day I will have a daughter-in-law who is a doctor.

Carl stays in Philly and I have started dating again. There isn't anyone special yet, but when I do meet someone, I will make sure he is Kadir approved.

Chapter 79

Tiffany

My days are consumed with the morning news, game shows, reality shows, and then repeat. One day I dream of living on my own again, finding love, making my own money, but not right now.

I have not left my home in six months for several reasons. One, being afraid that someone would see me. I've gained one hundred and thirteen pounds. My mother and I don't speak. She is repulsed by me. She probably wishes Damien had killed me or that I was in jail with him so she wouldn't have to be bothered with me.

I don't know what haunts me more, him or my conscience. I hear Damien's voice every night when I'm resting. Him saying, "Don't leave me. I need you, Tiff." I knew he had abandonment issues and maybe I shouldn't have left him.

I knew he didn't have any real family and yet I still bailed on him when it got rough. But part of me feels like I didn't make him do anything, especially not rob banks.

With all that said and done, I take full responsibility. No matter what anyone says, I should have never left him. I should have helped him manage his money better when we had millions. I should have been working and helping him build businesses; instead I spent and spent.

As for Warren, I always knew he was gay. I asked him when we were in college, and without hesitating he said he didn't know. He told me he liked both. Once I caught him with my bi friend. I was okay with it, because he promised me he would only do it with me there. And I believed him. Until I caught him again, and that made it easy for me to leave him to be with Damien. He always wanted a beard and he got one. I'm not a beard, I'm just a secret keeper. He pays me monthly for my silence and I'm glad to have income.

CHAPTER 80

Shanice

A few hearts had to break for us to be together, but shit happens. Jabril had to see me with Deuce to appreciate me, and I had to leave Deuce to be with Jabril. And none of it would have happened if Zakiya had stayed with Jabril.

That was her choice to leave. He wouldn't have ever put her out or left her. She just should have known that Jabril is never going to be a traditional husband, though. He's into a lot of shit that she isn't. You got to be able to be yourself in a relationship. In me Jabril had a confidante, a freaked out chick, his lover, his side chick, and wifey all rolled into one, and I wasn't faking. I was really who I was.

He can go out with his friends, flirt, smoke, drink, and be himself. I don't mind Jabril doing whatever he wants, because I know that his dick and paycheck come home to me. And because I don't trip on him, we don't have any cheating issues. He's never stayed the night out on me and he calls me when he's going to be late.

And Deuce. I tried to call him to make peace and thank him for all he did for me, but he has changed all of his numbers. I even went to apologize in person and he had me escorted out of the building. It's for the best anyway. Jabril wouldn't have gone for me being friends with an ex.

Last night Jabril and I were filming the second season of *Eye Candy Queens: The Come-up*. Now that he is divorced, he doesn't have a problem being on the show. I think he might even like all the attention.

Now that we are officially together, I could sit back and rest, but I'm not. I have a mother and daughter to provide for and I like having my own money. I'm still out here hustling like I'm broke and my man doesn't make seven figures. He was traded again to the Celtics and is doing well on that team. It's a much better fit for him. I have the reality show, hosting nightclub dates, my "Twelve Months of Shani Amore" calendar, Ms. Amore dress line, and I'm the new face of Charms Moscato.

The moral of the story is that men don't change. They like what they like. No matter how bad you want to change a man, he won't change unless he wants to.

What I do know is that good girls don't always win, but bad girls always get what they want. I wanted Jabril and I got him.

CHAPTER 81

Zakiya

The only man I ever loved was Jabril Smith, but he didn't love me as much as he loved himself. He doesn't love his daughter, either. He can't. If he did, he would have never chosen Shanice. He said he wanted his family, but his actions proved otherwise.

He's back having his picture taken with bottles of alcohol and women half dressed in the club.

I love him. I want my daughter to have her father, but to actually sit back and tolerate being cheated on to my face—I couldn't do it. So I filed for divorce and he didn't contest. I wasn't worried about his money, I knew Jabril would make sure that Jabrilah and I were well taken care of and he did.

Some people, including my own sister, said I was crazy for letting Jabril go. She said I'm handing him over to the side chick. She said I should have stayed and fought for my husband, but you can't fight for someone who doesn't want to be with you. When I moved out, he immediately moved her in, instead of coming to Philly to get me.

Yes, I miss my husband and being Mrs. Jabril Smith and the perks that came along with it. But I prayed and prayed and in the end, I'd rather wake up happy and single than married and miserable.

I'll take peace of mind over a name and a title any day.

CHAPTER 82

Adrienne

"Adrienne, Adrienne! Mrs. Joseph, over here." Several entertainment stations were competing for my attention. I walked over to a friendly reporter from *Access Hollywood* and smiled.

She pointed the mic in my face and said, "What do you think about your husband's performance in *Last Chance*? He's playing a dying detective, his first serious role. What were your thoughts on him switching from comedy to such a dramatic role?"

"I think it is incredible and his passion is amazing. He loves acting and every character he gets to become. What can I say, I'm just proud of him."

"The movie is getting Oscar buzz. Can you see him with an Oscar?"

"We will see." I smiled and walked away coyly.

I stopped for a few other reporters and then met back up with Warren and we posed together at the end of the carpet. We sparkled together and looked like red carpet royalty. He was wearing a dark blue custom Dolce and Gabbana suit and I had on a white and navy Yves Saint Laurent gown.

I was becoming used to all the flashing lights and the red carpets. Life in Hollywood was busy, but I enjoyed it. Malaysia is going to one of the best private schools in the country. *Falcon Hall Boys* has been greenlit and we are in pre-production and I am going to be the executive producer. My life is going extremely well and can only get better.

After the movie and after party were over, I remembered that none of it was real and my husband was indeed an actor and I was forced to deal with reality again.

"I'll see you in the house later," Warren stated, opening the SUV door.

"Where are you going?"

"I thought I told you. Edwin's in town tonight. I'll be in by the morning."

As much as I loved being Mrs. Joseph, it hadn't exactly sunk in that I would always be sharing my man. I am attracted to Warren, but we're more like roommates than lovers. We lie in bed together, we talk, we go out on dates; but no sex, not as long as he is still having sex with men. I can have another relationship on the side, if I choose to. I just can't hold his hand in public or let the world know that I'm in love with someone who is not my husband.

I came to Hollywood with the intention to sell a script, make some money to take care of my child, and maybe rebuild my life. I was able to do all of the above. Most women couldn't do what I'm doing, but I'm not most women. In life you have to make decisions and I know being Mrs. Adrienne Sheppard-Joseph is the best choice I could've ever made. I have my daughter, stability; I'm completely out of debt and have a wonderful life. And the bonus is designers call me to wear their clothes, I have a closet full of shoes, new cars, and access to whatever I want.

It's not ideal, but it is worth it. I would not give up his last name, because it has opened so many doors I wouldn't have been able to touch on my own. Is this forever? I don't know, but I think I can at least give it five million dollars' worth of my time.

Don't miss Cydney Rax's

Revenge of the Mistress

On sale in January 2017, wherever e-books and
books are sold!

PROLOGUE

A short man stood over Rashad pointing a semi-automatic pistol. It weighed only one point six pounds but to Rashad it looked like it weighed a ton. He stared at the barrel of the gun and quickly lifted his hands. "What did I do? What do you want?"

"You. I want you."

"Who are you?"

"Just call me Death."

"What?"

The man was only around five foot two. Rashad thought he could take him. But the man jumped on a chair that was next to a Rashad and pressed the steel tip of the barrel against his head.

"You are Rashad Quintelle Eason. And one of the women in your life asked me to send a message to you."

"What woman? What are you talking about?"

"Be quiet. Listen."

The man had a crazed look in his eyes, piercing black eyes that blinked rapidly.

"She said to ask, 'Why did you let Satan use you like you did?' "

"I-I don't know what you're talking about."

"She said you should know everything that she's talking about."

"But who is she?"

"Shut the fuck up. Right now. Do as I say and it won't hurt as bad, or take as long."

The man, although short, was strong and powerful. He first duct-taped Rashad's hands.

Rashad struggled to loosen the tape but couldn't.

"Please."

The man ignored him.

He reached in the back of Rashad's blue jeans and took his wallet.

Then he wound a wide dark piece of cloth around Rashad's eyes. It felt so tight he could no longer see. Rashad's shirt was soaked with perspiration. Was this some type of joke? Was someone trying to scare him just to make a point?

Rashad inhaled the breath of the little man. It smelled like sour milk. Then his mouth was being pried open with little hard fingers. A thick sock was stuffed inside Rashad's mouth. He instantly felt like he could no longer breathe. He felt as if he was choking and began to gag. The fibers from the cloth sucked all the liquid from his mouth and the dryness made him want to throw up.

He couldn't believe this was happening. Who was this guy? What else did he plan to do? Rashad felt nervous and wished his arms weren't trembling so much. His brain felt cloudy. He didn't understand. He felt sorry but it was too late.

The black steel pistol was shoved deeper against Rashad's temple.

Right then he heard the voice of his son, Myles, in his head. He heard his laughter. He saw his smile. He missed Myles. He wished he could see his daughters: Hayley, Emmy, and Jazz. He imagined what would happened if he could never hold his children again. He knew that his cell phone was only inches away. He remembered that it fell out of his pocket when he got startled by the man who suddenly burst into the warehouse.

Rashad wished he could get to his phone. Make a phone call. Tell the people he loved good-bye.

But he had a feeling he'd never talk to them again. They'd never know how sorry he was. He thought of his mother, Beeva Reese. She'd be brokenhearted. And so would his girl, Nicole. A weird animal sound escaped from his mouth as he began to sob.

"Please, sir, I'll do anything."

The man only laughed.

Rashad wanted to scream, but he was growing weaker and weaker.

He wished he could pray.

But it was too late.

Seconds later a loud blast sounded in the hollowness of the room. The pain in Rashad's head was excruciating. He felt he was going blind, it hurt so terribly. Instantly, a fountain of blood flowed from his head and formed a dark red pool on the floor beneath him. He fell over in a heap.

As Rashad lay on the floor he wondered about his killer's words. What woman was he referring to? Who caused this?

Was it Kiara, Alexis, Nicole, Remy?

Within minutes Rashad Quintelle Eason's life flashed before him. Everything grew eerily dark and eternally quiet.

He finally took his last breath.

And he nursed one last thought. *What caused this?*

Connect with U s

Visit us online at
KensingtonBooks.com
to read more from your favorite authors, see books
by series, view reading group guides, and more.

Join us on social media

for sneak peeks, chances to win books and prize packs,
and to share your thoughts with other readers.

facebook.com/kensingtonpublishing
twitter.com/kensingtonbooks

Tell us what you think!

To share your thoughts, submit a review,
or sign up for our eNewsletters, please visit:
KensingtonBooks.com/TellUs.